About the Author

I came to writing later in life after a successful mid-management career in big build in the UK and mega-construction in the Middle East. A chronic injury forced an early retirement but I prefer to be positive — that opened the door for me to start writing, resulting in this, and my debut novel.

Happily married for over seven years and living in South-East Asia for over a decade, I have had exposure to many rich and diverse cultures. I hope to include some of these many observations in my books.

JASON

Mark Laverack

JASON

Vanguard Press

VANGUARD PAPERBACK

© Copyright 2024
Mark Laverack

A CIP catalogue record for this title is
available from the British Library.

ISBN 978 1 80016 934 0

Vanguard Press is an imprint of
Pegasus Elliot Mackenzie Publishers Ltd.
www.pegasuspublishers.com

First Published in 2024

Vanguard Press
Sheraton House Castle Park
Cambridge England

Printed & Bound in Great Britain

To my wife, Joy, who supported me for the year it took to write the novel and who believed in me from day one.

To my dad for instilling his word and writing skills and my mum for always telling me to follow my heart. Both are now gone but never forgotten.

Lastly, to my son, Matt, who offered encouragement and advice throughout the whole writing journey.

Acknowledgements

My BETA readers: Richard Green, Kate Coles, Matthew Laverack, Yasmin Ali and Mahmoud Abougabal.
Technical research contributors: Nia DeFreitas, Nick Snell and Matt Pedley.
Thanks to all for your input and suggestions.
Appreciated.

Prologue

A year after Liam had started his quest for revenge, it was nearly over.

His mission was completed. He sat back in his seat as the train paced monotonously through the countryside and took a mouthful of water. Damn. It had lost its cool edge. The ticket inspector had just passed by, so now he could sit back in his seat, relax and think.

He thought about the team.

The police investigation team. Even now, fruitlessly searching the bus station or even better, chasing after a bus that had departed to... who knows where, his discarded telephone faithfully transmitting its location through the mobile network system. He imagined the look on the Detective Inspector's face. Frustration. Desperation. The dawning that, once again, he had been outwitted.

With a smile, Liam took his first bite of the sandwich he had purchased at the station shop, just before departure. Brie and cranberry — his favourite.

Over the past year, Liam had gotten to know about Detective Inspector Graham Tonnick. The Detective was a single man but there was a girlfriend, Gemma — she was possibly even the fiancé. Tonnick himself was pretty nondescript and looked like he would not say 'boo to a goose'. He certainly didn't stand out in the crowd or draw attention to himself, but Liam was not stupid. He did not make the mistake of underestimating the detective.

Graham Tonnick had not become the lead detective on this case by chance. Liam had done his homework. With an impressive resumé of investigations, collars and busts, the detective was very hands-on and liked to be on the front line and in the thick of it. Tonnick was well-respected as a professional who 'got the job done'.

Liam had observed that Tonnick was also a man of routine. He dressed in similar, drab clothes every morning and picked up breakfast from the same street stall most days on his way to the station. The detective rarely went out socially. He used public transport to get around, and he took the same train to work.

Liam was familiar with other members of the team, too. That old Laboratory guy, a manager he thought, with the amusing name. What was it? He had forgotten. The Detective, Geoff and the enthusiastic, and yet somewhat amateurish Detective, Max. Then there was the lab assistant, Liam thought her name was Lucy, or maybe, Lizzie. The young girl Mandi, a junior Detective, if there was such a thing on D.I. Tonnick's team.

Liam shuddered and sucked in a breath sharply as he remembered Mandi. He felt a twinge of guilt when that thought came over him. Yes... he was familiar with the team, and one of them was too familiar, but Liam had done what he had to do to survive. He had come this far. Come through it all. No way was he going back and no way was he getting caught.

Now, he was concerned. Had someone seen his reaction? He glanced around. No one was looking at him. Everyone was minding their own business. There were not that many people in the steadily moving carriage. A medical-looking person, a private nurse Liam assumed, was attending to an elderly lady in a wheelchair at the front of the carriage. A couple of people sat back in their seats, reading newspapers. A man with his laptop was trying to look like one of those city types. Maybe he was but Liam thought what a cliché *businessman-on-train-with-laptop* had become. He had a bet with himself that if he got up and went closer, he would see that the man was actually playing *Solitaire*.

Other passengers had headphones on with the tinny beat, just audible, leaking out from their ears. Liam knew that only happened if the volume was too high, and he did not fancy hearing trouble later in life — any hearing damage was almost always incurable. Tinny sounds lead to tinnitus. Liam laughed at the play on words. He felt pity for the headphone-clad music-lovers.

Of course, most of the remaining travellers were in a world of their own, playing with their phones. *What did everyone do before the mobile phone*? He thought about that, glancing down at his own replacement phone, still shiny and new from when he picked it up in the station shop before boarding the train and as yet unused, with its battery not inserted.

The wheels of the carriages continued their rhythmic clicking over the joints in the track.

No... you won't get me by tracing my original phone, Detective Inspector Tonnick. He smiled to himself. *You will get someone, but not me.* Ditching that old phone in the toilets of the bus station was planned. It bought him time. Time to make his real travel plans on the train, which right now he was executing.

Another hour or so on this train until the station where the connecting train would be waiting, and then he would be free.

***

In the bus station, Liam's old phone had been found, just as he had hoped.

But instead of keeping it, the finder had handed it in to the bus station's Lost and Found. Messages were broadcast over the public address system, hoping to find the owner. The owner did not come forward to recover the lost phone in the bus station, mainly because the owner was already ten minutes away on a train.

However, one person did come forward to claim the phone... Detective Inspector Graham Tonnick.

The detective had only one thought on his mind, as he looked at the phone in his hand — *the tables are turning — we are right behind him*, and after a year, he believed they were, at last, getting close to apprehending William Granger.

JULY

Chapter 1

It was the start of July and William Granger was driving purposefully towards his destination. He was about sixty miles from home, in a town he rarely visited but he knew the town had what he wanted. He had looked on the internet. What a magical resource it was. You could find just about anything.

You could research almost anyone.

With so much free information, it was easy to see why there were so many online scam artists. Everyday folks, who were oh-so-careful with real-life security, were lax when it came to information online. Lax and gullible. William was smart and saw right through it, most people would but he wondered just how many desperate people did fall for it.

William, or Liam as he preferred, took the ring road to the right and followed along until he came to the large DIY store that he had seen on his *Google* search. He pulled the hoodie up over his head, adjusted his sunglasses and walked towards the store entrance foyer. He did not want to appear on any CCTV recordings today.

'Hi. Good morning. How can I help you?' The welcoming committee of shop assistants were clustered around inside the entrance, shaking Liam out of his insular world and forcing him to respond.

'Err… yes… point me towards the power tools.'

'OK, follow me, please.'

When they arrived at the aisle, Liam started looking at drills and told the assistant he would call him if he needed further help.

As soon as the assistant had left, Liam walked along two aisles, to where the hand tools were. Rows of spanners, screwdrivers, hammers and pliers.

Just after the wood clamps near the end of the aisle, Liam found what he was looking for — a hefty wooden mallet, perfect for what he was planning.

***

The following Monday Liam waited and watched a large, four-bed executive detached house, located on a gentle hill on the Sunnyhills Estate. His Ford SUV completely blended in with the surroundings.

He knew that there was not long to wait. If his previous observations were correct, any second now, Madeline Torrey would exit from the rear of the house for her morning run. At 0802, as expected, a chic-looking Madeline, in purple leggings, a pair of black shorts, and a sports top, plus some expensive Nike trainers, walked to the pavement at the front of her house and set her smartwatch. With a press of the button, she set off, a loose jog bordering on a run. Not high intensity, but Liam knew she would be out for about forty minutes.

He also knew that she did not call herself Madeline any more.

Forty minutes was more than enough time for what he was planning. He waited for another ten minutes because from his observations of the routine he knew the next-door neighbour would leave for work at 0805, and that there was a school run which passed at about 0810. Then there was a gap of ten minutes. No need for anyone to see him crossing the road to the property.

At 0812, Liam exited the vehicle.

He was wearing workman's overalls, cheap trainers, a peaked cap and sunglasses, and on his hands were a pair of latex gloves. He was carrying a small, khaki canvas tool bag.

Liam walked to Madeline's house and following a quick look round, he quickly walked down the side of the property and into the back garden.

As he expected, the back door was not locked but he had come prepared to break in, had it been necessary. Liam swiftly entered the house and checked around. He not been inside before. There was a heightened excitement at being somewhere he should not be, prying into the personal and private life of someone… a lady.

He had glanced in the dining room, which looked unused, then checked the living room. The TV was on, with a 'good morning' magazine program showing some feature about winter fashions. *Winter? But it's July.* Liam watched for a minute, then went upstairs.

The layout had been pretty much as expected. Standard modern house, albeit with better quality finishing and slightly larger rooms. Liam thought about 'box living' — a term he had heard used for modern estate houses The main bedroom, and bedroom two had full en-suite bathrooms, with a shower room in bedrooms three and four plus another downstairs cloakroom. Yep... an expensive box, but in his mind, a characterless box all the same.

The master en-suite had a large Jacuzzi bathtub. Liam already knew it did. He had checked this from the online Sunnyhills Estate brochure for this house type, on the developer's website. Good, his plan was coming along nicely. He scoured the other bedrooms, on the hunt for something, and in bedroom four he had found what he was looking for. After checking that it worked, Liam Granger went back into the second bedroom to wait.

His only other action, while he was waiting, was to open his tool bag and remove the large wooden mallet.

Madeline returned from her run around the roads. She felt good. Despite being out for over thirty minutes she did not feel tired or ache anywhere. Her trainers had that air cushioning and this was like a suspension, protecting her joints. For once the advertising hype actually worked. She checked her watch. Oh good. 345 calories. She walked up to her front door but as she passed the living room window something made her stop and look in.

Yeah... not bad for forty-two. She smiled to herself, moving away from the reflection and on to the path leading to the back door...

Just need to get a man in the house with me, now.

Liam heard the back door opening and tensed up from his position behind the door of bedroom two. He squeezed the handle of the mallet. He heard the noises from the kitchen as the fridge was opened and a drink was poured, though he had no idea what it was. *Maybe she was an alcoholic and that was the first of the day*, he speculated. Some more noises from the kitchen and for Liam, the wait seemed endless. He needed to pee.

Then he heard the footsteps coming up the stairs.

The unseen body passed by bedroom two and Liam tensed again, expecting the bedroom door to open. Instead, the sound carried on into the master bedroom. Although a thin wall separated them, she was within an arm's length of him at that point. The next time that happens, he thought, there will be no wall.

Madeline went through her bedroom and into the en-suite. She turned on the taps to the tub. While that was running, she went back into the bedroom and started to take off her running clothes. She pranced about the room naked for a moment, the carefree actions of a woman alone in the house and with no witnesses, before reaching for her thin robe.

Unbeknown to her, there had been one witness. William Granger had eased the door to bedroom two open just a crack, and although he was not there for it, he had seen the whole show.

Silently he opened the door, Madeline Torrey now had the robe on, and was sitting on the bed with her back to him. He quickly crossed the floor of the master bedroom and struck her hard on the back of the head with the wooden mallet. As soon as he had done it, he knew that it had not been hard enough. She was disorientated but did not fall unconscious from that blow. Shocked and dazed, she collapsed onto the floor. The adrenaline was pumping as she struggled to turn and see her attacker.

'Why? Why did you do that?' she shouted, trying to focus her eyes on her assailant.

Liam cursed. There was supposed to be no interaction. He had not struck her hard enough and now, this.

'You have to pay for what you did to me, Madeline.'

'Madeline? Who is Madeline?' Her head really hurt, but her eyes were focusing more now, and she could see the man in front of her. 'My name is Sue. Susan Bailey. I think you have the wro… '

Her voice had trailed off as she half-recognised Liam.

'Oh my God. I think I know you. Is it Nicholas? Nicholas err… Roberts?'

Liam had forgotten that he was Nicholas Roberts back then. He half smiled at the thought that they had both changed their names.

'Your name might be Sue Bailey now, but to me, you will always be Madeline Torrey, my teacher.

'You have to pay for what you did, Madeline.' Liam spoke like a robot. Cold and emotionless.

'I didn't do anything.' Susan Bailey tried to think about what she had done, why she had been singled out.

She was trying to buy time.

'Exactly. You did… nothing. MS. Torrey.' He emphasised the 'Ms', as if back in the classroom, but in a sarcastic way.

'When I came to you. When I was being bullied in the playground. I came to you. You? You knew about it already, and yet you still let it happen. As you said… you did nothing, and let's not forget your role in the killing of my parents… any idea what it's like to grow up without your parents, Madeline?'

'I did nothing? Err… and what did I do to your parents?' She tried to imagine the grief of losing loved ones. 'No, I don't. I'm so sorry, Nicholas.' Susan fell silent. Her head was extremely painful now and she was unable to get up off the floor. She remembered back, fifteen years or so. She had been a good teacher, everyone said so. But that relationship with Quinton. She had known it would come back to haunt her. The accident. She remembered now. Memories she too had tried to put to the back of her mind. He had told police he was rushing to an appointment, but the 'appointment' had turned out to be a love tryst… with her. And after he had come out of jail, she had stupidly taken up with him again, even after he had faithfully promised his wife. She had continued the deceit. He had been insistent but she could have said 'no'.

It was only when his wife had threatened divorce that Quinton Chambers had realised what he stood to lose, besides the marriage. His money, his factory and his prestige. No affair was worth that. The parting settlement with her had been extremely generous — he had always said he would take care and it was clear he really loved her. He had sacrificed the relationship, but Madeline had sacrificed too. She had quit the teaching job she loved. She had moved away and legally changed her name. Clean break. Bye-bye to the past as Madeline Torrey, hello to the future as Susan Bailey.

Her mind came back to the room and the current situation, with a much clearer understanding of why.

'Do you have to do this?' Her voice sounded pleading, almost.

Liam moved closer and now stood in front of the prone woman. 'Time to say goodbye, Madeline.'

Liam raised the mallet once more. At that moment, a noise came from the bathroom, the sound of water going out of the overflow. He turned to look.

'Oh, that's my bath. I need to turn it off.' Sue was desperate to put space between her and Liam.

'Don't worry about that, you cannot even stand, but you will be in the bath, soon enough.'

Susan looked confused. She tried to stand.

With one swift movement, Liam again brought the wooden mallet crashing down on the back of Susan Bailey's head. She slumped to the floor, unconscious. Blood started to ooze from the wound.

Liam sprang into action. He went to the bathroom and turned off the water. Then he drained about half of the bath out. Next, he lifted the unconscious Susan and carried her to the bath. She was small and light so the task was not difficult. He put some soap on her right foot, then put her over his shoulder and moved her foot over the bathroom floor tiles, leaving a slip mark before sitting her on the side of the bath and letting her fall into the water. The water level came up but was not high enough. He turned the taps on again for a minute.

Next, he went to recover the item he had searched for, and found in bedroom four — a small, old portable TV. He also picked up her dressing table chair and took it into the bathroom, then placed the TV on the chair. There was no 220-volt power outlet in the bathroom, a safety feature in modern housing and he needed an extension cord. For a moment Liam panicked. Was his meticulous plan about to fail because he had forgotten to organise a cable?

He found what he was looking for in the garage. A 10m cable with a plug and socket. He connected up the TV to the bedroom wall outlet and turned it on. The same morning TV show was airing, but now they were talking about autumn mini-breaks and places to get away to. Again, Liam watched for a minute, as he scratched the letter 'J' into the bath panel, with a circle around it.

Then he pushed the TV into the bath.

***

It was approaching lunchtime on that same Monday. The desk phone rang and Graham Tonnick picked it up.

'Got one for you, Gray,' said the desk sergeant. 'Death up on that new estate.'

Tonnick couldn't help but notice the disdain in the desk sergeant's voice, referring to 'that new estate'. He could not bring himself to name it. Sunnyhills Estate had caused much controversy when it was approved, and even more when it was built. Dark murmurings of backhanders, and even organised crime involvement to get the approval, did the rounds. There was more dismay in the city when residents realised that the walks and recreation that they had enjoyed in those hills at the weekend were now gone, under the concrete, tarmac and brick of the Estate. The fact that the developers had carried out extensive landscaping did nothing to cool opinion. Houses for the rich only. Another green space lost forever.

Suppressing the need to get side-tracked, he got the details and the address from the Sergeant. *Female. Forties. Head injury and electrocution. In the bathroom.* Tonnick couldn't help thinking of *Cluedo* and added, 'with the rolling pin' under his breath.

'Is there no one out there already?' he asked, hopefully.

'No one who's available,' came back the reply. 'This shouldn't take long, though. It seems to be pretty open and shut, if it was an accident, that is, but you can decide that after taking a look. I'll log this one to you.'

The call cut, preventing further conversation.

Tonnick let out a long breath, staring resignedly at his laptop. It was just before lunchtime and he had planned to check out holiday destinations. After nigh-on two years of engagement, he was starting to think about honeymoon arrangements and at last, making wedding plans. His mind wandered, briefly, daydreaming about somewhere exotic and a palm-tree-lined swimming pool. It was only a moment though before this new job came back to mind, and he hurriedly left the office.

He met with his detective sergeant in the motor pool.

'A death over on Sunnyhills.'

The DS looked hopeful but was knocked back with a glance.

'Whoa! It's probably an accident. The initial report says electrocution. Let's go and check out what happened. You drive.'

They arrived at the address twenty-five minutes later. There had already been a call from the lab who were on the scene. *Yes, they were on the way.* That irritated the Detective. He hated being late for anything, probably the Aquarian in him. God, he was not even late. Twenty-five minutes to Sunnyhills Estate from the station? Not bad. But still, the suggestion that he was, somehow, slacking and wait… forensics? For a simple accident, on the face of it? He knew there were procedures, but it irked him that he was perceived as late and everyone was waiting for him.

The detective lightened up on seeing Raymond.

Raymond Gunne. The elder statesman of the forensics lab. He smiled, same as he did every time, remembering the last occasion he witnessed some officer referring to the forensics boss as 'Ray', followed by the realisation of the full name in that format, followed by the withering look from Gunne and quiet but firm correction to the young officer, the smile wiped from his face instantly. His name was Raymond… never 'Ray'.

Raymond Gunne had been in charge of forensics for… well… forever. As long as Tonnick could remember, certainly all of his career in the force. He must be up for retirement soon? Tonnick made a mental note to check on his retirement date when he got back to the station.

His DS had already walked over to the forensics chief, but Gunne waited until the Detective Inspector was with them.

'All the big guns here for this one… what's so special, Raymond, and more importantly, where's that lovely assistant of yours?'

'Lucy is safe in the lab away from lecherous old men like you. I'm scared to let her out. Hey, aren't you engaged? How's Gemma?'

The men were smiling along with the banter.

'As for, *what's so special?* The answer is… nothing. I think it's a false call. Seems pretty clear what happened. The victim, Susan Bailey went for a bath and somehow knocked the TV into the tub. I think she slipped. There's soap on the floor and she's got a head injury.'

'Husband involved?'

'She's not married. We think she's forty-two. Not sure yet what her work is.'

Gunne was relaying the background information to bring Tonnick up to speed. They walked into the house, while the DS went back to speak to the police officer in attendance. The detective was looking at the house and the Estate. They weren't joking. You needed money to live here. Not detective money only, that was for sure. *So, the deceased was unmarried, was she?* Tonnick was curious how a single forty-something afforded the place. He wondered what her line of work was. This was the sort of house he hoped to set up in when he and Gemma married. Again, his thoughts ran back to the honeymoon options.

'Graham?' Gunne was addressing him, with a concerned look. 'You OK?'

'Yes. Sorry.'

Tonnick snapped out of it and focused. They went through the house, upstairs and into the master bedroom, then through into the *en-suite*.

Everything was just as it was found. The bath was now cool and the bubbles were all but gone. The TV was in the water. The chair that it was supposedly on was laying on its side on the floor. As he looked around and started to appraise the scene, the detective noticed the soap on the floor, and the skid mark in it where, he assumed, the victim's foot had lost control.

Mostly though, he noticed the eyes.

Susan Bailey was staring straight at him. Wide, lifeless, frightened eyes. The mouth was also open, slack jawed. She was sitting, sideways in the bath, with her back against the opposite wall and her feet dangling over the side of the tub. She was wearing nothing but a thin dressing gown as if she was indeed about to bathe.

It was not the first dead body the detective had seen, far from it and yet this one — there was something about it. He thought back to his first homicide eighteen years ago, a shooting, when he was a grunt on the force, just starting out. *You never forget that first one*.

'When are they taking the body, Raymond?'

'They are outside waiting to do that now. Just wanted you to see the scene first. I don't think there's much more to say, do you?' Gunne replied.

Tonnick noted, with more than a little surprise, that the lab chief, who had not got where he was today by skipping over the investigation, seemed to be doing just that with this one, but he kept that thought to himself.

'Yeah. I'm surprised they called you out for this one, Mr Gunne.'

The DS had also heard the stories of those who made a mistake with Raymond Gunne's name.

'I was passing when the call came so I diverted. Save the 'resources' and all that,' chuckled the forensics' boss.

'The angles, do they line up for how she slipped? I mean, she's sideways and backwards. You don't get into a bath backwards. And how did the TV fall into the tub, anyway?'

Tonnick was warming to the scene now.

'I think she was adjusting the TV position, so she would have her back to the bath, right?' Max chipped in with his views of the incident.

Both the senior officers stopped and looked at Max.

The DS dipped his head. 'Just saying.' He shrugged his shoulders. 'It's a possibility, right, Mr Gunne?'

Tonnick also weighed the suggestion up. It was a possible, a pretty good one. 'Any clue as to which way the foot was facing when she slipped?'

'Thought you'd never ask!' said Gunne, chuckling. 'See here, the skid mark is away from the bath, with a big print from the ball of the heel and it tallies with the injury she sustained.'

Tonnick had noted that skid mark but it took the forensics professional to analyse it, read the clues and come up with the facts. Then he stopped. Oh my God! The head injury! He had completely forgotten about that. Raymond had spoken about it when they got there, and the desk sergeant had mentioned it, too. How could he forget? He was being distracted by something with this case, a case which, on the face of it, could have been handled by any detective in the office. It did not need him… on the face of it.

'Let's see that injury,' was all he could respond.

Raymond Gunne looked sideways at him again. Longer, this time. He moved to the body and tilted the head away.

'Yes… right here. Do you see? On the back of the head. And there's corresponding blood on the back wall above the bath. Seems like our Susan here was adjusting the set, slipped and fell back, grabbing at the TV for support, and ended up pulling it into the bath with her.

There's no sign of a break-in, but then again, the door was unlocked, that's how the friend got in and found her.'

Tonnick had neglected to ask how the force came to know.

Raymond Gunne had worked with the Detective for many years and always found him very thorough. Today, however, he noticed that Graham Tonnick was not on his game. He tried to steer the conversation.

'The friend was due to meet Ms Bailey here today. She arrived, as usual, rang the bell at the front a few times, then walked around the back, but there was nobody in the kitchen. She tried the door which was unlocked and went in, calling her friend but again got no response. Eventually, she found Susan upstairs, here in the bathroom, and called us.'

The detective was still processing this information, looking for any other angle. 'Where is the friend, now?'

'I believe still outside in her car with the police officer.'

Tonnick turned to Max. 'See if you can find the friend and get something down on paper. She's our only witness.'

Although he did not know it, that last statement was untrue.

The DS went back downstairs again.

'What a way to go. What was she even doing with a TV in a bathroom?' Tonnick was thinking out loud.

'No telling with folks.' Gunne was replying as a man who had seen it all before, in his almost forty years in the lab. 'Maybe she likes the morning magazine programs.'

Graham Tonnick was already walking out into the bedroom but then something made him stop. Something he had seen in the bathroom, but not really assimilated. He turned sharply and went to walk back, almost walking into Gunne, who was coming out of the bathroom behind him.

'Ooof! Graham, what's up?'

'Something. Let me look again.'

The detective was already past Gunne and back at the scene of the accident.

He had to move to get the light right, but once he did, it was plainly there, even though it was quite small. That might explain why it had been missed until now. Scratched into the side of the bath, in the top corner furthest from the door, was the letter 'J', with a circle or 'O' surrounding it. Gunne was still looking, and Tonnick helped him by pointing at the location.

'Well, I'll be… ' the lab boss's voice trailed off.

'It looks new,' said Tonnick, 'You think she… ?'

'Odd if she did. Maybe it's older than we think? Let me get the camera and I'll dust it also, just in case.'

Gunne left the room, leaving the Detective Inspector pondering. It had looked pretty nailed-on as an accident. 'J' for… what? Any connection to her? He would of course be checking the facts. Family. Friends. Boyfriend? Any connection to 'J'.

He went downstairs and outside, meeting up with Max who was walking back towards the front door. Susan Bailey's friend had just left. Damn. He had hoped to ask her about 'J'.

'We have her details, so we can call at any time, or we can visit her.'

The DS was matter-of-fact about the situation as he cross-checked his notebook.

Graham Tonnick was already walking to the car, thinking. *Surely this was not murder… was it*?

Chapter 2

It was murder, and it had been surprisingly easy for Liam to do it.

He had watched and waited. Blended in. No one had noticed or suspected. Speed was of the essence. No need for discussion, no need for explanation. In, finish it, and out. That's what he had planned.

He had used the previous few weeks to learn all he needed to know about Madeline's movements. The thing was, he was not starting from scratch, oh no. He already knew plenty about Madeline Torrey, from years ago, when it had all started. Those terrible events that had forever changed his life. He was a young boy, just ten years old. Those around him had thought he was probably too young to fully understand what had happened, but he was smart from an early age. He knew, and he never forgot.

From his observations, he had discovered that Madeline had tried to hide her past. Yeah… funny how she had changed her name, the same as he had. We are alike, Madeline. He smiled briefly then got serious again. *It made no difference, Madeline. I found you anyway, Madeline.* The Internet. So useful.

What you did, all those years ago, could not be forgotten, and could not be forgiven.

He had honestly tried to suppress it. He thought he had, but finally, it come back and overwhelmed him. Nicholas Roberts, or… William Granger, as his name was now, was on a mission to put those demons to rest, and Madeline Torrey was going to have to pay. He knew that Madeline did not work. That she socialised with other 'ladies who lunch'. He smiled when he mouthed that clichéd phrase.

He'd gathered information. She'd had a boyfriend but it had finished a short time ago. Liam had seen a photo in the social activity column of the local paper's supplement, from some charity function, a smiling Madeline with a bearded, older gentleman and again, about a month later at a Spring ball, resplendent in a long red gown, with the same man in a smart tux and a shirt with one of those wing collars.

***

If Liam had to put his finger on when things had changed for him, it was six months earlier. He had been called to the factory office. It was eight AM, and the boss was not usually in until nine, so Liam started to get a bad feeling, but still, he had no idea what was coming.

The boss was there waiting for him.

The MD and owner, Chambers, or Quinton Charles Chambers to give him his full name, and one which he liked to use as much as possible, had an office suite at the back of the factory administration building, near to his private parking space, containing his very nice, new BMW 750i.

Liam thought briefly about the mentality of a man needing to puff his image up. Not 'Chambers', or 'Quinton Chambers', or even 'Quinton'. No, he was always announced with his middle name included. It was on his LinkedIn. It was on his Facebook. It was, of course, on his business card. Liam assumed it was a validation, to distinguish himself from all the other 'Quinton Chambers' out there.

Liam did not like Quinton Charles Chambers and had only taken this job just to find out more about the man. Chambers' past was linked inextricably with ten-year-old Nicholas Roberts. Nicholas was old enough to understand and had had to experience the ultimate loss. Both his parents were killed in a motoring accident. A drunk driver racing to an appointment had lost control, struck an oncoming car and careered into Jim and Alice Roberts who were walking on the pavement. They were killed instantly. The driver was quickly apprehended. The driver was found to be in no state to be coherent, let alone apologetic. The driver was Quinton Charles Chambers.

Throughout the court case, Nicholas Roberts was kept out of the papers, and his photo was not published, just a reference to *the Roberts' only child, Nicholas*. Chambers never met him, and as he was not allowed to attend the private funerals, he never saw him. It was not high on

Chambers' priority list anyway... Quinton Charles Chambers was more than four times over the limit when he was breathalysed, and desperate to avoid jail time.

Now, as he entered the inner sanctum of the boss's office, thoughts were racing through his mind. Is he going to follow up about the workplace bullying incidents? Had Liam got the blame for what had been happening? Or, God forbid, had Chambers discovered his true identity? Until now, Chambers had not made any connection between him and the past, when he was Nicholas Roberts.

'Come in. Sit down.'

Chambers was brusque. Liam noticed that as he walked forward. June Davis the HR Manager silently followed him in. *Where had she been hiding?*

'Have you got the records, June?'

Chambers was informal with his senior staff. Davis came forward and passed him two sheets of paper, then stepped back to lean against the office wall.

'Good morning, Mr Granger. I'm calling you today to follow up on what you and I spoke about before.'

It was true there had been a conversation in the office before, about a month earlier. William Granger had been the subject of relentless 'horseplay' bordering on bullying while on the factory floor. With about five of the factory workers against one of him, it had at times become overpowering and his timekeeping had suffered. He had spoken to the HR department about 'what to do'. They had been sympathetic but to go further, William Granger had to name names.

Liam had thought about that.

Naming names might feel good on the day but afterwards, it would not. Those named people would make his life hell. Even more of a misery than they were already. He would be singled out as a 'snitch'. Things would go missing, endless pushing and shoving, insults and vicious verbal abuse. It would spill out into non-work time. Liam knew what would happen. He decided not to pursue it, but to make matters worse, he had been issued with a final warning for his repeated lateness and absences.

Now, barely a month later and he was in front of the boss again. What this time? And what were those records Chambers had asked HR to provide?

'I'll come straight to the point,' Chambers began, 'When we met before, there were some timekeeping issues. If I remember rightly, you were issued a final warning?'

He glanced at June Davis, who nodded. Liam thought it was funny how people say *if I remember rightly* when of course, there is no remembering about it. They have checked and verified the facts. They know.

'Now I have had to call you again, and again there have been timekeeping and absentee problems.'

'Yes but,' Liam cut in, 'I was genuinely sick. Food poisoning. I called the office.'

'Genuinely sick?' Ahh, so all the other times you were not genuinely sick, then?' Chambers saw an opening for the conclusion. 'You were scamming it.'

'No, I didn't mean that.'

There was a slight air of panic in Liam's voice, as it tailed off.

'So, we have one claimed 'genuine' sickness. Did we see a doctor's note, June?' June Davis shook her head almost before Chambers has finished talking. They had reviewed all the possible angles. '…and a large number of, shall we say, not-so-genuine' absences.'

'Not a large number.' Liam was trying to state the facts but only succeeded in confirming that he had been absent more than once.

'What about the timekeeping? According to these records, you have been late to work on twelve days in the last month.'

Chambers was readying himself for the killer punch.

'My punch card keeps disappearing. When I go to punch in, the card is not there.'

In truth, Liam Granger was stretching things. His punch card had gone AWOL on only two occasions and had appeared within a minute of the normal clocking-in time. The other times, he had been on the end of some prolonged abuse the previous day and had woken up unable to face the factory. He had forced himself to go but had been late as a result.

'Look, facts are facts.'

Chambers was in *endgame* mode and not listening.

'One genuine absence but no Doctors note, which is a company requirement. Several other absences. Poor timekeeping. Did you report the missing punch card?'

Liam shook his head.

'No? Well, we cannot take it into account, then.'

Chambers' voice had become very authoritarian. 'You were warned what would happen if this continued — you had a final written warning and that was only a month ago. You leave me with no choice now. You are hereby dismissed from the company, effective immediately. I have already spoken to Ms Davis and we have agreed to pay you until the end of this month, plus any other accrued payments. Can you take care of that, June?'

'Already done.' As soon as she said it, she wished she hadn't.

Chambers jumped in. 'OK... go with Ms Davis now. You need to return everything that was issued to you and sign off on that. Then you can collect your stuff and security will escort you off the premises.'

Liam grimaced. Not even a chance for leaving quietly. This departure would be in front of everybody.

'I think we can trust him to leave in a dignified manner, Quinton. No need to draw attention with security.' She glanced over. 'Right, William?'

Liam nodded, thankfully. Maybe Ms Davis had just been doing her job earlier.

'Right. I have a meeting so can we conclude? Anything you want to say?'

He was looking straight at Liam.

Liam resisted saying that this disciplinary meeting was a total shambles and he was treated unfairly. No notice beforehand, no person to support him, etc. but instead he just shook his head.

'Follow me.'

The HR manager was already heading for the door. William turned to say something, but Quinton Charles Chambers had already rotated his chair so he did not have to see him leaving.

***

Liam was in the bar with a couple of his factory mates. They met regularly, at least once a fortnight, sometimes more. He was in a comfort zone and they used this bar quite often. It was agreed not to talk about work and here he could sort of relax, but this was the first get-together since his dismissal from the factory.

'Apparently, Jimmy comes in here too.' Liam stiffened. Jimmy was the chief tormentor he had faced when at work, although with the sacking, that was now over. What his friends did not know was that the same Jimmy had made his life hell earlier, when they were both schoolboys.

'Relax, he never comes in on a Monday, so we are fine. He comes with his wife before they head to town.'

'I didn't even know he had a wife.'

'He does. How are you, anyway, Liam? I know we are not talking about work but I'm interested in your well-being. Those bastards did one on you. Can't we do something?'

Though it was early days, Liam was already planning on 'doing something.'

'I have some plans,' was all he said, then Liam ordered some more drinks and they moved over to play pool and the topic died away.

***

Liam was still out of work, but he was not out of money. The trust fund ordered by the court, which was set up sometime after his parents were killed, saw to that. It had started this year, and Liam had already received three payments from it since he had been fired.

Those monthly payments had come in very useful. He already owned his house, bought and paid for thanks to the money he had received directly from his parent's death. He did not need to rush out and find another job.

He had enjoyed the factory job before things had started to go sour. Why had Jimmy come to the factory? His workplace. Before Jimmy had come, Liam was settled, with his past very much behind him. The bully's arrival reignited feelings he had suppressed. He became more agitated as time went on and when the day came that he was dismissed, Liam was positively burning with anger and resentment.

Now, with no job to distract him and all the events of the past once again fresh in his mind, Liam had both the time and motivation to settle scores. He had not been out much in the past six months. Instead, he had become somewhat of a recluse, just surfing the internet at home, finding out about all the people involved in his family tragedy. He had become obsessed.

With that obsession, Liam had built himself up to get revenge. The more he had locked himself away with his computer, the more he had looked, the more he had gathered the information... the more he hated all the people involved.

He had suppressed his feelings all these years, but after everything that had happened and with six months of planning, Liam experienced feelings that he had not had since he was a small boy.

Growing up in a family. Trips to the beach. Summer weekends spent in the family's wooden cabin by the lake. Liam remembered the boat, and fishing with his dad. Going for forest walks and a picnic lunch. His mum tucking him up in the cabin's small second bedroom, with the scent of the wood fire and the clean air of the forest all around them. He never slept as well as he had done on those holidays. Then waking up to the smell of Mum's fry up breakfast every morning. The tears welled up and for a moment, Liam was inconsolable.

He missed his parents.

***

Once again, Graham Tonnick was on the computer during his lunch break, researching. He appreciated the ease with which he could find out information about locations, sights, restaurants, hotels and of course, prices.

It had become a bit of a ritual every lunchbreak. Well, every lunch break he was in the office. Do this research. He had eliminated a lot of destinations. He was looking for ultimate relaxation, with quality time for himself and Gemma. Never mind a honeymoon. He needed a holiday.

He glanced out into the main office, something he did regularly. It was quiet. A couple of the team were working at their desks, sandwiches in hand. He chuckled. Maybe they are planning their holidays, too. It was nice to have a bit of a lull in the workload, though to be honest, the detective relished a good case. More work rather than less, he decided. He knew it would not last.

Lately, he had been focusing on the Maldives, that group of paradise islands in the Indian Ocean. '*No news, no shoes*' seemed to be the mantra, and that struck a chord with him. He liked the idea of a high-end yet carefree vacation. So many islands, all offering different levels of luxury and cost.

He started trying to whittle them down. Take out the ridiculously expensive. Take out the cheapest ones. Take out the larger ones — too many people. Seaplane access? Maybe… could be fun. Leave that in. But wait… what if the weather turned bad? They would not get to the island… or get off it if it was bad when they went to go home. Hmmm… something to think about. There were still plenty of islands to choose from, even without the seaplane ones.

He continued to narrow it down but in the back of his mind, the Susan Bailey death would not leave him alone.

Yes, it looked accidental but… something. That scratched letter. The ridiculousness of carrying a small TV to the bathroom requiring that lengthy extension cable. The soap on the floor on the same day as the TV's use. Tonnick was not a fan of coincidences.

He gave up on the holiday search. Something was not right about that death.

AUGUST

Chapter 3

'There is not much in the report, Gray.' Gunne was verbally outlining the document he was at the same time passing over to the detective. He had stopped by to personally drop it off. The detective took the thin report and scan-read it.

'So, you're saying it was an... accident?'

'Can't see it another way. There's nothing else to open it to anything further.'

The lab boss was checking his watch. 'Have to excuse me. I'm needed. If you have any questions, give me a call or, why not come and see me?'

Gunne turned to go. Once again, Tonnick got the feeling that the lab boss was, uncharacteristically, pushing it to closure.

'One question, Raymond. That 'J'. Relevant? Or unconnected?'

Tonnick was trying to cover everything in his usual thorough manner.

'You spoke to that friend, right?' Gunne half turned, 'She said there was no connection between Susan and 'J'?'

Tonnick nodded.

'There is nothing else connecting that 'J' to the evidence for this accident. She did not buy the place new. Maybe some kids from the previous owner? I'm struggling to link it, based on everything we have, which admittedly, is not a lot.'

Raymond Gunne started once more for the door.

Detective Inspector Tonnick continued to stare at the photograph of the bath side with the scratched letter, as the door closed.

Still… an accident. He looked at the door and smiled briefly. Door closed, case closed.

***

Liam was outside in his garden. In case there were any spectators, he had made a show of clearing up, forming a small pile of garden waste in the brazier to burn up. When he was ready, he went to the kitchen and collected a small canvas bag. He lit the fire and waited until it was burning well. Then he added some wooden off-cuts that at one time may have formed a mallet, together with some cheap trainers, now in six pieces, a pair of coveralls cut into a bundle of rags, some used surgical gloves and a baseball cap. Lastly, he put the canvas bag into the flames. The fire flared and burnt efficiently — the items he had added were all dry. Soon, only the wooden off-cuts were still burning, but they had become charred and rounded and were unrecognisable as a tool. Everything else had turned to ash, even the trainers were gone. He had been careful to choose a canvas bag with plastic fastenings, not metal. Nothing to be left over. The fire was making next to no smoke so Liam decided to let it burn and go in. He would check that all the evidence had been destroyed later.

***

Tonnick remembered he had something to do, following that meeting at the Susan Bailey house. He opened up the police personnel database and spun the mouse wheel down to 'G'.

Grant... Groover... Gulliver... Gunne.

The detective inspector clicked on the record. Gunne, Raymond. No middle name. Length of service. Date of birth and age. Tonnick let out a long soft whistle. Age: sixty-eight. He was well past the normal retirement age. In fact, with that length of service, the Lab manager could have retired years ago. He called Personnel.

'Hi... this is detective inspector Tonnick. Yes. Quick question for you. Can you give me any idea as to when Raymond Gunne plans to retire? We want to organise something for him. Yes. Yes, a leaving party. Yes, sorry. Retirement party, I mean.'

There was a pause as the assistant looked through the personnel files and records.

'About a year-and-a-half. We are pushing him for this actually, due to his age, but it's not yet finalised.'

The detective thanked her and put the phone down.

***

Back in his home, Liam was already working on the next part of his plan. This one would not be so easy. The target knew him from the past and had had dealings with him about half a year ago though he did not know that William Granger was not his original name. Liam would have to be smart, to get his target in the right place at the right time.

As before, he had watched his target's movements, which, like Madeline, were fairly regular. He left home at 0830 to arrive at his work by 0900. He often went to a local restaurant for lunch, something he had been doing for over fifteen years. He had met a certain younger lady there on a lot of occasions, but Liam already knew that he would never do that again. He went home to his wife and family at around 1745 every night. Apart from Friday, that is. Fridays he went to an off-licence and a bar, before going home.

Just over a week earlier, Liam had been to that same out of town DIY store he had visited to purchase the wooden mallet, this time to buy some bolts — a hundred in a bag. He had bought washers and nuts too, so as not to arouse suspicion, though he had no intention of using them. Then, for the next five nights, Liam had been making changes to some barrier railings, part of his plan for that next target.

***

Graham Tonnick was on the Metro, travelling home. He was due to meet his fiancé later for dinner, but today, he was not really in the mood for it. He had thoughts rushing through his head… about his fiancé, about the Bailey case… *it's true what they say, for detectives… married to the wife or married to the job*. One or the other… but not both. It seemed to be for him, anyway. He pondered. I'm a good detective, I think. No… I am. I enjoy the work so does that mean I will not be able to live with my future wife?

The metro had been stopped at a station but was now moving again. He looked around the carriage. People lost in the world of the mobile phone. He saw one man who had just got on the train attempt to sit down on one of the benches, next to an Asian girl. She was sitting in a way to make it difficult for someone to sit down, spreading herself out with a small rucksack to take about one and a half seats. The man persisted, asking if she could move. She pretended to not hear, her earphones in. He tried to attract her attention and moved a hand in front of her face but she had carefully closed her eyes, closed to the world, or at least closed to being sociable. Eventually, the man just attempted to sit down. The look of annoyance confirmed it — her plan for 'VIP' seating had failed and she reluctantly moved her rucksack and made just enough of the seat available for the fellow passenger to sit.

Inwardly, Tonnick gave a fist-bump of victory for the man. It was clear the girl thought she was too important to have anyone sit down next to her, or was it that, like so many others of her generation, she had lost the basic social skills of real life and felt annoyed that the space she perceived as being 'hers' had been invaded. She scowled for the next five minutes, staring straight ahead, across the carriage towards Tonnick.

What had made Graham Tonnick laugh cynically was that he had seen the girl ten minutes earlier. Then, she had been all smiles, fake smiles in fact, as she clicked away taking selfies. The usual 'V of victory' hand gesture, another with that same Vee but with the fingers over one eyebrow like a crazy salute, the one with the tongue sticking out of the corner of the mouth, the one with one eye screwed up. The cross-eyed look. The pretend kiss. Tonnick ticked the poses off in his head. He had seen them all before. The same formulaic poses practised by a thousand Asian girls in every city, every day. Everyone copying everyone else, trying to look cool. Those poses had become so clichéd. What was it with those endless V-signs, anyway? Aside from the fact that half of them had the hand the wrong way round, and were seemingly telling the viewer to 'fuck off', what exactly was this 'victory' that was being shouted about?

He knew where those pictures were heading, too. Straight to social media, with suitable captions. 'Living it up in the city!' 'On the way home after a long day!' 'Got the seat to myself!' *#busygirl, #asiansatlarge, #onthetownwiththegirls, #asianmafia.* Along with the obligatory exclamation mark after every caption, Tonnick imagined the mandatory hashtags accompanying the uploaded pictures, each one carefully crafted to make the girl seem like the life-and-soul of the party, a successful, sociable darling with loads of friends and a very busy social life. The image of getting away from the homeland and somehow 'winning', and at the same time hoping to make a couple of her followers a little jealous.

He compared that image to the sullen, scheming anti-social girl he saw ten minutes later when someone tried to use the same seat she was sitting on. The whole thing was phoney. She was living life through the phone and social media but could not cope with real interactions in real life. The often used saying '*slave to the phone*' sprang to mind.

His thoughts drifted back to that holiday he was looking forward to. Somewhere hot and sunny. He had got the choice down to one of the Maldives islands, or maybe Seychelles. They were hot and sunny. Exclusive, too. He smiled. Lots of lovely photo opportunities. Swaying palms, soft golden sands and turquoise waters. Luxury accommodation right on the beachfront, fishing, swimming, eating, relaxing. Tonnick allowed himself a moment to dream about relaxing. He could fill an album of happy memories, just the two of them, and the location, the ambience all captured with the camera.

Then his thoughts were drawn back to the selfie brigade. Those self-promoting girls, even assuming they managed to get to the Maldives... walking around in mismatched swimsuits of lurid pink and green, a selfie stick glued to the right hand, clicking away. Back at home, they had five hundred photos to show, four hundred and fifty of them selfies and groups of faces and bodies with those obligatory poses, and showing nothing of the beautiful location, and the other fifty of food, accompanied by the captions 'burp!' or 'time to sleep!'

And don't forget the all-important exclamation marks.

***

Liam had watched his next target enough to gather all the information he needed.

He had made his plan, and now it was almost time. As before, he wanted to be in, act, and get out quickly. No chatting this time. No matter what the target said. No responses. Keep it distant.

He had made a trip out to Sunnyhills Estate the previous day to double-check one part of his plan. Once satisfied, he returned to the top of a nearby hill and hunted around for somewhere he could conceal his getaway equipment. A bushy outcrop just off the road was perfect. It was only for less than one day, no one would find his stuff. He pulled up next to it and deposited two items, then made his way back down to the run-off area at the bottom of the hill and parked his car to obstruct the view of what he was doing. He had been there a few times before — it was a big job to make all the adjustments he needed and today was only a last check to make sure his modifications to the barrier were all still in place.

Liam knew his target liked to stop off for a couple of drinks on a Friday evening, before heading home. He also knew that before that, the man went to the off-licence for a bottle or two to take home for the weekend. Once an alcoholic, always an alcoholic, Liam decided.

He thought back to the pious promises made by that same target when he was standing in front of the judge. Although Liam had not been in court himself, he had read up on the case and learnt how his target had stated that he was giving up drink. How he saw the tragedy of what happens when an alcoholic is out of control. He had made those promises. The judge had seemed moved. The sentence was shockingly light. A slap on the wrist. For two lives snuffed out, for a lifetime without parents, the sentence was a joke. An insult. The target had got off virtually scot-free. The anger started to rage in Liam once again.

Now it was obvious. Chambers did not keep those promises. He was still drinking, and still carrying on. That upset Liam Granger. The time had come to put it right.

He had already dealt with one half of the problem. Now it was time to deal with the other half, and for Quinton Charles Chambers, the time was almost up.

Chapter 4

Detective Inspector Tonnick had arrived home and was getting ready to go out again. He had showered and shaved and was picking out something to wear. He looked critically at his wardrobe. A lot of the clothes were old, and a bit drab. Graham Tonnick realised he had got stuck in a rut. The same thing every day. Same boring clothes, same routine. He would be so easy to suss out if anyone had decided to watch him! He smiled. *Yeah... like that's going to happen*, he thought to himself while looking in the mirror.

***

Liam was also looking in a mirror. A car mirror that was focused on the off-licence. It was Friday night, seven PM, and if true to form, any second now, a black BMW seven-series was going to pull up outside.

The seconds ticked past.

Damn. Where is he? What seemed like forever was in reality only a couple of minutes past the hour. Liam started to panic. Was his plan going to fail? Then he relaxed. *There was always next week.* But no longer than that. Chambers had to die this month.

Even as he was contemplating those timescales, the BMW glided past him and pulled up. Liam breathed a sigh of relief and noted that Chambers was always lucky with the parking. He had watched for a few weeks and every time, the BMW was able to park almost in front of the off-licence.

The door slammed and he could see Quinton Chambers entering the shop.

***

In the mirror, Tonnick caught sight of his bathtub and immediately thought of Susan Bailey. Something was not right about that whole incident. Why would she have the TV in the bathroom? He still could not comprehend that one. Although he was working on another case now and the Bailey incident was already a *case closed*, it would not go away.

He usually got a sense of satisfaction when a case was investigated and concluded. But he did not feel closure with the death of Susan Bailey. The bathtub again made him think about that letter 'J' scratched into the upper left side of the front panel. No real explanation for it had ever been provided.

Maybe that was why he could not close it out.

He was still thinking about it when he called his fiancé to tell her he was on the way.

***

Liam knew that Chambers would be a matter of minutes only, just enough time for him to turn his car around and head to the bar. He started his car and did a U-turn. As he passed the off-licence, Chambers was just coming out. Perfect timing. For once Liam did not worry if Chambers saw the car. The man was preoccupied with getting a drink same as every week. Head down, walking to the BMW, oblivious to his surroundings. Focused on only one thing. Ahead of him, Liam drove to the bar, which was close by, found a parking space and waited.

***

Tonnick was in a taxi, five minutes out from his fiancé's house and again thought the same thought he had had many times in taxis. If only she was a live-in fiancé. There had been many discussions about that.

They were living together in every way, apart from under the same roof. She was adamant… *only if and when we marry*. The convenience would not sway her, nor would the cost-saving of giving up her apartment. *Who said it's me who has to give up my home!?* was the response, even though she flat shared.

Tonnick thought that maybe she liked the conversation and socialising with her flatmates. Could it be because she feared loneliness when he was giving his all to police work? Oh my God. How would it work when they were married? Tonnick figured he only had a few more years before he could retire. He would make it work, whatever was put in front of him.

**

The BMW cruised past about five minutes later. Liam was just starting to think, *what if he goes straight home?* Then he remembered. This alcoholic was a man of routine. Get the bottles. Go to the bar. Go home. Liam's plan hinged on this routine.

Chambers had parked somewhere behind him, meaning he would have to walk past Liam's SUV. A short while later, Liam heard the footsteps approaching.

He glanced around and realised he had cut the engine but had left the lights on. Swiftly, he reached out and turned the knob to switch them off. Had Chambers seen? The footsteps grew louder, measured, firm, in control. Liam slid down in the seat, almost trying to ball himself up in the foetal position. The footsteps were very loud now, right next to the car, and then... they stopped. Liam froze, eyes closed, waiting for the tap on the window. Then he heard the lighter, followed by a cough as the first draw was inhaled. The footsteps again, the sound lessening as Chambers walked away, cigarette in hand.

Liam exhaled slowly. His plan was still on track.

**

Graham Tonnick and his fiancé were at the restaurant. He opened the door to let her in. He thought, *who said chivalry was dead*? Tonnick was a firm believer that good manners cost nothing, but he was also aware that there was a feeling in some of the younger generation that opening doors etc. was somehow 'sexist' and women were equal to men and such actions as opening the door was almost an insult to that equality. He was pleased he did not belong to that generation.

They were shown to the table, and the menus were passed over. A couple of drinks were ordered and at last, they could relax together.

Gemma spoke first. 'What are you working on today?'

She had a small idea of how the investigations worked and thought… new job every morning.

'Same as yesterday actually, that body that was found on the school playing fields. We have a couple of leads so it's a case of following up. There's some CCTV footage so maybe we can tie everything together. Her boyfriend has 'disappeared' which could point to something.'

Tonnick was aware he was talking to a civilian about an active case. Have to be careful. He kicked himself for saying 'her' and 'boyfriend' instead of 'the victim' and 'partner'.

Gemma warmed to it. 'So how do you solve one like that?'

He had just told her about leads, CCTV and the missing partner, but Graham was patient.

'Same as all cases. Follow up on everything, and the evidence should lead to the result. We deal in facts but establishing all the facts is the trick.'

'So… just like Matt Lindon, then?'

Tonnick thought back to the movie and smiled.

He sipped his drink. He wanted to get off specific cases and generalise, but the one specific case in his head would not go away. It was his turn to speak.

'How's life in the world of publishing?'

'Oh wow! You know that author who did the series of *Detective Judith* books? The books where—'

'…where the evidence always seems to unfold right into her lap, and no one else sees it?' Tonnick cut in, smiling.

'Yeah, well anyway, she came into the office this morning with her agent. I did not speak to her but there was a definite air in the office of, maybe, something big. The agent did most of the talking. I gather she's looking for a new publisher, so… well… we will see!'

Tonnick had read one of those books. The main character, Judith Hadd, solved the cases with nauseating speed, often in the face of put-downs and insecurity from her boss.

Tonnick thought for a moment. Hell… that situation seemed to feature in a lot of detective books, and films too. The rebel detective doing it the 'way-to-get-results' way, facing opposition from the superior who always seemed to have an eye on what the powers-that-be above them would think of the 'methods.'

Always the methods, never the results.

Always a thought for the criminal, seldom support for the detective. The detective always seemed to be up against everyone including the boss. But and as it was with these books too, that 'rebel' character always triumphed in the end, and usually with a 'told you so' look on their face. The readership loved it. All her books were bestsellers and the author had a huge following online.

Then, Tonnick remembered one other detail.

In nearly all the detective books and films he had seen or read, the detective, male or female, was single. Either they never married or they were divorced. That too was a bit formulaic. He snorted. Out loud. If only the books followed real life. Real detective work. It simply was not like that in reality. He was staring at the ceiling. He was a detective and he had a fiancé and…

'Are you OK?' Gemma was looking at him in alarm.

Tonnick also looked confused for a second, like he had forgotten where he was. He had forgotten. He saw the food had already arrived. God, how long had he been daydreaming? His head spun back to this reality immediately.

'Sorry, just thinking about reality and detectives. Listen. We need to talk about holidays. I have some ideas for—'

Gemma cut him off. 'I need to see what the lie of the land is first, what with 'you-know-who' dropping in before I start asking for time off. Let's chat about it in a week or two, once I know what's going on.'

And to think, it's always the police force putting job before pleasure… Graham Tonnick smiled the smile of someone who now knew what it was like to be on the receiving end.

There was a silence as both started their meals.

***

With Chambers safely in the bar, Liam grabbed his small bag, got out of his car and walked up the road to find the BMW. It was parked at the top of the street, and Liam noticed, not directly under a streetlight. Perfect. He scouted around quickly to find a place to emerge from when Chambers returned. He had about another twenty minutes. The bar stop-off was not a long one, as Chambers needed to get home before the alcohol kicked in.

He backed into the shadows and got ready to meet Quinton Charles Chambers for the last time.

He did not have long to wait. Barely more than twenty-five minutes had passed and he heard those footsteps again. Not so self-assured this time, a little wobbly and uneven, no doubt caused by the drink. Of course, this was exactly what Liam wanted. He peered out from his secluded spot to see his target moving unsteadily towards the BMW. He had put on the latex gloves and in his hand now was a large pebble. In his pocket, some cord and a gag and in his bag was a plastic pipe, some Gaffa tape, and a funnel. Just the kit for siphoning petrol, maybe?

Liam allowed himself that one digression. Then he focused.

Chambers was almost at his car and was fumbling for the ignition key in his pocket. He retrieved it and moved towards the driver's door. Silently, Liam moved out of the shadows and came up behind Chambers. A quick look round. No one on the street, no cars, it could not have been more perfect. Just as Chambers got the car door open, Liam made his move. The pebble in his hand struck Chambers a blow to the forehead and he sank to the ground like a sack of potatoes.

Swiftly, Liam pulled his ex-boss's hands behind his back and tied them with the cord, then repeated the action with his feet. Liam opened the passenger door, got in, and pulled him over and into the passenger seat, then went round and got in at the driver's side. He started the car. Chambers was groaning until Liam silenced him by securing the gag.

Quinton Chambers was dimly aware of his car moving but… he was not driving it. His breathing was difficult like his nose was blocked, and he did not seem to be able to move his arms or legs. His head hurt, a combination of the blow and the drink. The car came to a stop, and Chambers tried to look round but his eyes were not working either. It was quiet. He tried to talk but no words came out just muffled sounds. Then he heard a sound he did recognise. The unscrewing of a whiskey bottle cap. He brightened up — all was not so bad if he was getting another drink. His face seemed to pull around as if his nose was attached to a lead. Why was his breathing so difficult?

Just as he was trying to work that one out, the first taste of whiskey splashed into his mouth. He had no glass? He did not lift the drink? He swallowed. What's happening? Another splash. He swallowed that one too. Then a lot more, at least a mouthful. Chambers coughed but even that was difficult. Another splash, larger this time. Even in his relaxed state, Chambers had worked out that he was breathing only through his mouth and if his mouth was obstructed by whiskey, he had better swallow it if he wanted to breathe.

Another splash, slightly bigger this time. Chambers managed to swallow it without coughing. Immediately there was another one.

Chambers was in a position he was not used to. He was not in control.

Another slug of whiskey

And another. Chambers swallowed.

And another, bigger again.

He tried to speak but started coughing again as the words he tried to utter met the whiskey coming the other way.

A pause until he had regained regular if rapid breathing.

Another splash, much bigger this time. He had to swallow twice to clear his mouth and breathe again.

Another, same.

Another.

A pause.

Chambers thought the drinking game was over until a lot of whiskey entered his mouth. He had to swallow four times, gulping the spirit down to clear the way to breathe. He sucked in a breath and started to panic. Even in his muddled state, he could see that this was no game. He was bound and helpless and under an unseen assailant's control. Who the hell could it be?

He barely composed himself when another large slug of scotch entered his mouth. Again, he barely managed to clear the airway before he was again gasping for breath.

'Please… let me breathe.' He tried to speak but nothing came.

Another large shot of whiskey. Chambers started to hate whiskey. He swallowed it and immediately there was another one.

Oh my god… he's making me drink the whole bottle. At that thought, Chambers' heart sank — he remembered he had bought two bottles at the off licence.

***

Chambers was now in a drink-induced stupor, unable to talk or move. He was breathing with difficulty.

He had been made to drink two full bottles of whiskey. That was thirty minutes ago. The pipe had been removed from his mouth, and his mouth and nose unblocked once the Gaffa tape had been removed. All his restraints had also been removed, but Chambers did not know that. He was completely out of it.

Liam had chosen Gaffa Tape because he had read somewhere that it was supposed to leave no adhesive residue, unlike duct tape. He wanted no evidence for the police to go on.

Chambers' phone had rung while they waited the thirty minutes, but no one answered. It was in Chambers' pocket and Liam was in no mood to even see who it was.

***

They had finished the meal on a high note, talking about the future beyond the author coming to her office, and now, relaxed and happy, they were heading back to Graham's apartment in a taxi. Gemma had already indicated that she was staying over, no if's and but's. She had also said she wanted to talk about marriage… they had been engaged long enough, she thought.

But not tonight. They'd had a great evening and maybe drunk a little too much — she was glad that Graham had not brought his car. No… tonight was just about the here and now, the two of them. Everything else was forgotten. She might be open to discussing that holiday, though. After thinking, she realised she had not been away for… months, over a year, in fact.

Graham perked up at the plan for the evening. Holidays, she 'n' me time, and marriage talk to come. What could be better? He leaned over and kissed her cheek. She smiled, shyly, looking at the taxi driver who was staring straight ahead. 'Not in the taxi', she mouthed. Graham pretended to look hurt, then he too smiled as she squeezed his hand.

They finally arrived and she got out as Graham Tonnick paid the cab. Yup… chivalry was still alive in his world. She had offered to pay but he was insistent. They went in and took the lift to the fourth floor and his apartment, an older but more spacious unit with higher ceilings and a separate kitchen unlike some of the more modern offerings, where the developer had worked out that he could get away with one room covering kitchen, dining and sitting, all under the guise of *modern open-plan living,* and save a shedload of building costs in the process.

He closed the door, and immediately she wanted to know about the holiday plans. OK, he thought. Holiday plans first. Then just-the-two-of-us time in the bedroom! He got out some brochures and the notes he had made and sat down with her on the sofa.

'Wait. What about some drinks?' She was up and pouring a couple of shots, as he laid the paperwork out on the coffee table.

***

Liam looked around outside the car. The night was still and dark — no full moon at the start of the month. He had planned that too, of course. It was silent and deserted. In the passenger seat, Quinton Chambers was having a lot of

66

trouble breathing. His eyes were closed, his arms hanging limply at his side. Liam had packed away the pipe, the funnel, the Gaffa tape and the cord. Nothing left in the car except Chambers and him… and two empty whiskey bottles. All Liam had to do now was get the car to the start of its final resting place, and that meant a drive over to the Sunnyhills Estate. He settled back into the driver's seat and started the engine. A low purring came from under the bonnet, as he put it into gear and moved forward. *Drive carefully, do not attract attention*. He set off for the Sunnyhills Estate, glancing at the dashboard clock… it was 2010.

***

Graham and Gemma were finished with holidays. They had finished the drinks and she had suggested that it was time to turn in. He let her use the bathroom first, while he washed up the two glasses. She had nightwear at his place but when she called from the living room door that she was finished he turned and was startled — she was wearing just a pair of socks, and a smile.

'Hurry up, I'm getting cold.'

He was about to say 'put your pyjamas on then', but realised what an idiot he would be if he did, and instead switched off the lights and quickly made his way to the bathroom.

***

Liam had arrived at his chosen destination.

He positioned the car at the crest and carefully aimed it facing down the hill. The road here was straight and level… nothing to make a car pull to either side, all the way to the bottom of the hill. It was quite steep, and ever since the new access to Sunnyhills' had been constructed it was not used very much. That suited Liam. He put the handbrake on, got out, went round to the passenger side and opened the door. Chambers was immobile. Liam thought for a minute he was dead, but as he started to push the drunken man over into the driver's seat, Chambers' arms flailed weakly. With his legs in the driver's foot-well, Liam gave Chambers a hard shove and the body moved over to the driver's side. Next, he closed the passenger door and came back to where Chambers was now sprawled, straightened him up and pushed him back into the driver's seat.

Liam stopped and listened. No car around the corner, coming up the hill. It was all quiet on the road behind the car, too.

As he reached to put the car into gear. Chamber's phone broke the silence, making Liam jump. The phone sounded so loud; he had to stop it. He put the car back into neutral, rummaged in Chambers' pocket for the phone, and pulled it out

The caller was Jocelyn. Liam had to think who it was. Then he remembered. Her name was Jocelyn but everyone called her Lyn.

Lyn Chambers.

Liam dropped the phone, suddenly conscious of what he was about to do to this woman's husband. Lyn was thinking he was late in the bar, meeting his friends, but in reality he was in a state in the car, and about to meet his end.

The call rang off. Liam noticed there had been four missed calls.

His guilt passed as quickly as it had come, replaced by steely resolve. She had given Chambers the ultimatum only because of money. She did not care about Nicholas, as he was, his parents or anything. She only cared about herself.

Swiftly, he checked the wheel alignment — pointing dead centre of the road, put the car into gear, placed his foot on the footbrake and released the handbrake. A quick last check at Chambers, sat bolt upright in the car, no seatbelt on and facing straight ahead.

Liam stepped back, out of the car, releasing the footbrake and closing the driver's door as the BMW slowly moved off, gathering speed.

The car accelerated rapidly, keeping its straight line. It was aimed at the safety barrier at the bottom of the hill. Liam watched, spellbound. Had his plan worked? Moments later the BMW reached the bottom of the hill, drove onto the run-off area then crashed into, and through the barrier and was suddenly lost from view into the night.

For the briefest of intervals, there was no sound.

Then there was the sound of an almighty impact and the screech of twisting metal and exploding glass. Liam did not wait to see the result. He calmly walked back to the outcrop of bushes and retrieved the bicycle he had hidden there earlier. He switched on the cycle lights and put on the helmet he had hidden with the bike, and then with a last look round, he slung the rucksack over his shoulder and pedalled off in the direction of the city.

***

It was the middle of the night and all was peaceful. Graham Tonnick was in the bathroom, splashing some water on his face. He had relaxed again, after the exertions of earlier. Gemma was sound asleep.

He walked to the kitchen to get a drink. The iced water revived and refreshed him, same as the splashed water on his face. He savoured the moment. The cool water. The stillness of the night. His fiancé tucked up in his bed. He allowed himself a happy smile, then walked back to the bedroom.

***

Liam had made good time and was almost back at his car. He slowed to get his breath back. He briefly imagined Chambers trying to cycle that distance with a skin full of whiskey. Ahh… he was gone now so no need to dwell on it.

He arrived at his SUV and looked around. Just a couple, walking along the opposite side, and a car racing too fast along the road. An image of a similar scenario crossed his mind, one he had played out all too often, with Chambers racing to his 'appointment' and killing Liam's parents.

But now I have avenged you, Mum and Dad.

He popped open the back of the SUV and loaded the bike in quickly, removed the cycle helmet and rucksack and tossed them in next to the bike, before closing the tailgate.

Job done.

Chapter 5

The dark, still of the night of earlier had been replaced by headlights of stationary vehicles, flashing lights of the emergency services, flashes of the cameras and the noise of an ongoing investigation.

'He looked so relaxed. It's hard to believe he could have been unless he was unconscious.' Max was talking to a police officer at the scene.

They were standing close to the overturned car. The driver, who was through the windscreen, was dead. That had been confirmed. The car was a wreck, but the airbags had all gone off correctly. The driver looked undamaged except for a cut to his head. He smelled strongly of alcohol.

The BMW was at the bottom of a long hill, with a road above it that ended at a run-off area with safety barriers, and gentle right-hand turn, or if you chose to go straight on, as the BMW had, a hill that sloped steeply down and away from the road above with some sizable trees at the bottom.

It was near to the Sunnyhills Estate.

A fat lot of good that barrier did he thought. He glanced up and the investigation taking place in the run-off area above.

'Better get the municipality to check it for strength, etc.'

Max reviewed what they knew of the driver. The deceased was a well-known businessman in the area, a major employer and a supporter of local charities and events. His wife was also into the community, sitting on various residents' and causes committees.

Max thought of how it had ended for the driver, the car careering down the hill, the driver not in control, the failure to slow or turn, the thud of the car as it burst through the barrier. The airbags deploying, uselessly it seemed. Then the silence as the car left the road and flew, in a graceful arc towards the trees at the bottom of the hill. That final sound of metal and glass on wood as a hundred-year-old hardwood tree brought the car to a dead stop. Then a secondary crunch as the car fell to the ground and rolled over.

'At least there was no fire,' the officer was trying to find something to say, 'and he was alone. There was no one else involved.'

The medics began recovering the body, and Max started to work the scene. Quinton Charles Chambers had more than most to live for, so why let this happen?

In the car, Max found two empty whiskey bottles. That, maybe, would explain the breath. Max wondered what it would be like to drink that much. He shuddered. This kind of drinking was from a different world to his.

He turned… and there was Lucy.

He suppressed thoughts of loose undies and brightened up immediately.

'Yes… you have me.'

Max wasn't complaining.

'Raymond is at a function out of town, so here I am. What have we got?'

Lucy was not one for too much small talk.

'Car left the road up there.' He waved vaguely back up towards the road. 'And hit this tree with a drunk driver at the wheel. It cost him his life.'

Lucy was already looking at the car.

'His airbags all worked correctly but that would not have saved him in this case.'

'How so?' Max was keen to engage in any conversation with Lucy.

'Well… when an impact occurs, the bags deploy fully in around thirty milliseconds, just enough time to catch the inertia of the passenger moving forwards. That's assuming he was wearing his seatbelt, but in this case, he was not.'

Lucy had already spoken to the medic who confirmed that Chambers was through the front windshield.

'Even so, surely the bags would have helped?' Max posed the question to keep the conversation going.

'Maybe for the barrier strike… there was enough resistance when the car struck the barrier to deploy the airbags,' Lucy spoke as one who knew, 'but they don't stay inflated forever, in fact, they start to collapse again almost immediately, to aid rescue and evacuation, and to prevent suffocation. They would be non-existent by the time the second collision happened.'

'The second collision?' Max was too preoccupied talking to Lucy but recovered quickly 'Oh. You mean… the tree?'

'Obviously the tree. The car was airborne for more than enough time for those airbags to deflate. He hit the tree as if he had been sitting on the bonnet. Boom! Game over.'

Max had already given the BMW the once-over. Although it was a mangled wreck now, the car was almost new. Lucy noted that the tyres were all good. The brakes would be checked once the car was recovered from its resting place.

'Not so much to find here,' he said. 'We are trying to retrace his steps up to this point. You will be checking the blood alcohol, right?'

She looked at the empty whiskey bottles which were now in an evidence bag.

'Yep, the post-mortem will, and of course, we will look at any other injuries, just in case there is more to it.'

They made their way back up the hill and returned to the road and the run-off area.

'Did you notice?'

Lucy was looking at the broken barrier.

'What?'

'No skid marks. At all. Not even just in front of the barrier. He was in no position to do anything about this incident.'

Lucy chose her words carefully. She was clicking away with her camera and asked Max to help with the tape measure.

'Certainly, hit the barrier with force. See here... the impact has uprooted the post.'

They looked at the post, resting almost horizontally. She recorded it all. Then she videoed the scene too.

At that moment, a crew of municipality workers arrived.

She had all the photographs, and Lucy had taken all the measurements she needed. 'Just check it over for now,' Max spoke over to the group. The area had already been cordoned off with police tape.

He was standing near to the next barrier post and idly put his hand on it.

It gave way, unbalancing him.

Max pulled back. 'What the... ? Hey guys. This post is loose. What's going on?'

One of the municipality workers walked over, as did Lucy.

He rocked the post, which had little resistance. 'Weird. The rail should keep it from moving that much, even if it was completely unsupported.' He rocked it again.

With a crash, a section of the safety rail fell to the ground.

They all stared in silence. Finally, the municipality guy spoke, 'That's not supposed to happen.'

'Really?' Lucy was a little sarcastic but was already looking at the rails.

'Are these the standard bolts for this barrier rail?' She held up a short, stubby fastener.

'Err… no. Where did you find that?' The worker took it and looked.

'Well… here,' she said, pointing. 'In the next barrier rail.'

'OK… how did you undo that so fast? Where's the nut?'

'Exactly. Where's the nut?' Lucy was looking more serious. More… investigative.

'It doesn't have a nut and even if it did, it would not tighten on this bolt… the bolts' too short.'

Max started to get a bad feeling. Do we still say this was an accident?

One of the other workers came over.

'Five of the support posts have been loosened. I mean… the ground has been dug away to the concrete base block, and underneath it. See here.' He led them over. 'You can't see it immediately because the undergrowth was pulled back over the post. He moved the vegetation out of the way, 'But look, someone went to a lot of trouble to dig this out and hide it.'

A shout came from one of the other workers. 'Hey! Look at this.'

They hurried over. He was holding a similar bolt to the one Lucy found earlier.

'All the bolts in this section have been replaced, and none of them have nuts. There's nothing really holding this barrier together.'

Lucy photographed it all, then took a stubby bolt for evidence, and asked for a correct bolt for comparison. The correct bolt was produced and it was over twice as long as the bolt they had recovered from the broken barrier. It had a nut and washers too.

'I think we have more than an accident here,' Lucy surmised.

Max glanced at Lucy, who was looking at him. He nodded his head. Doctored barrier bolts. Loosened posts. Suspiciously unconscious driver. Unbelievable amounts of alcohol. She was right. This was no accident. This was increasingly looking like a deliberate act.

He reached for his mobile to update his boss but before he could make the call, the municipality worker was calling him again.

'Over here. Don't know if it's relevant?'

He walked over to the line of useless barriers again.

'See here?' he shone the torch. 'There. And there.' He moved the torch. 'That's on every loosened barrier section.'

Max stared, screwed his eyes up, and looked again. He said nothing. Lucy photographed the barrier sections, then set about dusting the barrier for any prints. When she had completed the first one, she asked the worker to carefully remove it for the lab.

Max made the call.

***

78

Tonnick had just got into bed and was settling down when his phone lit up and buzzed. He'd had the sense to put it on silent, so as not to wake his fiancé, but he still jumped when the light and sound cut through the dark and quiet.

People do not ring for fun, he reasoned. It must be important.

'Tonnick.'

'Boss, we have what seems like a suspicious death here over near Sunnyhills. Yes. Fairly near to the Bailey house. Yes. Sorry to disturb you but there's an element of this one I think you are going to want to see. If I tell you, it probably re-opens the Susan Bailey case, you can understand why I called.'

Tonnick was intrigued. 'OK, I can meet you. Where?'

'In the lab.'

***

Forty minutes later, D.I. Graham Tonnick got out of the taxi and entered the police compound. He made his way to forensics where Lucy greeted him and showed him through to an examination table.

Tonnick stared. On it were some short, stubby bolts, and a section of safety barrier.

Tonnick glanced briefly, then his eyes were drawn to the spotlight, illuminating a part of the safety barrier. Tonnick looked again, closer this time.

On the barrier was written something, not particularly clearly, but now he had seen it, it was like a beacon glaring out at them.

Tonnick and Max had seen something similar before, but this time it was the capital letter 'A' inside a circle.

'Oh. My. God!'

Tonnick let out a long sigh. Max looked at Lucy, then back to his boss.

'I called up the Bailey case documents.'

'Yes... thanks. OK, we need to revisit that case and cross-reference against this one. There is a connection, a link. More than those similar characters, I mean. This is undoubtedly more than just accidental death.'

***

Liam's plan was working.

Two down, and just enough for the police to think maybe 'something' but without anything coming back to him. There was no apparent link between the two victims — well... only from fifteen years earlier, and would they look back that far? And with the name change, too? Unlikely.

He had already 'lost' the large pebble in the river that ran past the city. One pebble taken from a bend in the river where there was a 'beach' of hundreds of similar stones. One pebble, like so many others. The latex Gloves burned easily, as did the cord. He waited until the brazier got hot before dropping in the plastic tubing, the funnel and the used Gaffa tape. All he had left was the unused tape roll, and some nuts and washers. Nothing linking those items to the two murders.

He sat in his kitchen with the brazier fire burning outside and began to write his first note.

***

Tonnick was back in his apartment, but his head was racing. He had only gone back to wash and change and to tell Gemma that something had come up and he had to go in early. She mumbled something, only half-awake, and he left quietly.

As he set out for the office in the taxi, he thought back to the pleasant evening, the glimpse of normality.

Then he remembered… they never did get around to talking about marriage.

***

Through his earlier observations, he already knew much about the detective's team, but the next part of Liam's mission was to gather information about the cases — his cases and for this, he had an idea. He would go out tonight, to one particular bar, and see if he could engineer a meeting with one particular lady.

Yes, he was on a mission but he was warming to this mission and found a sense of satisfaction that the first two parts of his plan had gone smoothly. He was in control. He needed to stay in control, and that included the need for information. Information on how the police were responding. Up until now, there was no real media interest, but once he sent the note, that would all change.

He relaxed for the rest of the day, a Saturday, then busied himself on getting ready to go out. Though he would never admit it himself, he scrubbed up pretty good. When he made the effort, some would describe him as handsome. He was still young, mid-twenties… in his prime, really.

And tonight… tonight he was 'on the pull'.

***

Tonnick had already been at the station for several hours when he pulled the team together and they had spent their Saturday poring over the two cases. A stay-at-home single forty-something, and a married businessman. Max joked that the two could easily have been having an affair, or even long-term lovers. The team smiled. A single lady. A happily married, successful businessman with a family. He had everything to offer, she had nothing, apart from the 'obvious' in those situations.

'Yeah well, of course, check that.' Tonnick wanted to cover every possibility.

Geoff revealed the events that led up to Chambers' appointment with the tree. He had retraced Chambers' movements, and after identifying it from the carrier bag that had contained the whiskey, had been to the off-licence. He discovered that Chambers was a regular, every Friday night, two or three bottles of spirits, sometimes wine as well. He was a good customer. The shop owner confirmed he purchased two bottles of single malt whiskey, and that he was alone in the shop, at least. He said Chambers had told them he was heading home for a weekend with the family, but that another assistant had told him that in fact, he stopped off at the 'Cheers' bar for a couple with his drinking buddies before going home.

Tonnick remembered the eighties sitcom and wondered how many 'Cheers' bars it had spawned. He imagined Quinton Chambers as a drinker in the TV bar. He would fit right in sat next to Dr Crane and 'chewing the fat' with Sam Malone and Diane Chambers. He smiled. Small World. Old 'Mayday' Malone was a recovering alcoholic, he thought, and Diane could be his daughter in the actual sitcom with a name like that.

'I went to the bar, too,' Geoff was continuing.

Tonnick shuddered, his image of the TV bar characters messed up with his detective in the cast.

'It was named after a TV show, would you believe? It's a bit run-down. The landlord told me that Chambers went there religiously every Friday evening and spent about thirty minutes, had two or three drinks then left again before the other patron's drinking got too much. The barman said the place was known as a haunt for heavy drinkers. He knew Chambers well and said he was not one for excessive drinking, just a few gin 'n' tonics, nothing else. He never came in with anyone, he confirmed that too.'

'Not a heavy drinker?' Mandi was aghast. 'Just the two bottles of scotch, only.'

'Has Sue Bailey ever been there? Just check to see if there IS some link. Get back there with a photo.'

'We can do that,' Max cut in, 'but I'm guessing she has not. We checked out her place after she died. No alcohol in the house at all. It was negative in the post-mortem, too. Seems our Susan was teetotal.'

'She's more upmarket than that place anyway,' Geoff added, 'She was dating that banker fellow and they went to charity balls and fine restaurants, not seedy bars full of heavy drinkers.

'OK, so we have a solo drunkard and a lady who likes electrifying TV shows.' The team groaned. 'At the moment, the only thing linking them is that 'A' in the circle that we found by the roadside, and the 'J' we found over at her place. There's got to be more.'

The senior detective was his usual thorough self.

'Full background checks on the pair of them, please. Take it right back. Did they grow up together as kids? There's something but we haven't found it yet.'

Chapter 6

Liam was out on the town and had made his way to the Bistro Wine Bar. It was already buzzing with happy people relaxing after a hard week of work, making the most of their Saturday evening.

Some football players were at the bar, being loud in a 'look at us' way, exuding a confidence that comes with wealth. Over in the corner was a group of girls out to celebrate an imminent marriage, the bride-to-be with the pre-requisite white bride sash, the 'virgin' hat and wearing a memento shirt that had already been signed by several male drinkers in the bar. Liam looked further into the room, but his target was not yet there. Elsewhere were suited groups of what looked like businessmen, with either wives, friends or, a few anyway, trophy girlfriends.

He went to the quiet end of the room, ordered a drink and sat on one of the stools facing the bar. How was he going to engineer the meeting and hopefully, more? For a start, he did not even know that she would turn up that evening. Liam looked around. He was no confident footballer. Maybe that was her type? He could pretend to be another one of those businessmen, perhaps. Or a business owner. Yes... he could model himself on Quinton

Chambers. He knew enough about him. Not the excessive drinking, of course. Got to stay focused.

The other stools filled up as he stared at the myriad bottles of spirits that lined the back wall behind the bar. First, he looked for drinks he knew. Then he looked for different single malts. He fancied one day, just sitting in a bar like this and sampling several different single malts.

'Excuse me.' The girl's voice came from behind his chair. 'Could I get to the drinks?'

Liam turned on the chair and looked behind and then down a little bit.

And there she was… his target.

OMG, she had come to him. He glanced along the bar, towards the gaggle of footballers.

'Not my type at all.' She saw him looking and cut in, 'My friends are all down there now, but I am more the library type!'

'So, these drinks… is it two… or three?' Liam picked up on her opening sentence.

'Ha-ha well… for me just one, though I am ordering for them, too. You're nearer. Can you order me a *Cuba libre*?' She had some money in her hand.

Liam leant forward and caught the attention of the barkeeper. He ordered, and another one for himself then turned back.

'What about the friends? If you are on ordering duty!'

'I seem to have that role a lot.'

She laughed, but Liam noticed she did not order any more drinks. Just then, her phone rang.

Liam turned back, and the drinks arrived. He paid.

She was still on the phone as he passed her drink over. She took it and the first sip.

'Cheers!' he said, raising his glass.

She clinked hers with his and mouthed, 'Cheers!'

The call ended.

'Work. Never get off the clock.'

She looked around to the footballer party, where her friends seemed to have melted into invisibility within the group.

'You need to go. Cheers! That one's on me.' Liam smiled again.

'No, no mister. I'll have to stay a little bit now, at least 'til we have another. They're OK over there and it's not my thing.' She was sipping quickly.

'OK in that case, here you go.'

He jumped off the stool and walked around behind her.

'W-what? Oh, I see, well... err, OK, go on then. Not that I would usually but I'm tired. Busy week.'

She sat down.

Liam noticed she was small and slim. Pretty, though. Much better-looking up close, and in casual clothes. They made introductions, with Liam telling her his name was Mike Kallin, and he went down the 'business-owner-relaxing-after-a-hard-week' route, but gauging her reaction, said this was not his scene and he preferred nice restaurants.

'WOW! You are young to be a big company owner!'

'It's not a big company!'

'So… these restaurants. Is that where you take your wife?'

She spoke with outward courage that only swiftly drunk alcohol could bring. She was twirling her hair with her fingers and giggling. Liam got it. She was flirting with him.

'No… No wife yet. Or girlfriend. I'm married to the business, but I'm going to ease up soon.'

Liam did not want to put her off by sounding like a workaholic, but she was already smiling at that last sentence.

Twenty minutes later and they were chatting and laughing like two old friends. One of the other girls came over just as they were ordering another round.

'Oh, Sam… this is Mike. He very kindly bought me a drink, and well… looked after me while you were feeling up the football stars!'

They all laughed.

'Well… we gave up waiting for the drinks from you and one of the boys got us some champagne. Then just now, I remembered we had lost you.'

Sam was smiling, probably at the thought of the champagne, Liam guessed.

'Look… if you need to go… ' Liam tried to sound genuine, but he hoped she did not take him up on that.

'Well, I just came to check you were OK.'

'I. Am. OK. Mike and I are putting the world to rights. I'm going to stay here a while longer.' She spoke precisely, as she took another drink. 'Cheers!'

'OK… I will come to get you later. Nice to meet you, Mike.'

Sam nodded then went back through the now crowded bar to the other group. Liam noticed that one or two of the other girls craning over the crowd of drinkers to see who he was. He recognised the code about *coming to get you*. This was to make sure she was not being led off somewhere if under the influence of the drink.

They chatted for another hour, commenting on the wedding party, footballers, anything and everything, then Sam came over again. 'We are going. Come on… time for food.'

'Not with those bloody footballers?'

'Nope. They are going somewhere else now. It's just us.'

They both stood up.

'OK, Mike. I'm going. Duty calls. Food-eating duty. I would invite you to join us but one guy and seven girls? No, you are not ready to meet this lot yet. They would tear you apart and I would not be able to defend you!'

She was still giggling.

'Another time, Mike.' That from Sam.

She said 'goodbye' and turned to go. Liam bid farewell and then turned back in his seat.

'Don't think you get off that lightly, mister!'

A hand came past him, a small feminine hand. In it was a business card. Liam glanced at the details.

'Call me, Mike. Soon.'

He turned. She had already walked away, but she turned back too, a big smile on her face.

Liam met it with an even bigger one of his own.

He gave it ten minutes to be sure they had left, then finished his drink and left the bar room. Another piece of the jigsaw accomplished, rather fortuitously in this case, but who's counting? Liam got to the outer door and glanced both ways up the street before striding purposefully outside and hailing a cab. The traffic was Saturday night busy, and it was now raining, making those colourful reflections from the night-time lights on the wet asphalt. He sat back in the taxi and was home thirty minutes later.

Once he had changed out of his bar clothes, washed his hands and face and put on something more comfortable, he went to the coffee table and picked up the pad. He read the note in his head and imagined the detective reading it out loud. Yes. It was good. Enough to stir them up but give nothing away.

He put on some latex gloves and drew out a piece of heavy vellum from the middle of an expensive pack he kept near his home printer. Using a cheap, mass-produced black ink gel-pen he had picked up from a stationer in town, he carefully wrote the note out again and printed a name at the bottom, this time resting his arm on a piece of kitchen roll, to avoid leaving any trace of... him on the paper. Then he carefully folded the note and placed it into a white envelope, one of a pack he had bought from that same stationer's store. He used a tissue, dampened with tap water to moisten the glue before carefully sticking it down. There. Once again, job done.

Now he picked up the business card he had received earlier in the bar. It seemed so long ago now, but Liam remembered every detail. The flirting. The scent of her perfume. The petite frame. The Cuba Libres. He wondered how the food was going. He imagined seven boisterous women in a downtown restaurant. The card had the usual information: Name. Job title. Mobile number. There was also an office address, which Liam already knew, and the landline number. He smiled again. It could not have been more perfect. He thought back to his surveillance of the work location and seeing her before, in work clothes. But that was from a distance. Last night was up-close and personal.

He reached for his mobile and made a call. The girl's voice at the other end was familiar.

'Good evening, this is Lu... how can I help?'

Liam smiled. She sounded all business-like but he knew the voice. He looked down at a paper on his table.

'Good evening, Lu. Nice to hear your voice again. This is Liam. Get me one chicken chow mein, one sweet 'n' sour chicken and one duck and pineapple. Oh... and one fried rice.'

The girl read it back then. 'Ahh... Mr Liam, at home, right? Liam confirmed. 'It's OK, we know your address.'

She told him the cost and said it would be about forty minutes because the traffic was busy on Saturday and it was raining. Liam smiled, remembering those watercolour effects on the road surface.

'No problems. Thanks. Bye.'

He looked at the business card again. That call… he would make that call tomorrow.

Chapter 7

The next day, Geoff set off to the Cheers Bar again, armed with a photo of Susan Bailey. The rest of the team was going over what they knew about Chambers.

'Quinton Charles Chambers, forty-five. Married to Davina Jocelyn Chambers, she's known as Lyn... two children, Robert age eleven and Mia, who's just coming up to nine.'

'He owns the Wilkins factory over on Broad Street. It's successful and Chambers lived a very good life. He had a very large, and I might add expensive house near to the river. He had everything going for him. Successful business. Family life and kids. Plenty of money. Flash car and she has one too. Everything seems to be bought and paid for. No debt we can see at the moment. We are checking on bank accounts for any hidden loans, mortgages and investments as well, in case there is blackmail involved. The elder kid is at an expensive private boarding school.'

Max tapped keys to see if they had anything on Quinton Charles Chambers in criminal records.

'Oh My God! Our Mr Chambers has quite a record. A parking ticket. Another parking ticket. Speeding, oops… four times and fines.'

The others were switching off, thinking there was nothing.

'Then arrested for driving under the influence of alcohol, so he has been drunk before. Oh, plus… manslaughter and jail time.'

The D.I and the others came over to the terminal, surprised, especially about the manslaughter.

'And yes… there it is… Quinton Charles Chambers was involved in an affair.'

Now they were focused on this new information. They learnt that Quinton Chambers, a rich factory owner, a married man and pillar of the local community, was having a secret affair with a local school teacher and had been for years.

They also read the account of the manslaughter of two innocent pedestrians, as he was driving to meet his affair while under the influence. There was a photo of younger-looking Chambers in custody, and a reference to a young teacher named Madeline Torrey. The paper mentioned a son, orphaned by the incident but there was no other detail.

Tonnick went back to his office and picked up the phone to get that case file from the archives.

***

Geoff had reached the Cheers Bar and once again was talking with the bar staff. There were a couple of customers having their morning coffee.

He showed the photo. 'Ever see this lady in here?'

'Well, I haven't but I'm new. Jack?' He called the bar owner as Geoff was showing the photo to the other staff. Blank faces all round.

Jack came over. 'Let me see… '

'We were wondering if she's ever been here.'

'Well, I'll be!' exclaimed Jack, 'Yes. Yes, she has!'

Geoff stared at him.

'You are telling me that you have seen Susan Bailey. In here. With Quinton Chambers?'

'One. It's Quinton Charles Chambers. Never forget. And two… sorry I was mistaken. I thought it was someone else in that photo, not this 'Susan Bailey'… here… let me see it again.'

Jack stared at it for some time.

'No… I was right. It is who I thought it was. When was the photo taken? She's changed a bit.'

Geoff looked confused. 'Well, this photo was recent, and I'm hoping you are going to tell me she was in here last month or maybe the month before.'

Jack laughed. 'You must be joking! Your girl here… she's not been in this bar for the best part of fifteen years. What's she up to now?'

'Oh.' Geoff looked deflated. 'There goes the lead then. Susan? Did you see in the papers about that electrocution in the bath up on Sunnyhills?'

The bar owner nodded.

'That was Ms Bailey.'

Jack was still thinking back.

'Oh, that's a sad tale. It's odd, anyway. That name? Susan Bailey, you say? But the person I'm thinking of wasn't called Susan. Her name was Madeline.'

***

Tonnick came out of his office

'So now… Susan Bailey. Mandi, do you want to fill us in with those details?'

He sat down to listen.

'Susan Bailey. No middle name. Forty-two years old. Unmarried. She lived on the Sunnyhills Estate, and she moved there just under eighteen months ago. She does not appear to have any job that we can identify, anyway. We are checking for family money or some other income stream. She was dating the banker Charles Dutworth for about a year but it finished three months ago. What is strange is… there is not much detail about Susan's early life. She was an Administrator for an engineering firm over in Druton but gave that job up when she moved here. She started that job about twelve years ago. Before that though, I can't find anything at all.'

'You mean she was created, not born?' Tonnick was exasperated. 'Births, marriages and deaths? Parents? Schooling?'

Mandi was ready for the response.

'Already searched. A blank. I checked with the Druton firm, too. No information to give apart from what we already have.'

'OK so… no link so far. Keep digging.'

The case file for Chambers' car incident came up. Max immediately started to look through the box. After ten minutes, he stuck his head around Tonnick's door.

'Two things from the Chambers case. One… yes… he *was* having an affair. Some teacher named Madeline, it says here. That was why he was speeding. To meet her. Two. He got an incredibly light sentence. It caused some rumblings back then. His lawyers did some kind of deal with the judge, the notes say but that's a suspicion, not a fact.'

Tonnick thought. 'Drink driving, dangerous driving, death while under the influence? He could have got fourteen years.'

'It went down as accidental death, and… try sixteen months.'

Max was visibly disgusted.

'And let me guess… out in somewhere around half of that?'

Tonnick knew the system.

'Eleven and a half actually. Not even a year. For two dead. Money talks.'

Max's voice belied the injustice he felt, even though he had no evidence that any deal has been done with the judge.

'Chambers was a pillar of the community, large employer, no previous, admitted everything to avoid dragging it out, and was remorseful in court, though he did cite stress at work trying to keep the business afloat and employ the hundred and fifty people there who depended on him, and home pressures at the time, as mitigation. It was never really explored. He did rehab and AA courses and of course, the civil case put a lot of money into the family of the deceased.'

'So… who were the beneficiaries, this… family of the deceased?'

Tonnick was joining the dots.

'Not many. There was a son, Nicholas, an only child. Would have been around ten years old at the time, according to the notes in the case file. Following the loss of his parents, he was cared for by Rosemary Hill, the sister of James Roberts, who was Nicholas' father. His mother Alice Roberts was also an only child. The money was put into trust for him and available after the age of twenty-five. There was a sum for Rosemary, too… maybe it's why she jumped in as the caregiver.'

'Or maybe because she was compassionate and was the only family the little boy had left.'

Tonnick was abrupt.

'Sorry, I didn't mean to imply that… '

'It sounded like you did. Not everything is money-driven.'

Tonnick cut him off with a glance, and Max rushed to finish the summary of Chambers.

'His trust fund has grown to about five million now. That's equivalent to around a hundred thousand per year, with a life span to seventy-five and assuming no interest.'

Max finished, and there was lull in conversation as everyone digested the latest information. Tonnick broke the silence.

'Right, Max... get those details of the car crash and Chambers' affair up on the board and also the trust fund for the son.'

He looked around at the team. Almost incomprehensible driving, with excessive alcohol plus the doctored fencing and posts plus the letter in the circle at the scene — same as the other one. It looked like these cases were no accidents. It looked like murder.

***

After his activity of the previous night, Liam had got up late, enjoying the sun at the window, and feeling on top of his game. ALL the pieces were currently in place. He would be making the call later this morning, and hopefully, starting to get a little information.

He swung lazily out of bed and went to put the kettle on before making his way to the bathroom.

***

Geoff had got back to the station and was filling in the team, but he was being interrupted.

'Wait so… yes she was with him, but no, not last month, it might have been fifteen years ago anyway, so maybe it's not the same girl?'

Max was trying to summarise it in one sentence.

Geoff corrected him. 'No. That's not quite right. Jack, the landlord, was sure he recognised the photo and he said she was with Chambers, but it was a long time back, not recently, and he thinks we have the name wrong.'

'So, nothing to link them now.' Tonnick was impatient. 'I'm guessing Chambers knew a lot of people in the area, his charity work, what was that phrase, *a pillar of the community*, wasn't it, Mandi?' She nodded. 'Maybe a charity function or maybe she was an ex-employee.'

'Who was an *ex-employee*?' Mandi asked in the momentary silence.

'Susan was. Susan Bailey. Who the hell are we talking about? What do you mean, who?'

Tonnick was looking at her with despair again.

'Because we have no record of Susan Bailey back then, remember? She's a ghost.' Mandi pinpointed what they had overlooked.

'OK. An easy way to check would be to just go to the factory. It's back open again now, right? Geoff… write up your notes on the case board.'

***

Max and Mandi arrived at the factory. She was still getting used to field enquiries, so Tonnick sent her along to observe.

They signed in at reception and were shown to the meeting room. After five minutes, June Davis, HR manager, entered.

'Ms Davis, thanks for sparing the time. We are following up on two recent deaths, one of them being Mr Chambers, and we hope you can maybe help with one avenue of enquiry we are pursuing.'

June Davis looked uneasy, and Mandi picked up on this.

'Are you OK?'

'Err… yes,' Davis answered quickly. 'How can I help?'

'We would like you to take a look at a photo. What do you know about this person?'

He handed over the photo. June Davis's hand was shaking. She had only glanced at the image for a second. That was enough for Mandi to realise she knew Sue Bailey.

'Ms. Davis. What can you tell us?' Mandi was careful to make the question open and wide-ranging in the hope of getting more information.

'Oh my… well… '

June Davis found a chair and sat at the boardroom table. Mandi passed her some water from the sideboard.

'Go on, please. How well did they know each other?'

Max looked alarmed and shocked at the question, but then caught a look at Mandi, then at June. He realised… she had something to tell.

'It went back such a long time, more than fifteen years. He became obsessed. Such a long affair.'

The detectives looked at each other.

'To be honest I thought it would end after the, you know, the accident. It did for a while but then he pressed her to start it up again. I think he loved her a lot. She gave in.'

'So, we are clear… the 'he' and 'her' — who exactly are we talking about?' Max was direct, and a little impatient.

'Who? Why Quinton of course. Who else?' Davis was pouring it out. 'He had the position and the money. He could easily accommodate his family and her. I guess he thought he was above the law. In my line of work, I know that people with money often believe themselves to be invincible. He certainly did. He only took the break in the relationship when his wife gave him an ultimatum — *chose one of us, and it better be me if you want to keep everything.* She was sickened by the affair but had turned a blind eye until those deaths. She could not hold it in any longer. There were a few of us having to hold that secret.'

'So, Mrs Chambers — Jocelyn Chambers was aware of the affair?' Max was taking notes.

'It's Lyn, and yes, she knew.' June Davis was almost on autopilot, unloading the burden she had carried for so long.

'Wait a minute,' Mandi cut in, 'you clarified Chambers but who is the 'her'?'

June Davis looked at them, standing over her. 'Madeline Torrey. She was a teacher in the local primary school.'

Max and Mandi had stopped writing. It was suddenly silent in the meeting room.

June looked at the ceiling. 'Ahh... she's dead now. I suppose it's not going to hurt if you know, one way or the other.'

'So, Madeline's dead, too?'

Max was talking out loud as he wrote, trying to keep up with who died and when. June looked at Mandi, then Max.

'Madeline has been dead for nearly fifteen years.'

The detectives were confused by that last statement.

'After the accident, she decided to make a break. Like a clean break, leave the past behind. She changed her name, legally and moved away. Max leaned forward, eyes wide.

'Her name was Madeline... but then she changed it.'

Davis paused, then looked again at the photo.

'Madeline Torrey and... Susan Bailey... it's the same person.'

Max let out a long breath. This was a breakthrough. One thing was still troubling him though. Again, he used the open question. 'And that house up on Sunnyhills Estate?'

June Davis stiffened again, her face anguished as if she was fighting with herself.

'If you prefer, we can come here with a court order. Y' know… start going through all the records. Hey! Who knows what we will find?'

Max knew how to apply the right pressure, and now, so did Mandi.

'Wait. OK. No need for that,' June jumped in. 'OK… yes, he bought that house for her. A thank-you for all those years. She got an allowance too. Mrs Chambers was livid when she found out about that, I can tell you.'

'When did she find out?'

'Recently, I think. I don't know, maybe six or seven weeks ago. I think she followed Quinton when he said he had to go to the office. She saw the house and she saw Madeline. There was an almighty row between Quinton and Lyn. It all came out and he said what's done is done and he was not changing anything, and it did not affect her at all, so let it lie.'

'That wouldn't have gone down too well, I bet.'

Mandi was thinking how she would have reacted to finding out her partner was still seeing an ex.

They said their goodbyes and left for the office. After driving for a while, Mandi spoke. 'That was a good morning's work.'

Max said nothing.

Mandi waited a minute then, 'Max, what are you thinking?'

'Just one thing, only.'

Max glanced over to her seat.

'We have a suspect.'

***

Geoff had been distracted with another case he was working on and was only updating the information they had with his contribution from *Cheers* bar two hours after the last team meeting. *Chambers had an affair with a young teacher*, he wrote, *but the landlord thought the name was Madeline, not Susan.*

As he was writing he glanced at the previous information that Max had added to the board.

Chambers. Road accident. Racing to meet girlfriend. Name — Madeline

He jumped and re-read it, then called out. 'Boss! Boss, it's a link, I think.'

He circled the names and drew a line between them. Tonnick came running.

'I got from the landlord that he thought the photo I took there was someone called Madeline, not Susan and here, see? From the police report of the DUI case. Chambers girlfriend was someone called Madeline Torrey.'

Tonnick's mind was racing. The same girl? Two different names? Or two similar-looking girls?

'So, Susan, or is it, Madeline? What can you tell us?' He was thinking out loud.

'That we are one and the same.'

Max and Mandi had come into the office at that very moment.

'Eh?' The Detective Inspector spun round.

Max related the conversation with June Davis, confirming the affair and the name change. When he had finished Tonnick exhaled slowly and loudly. This was the link they were looking for. He punched the air.

'Yes! Good work, the three of you.'

'So… a free house… and a very nice house at that. Plus, a free income? I bet Lyn Chambers felt stabbed in the back. I bet she was furious. She had been humiliated. I bet she might do anything to rid herself of this problem, once and for all.'

'Even murder?'

'Maybe, Mandi. That's what we need to find out, and quickly.'

'We need to interview Jocelyn Chambers ASAP. I will do it. Max, you can come too.'

Chapter 8

Another day passed, and Liam was getting excited. He would soon discover if his plan to get information was working.

He made a call.

A small but confident voice answered, just how he remembered hearing it the first time. After a little small talk, they agreed to meet for dinner at seven PM, and some more 'get-to-know-you time'. The call was brief but the meaning was big. She was interested. In him.

Again, the plan continued to work. Liam could not help laughing out loud once he had finished the call.

***

The Chambers' residence was every bit as you would expect. A high wall with large, imposing wrought—iron gates. These had some gilded detail added, a bit like those gates you find in some Qatari villa complexes in the Middle East. Anyone outside could not see anything as there, directly behind the road leading from the gates, was a large yew hedge, effectively forming an impenetrable screen.

Max had pressed the intercom and someone answered. They explained who they were and that they needed to speak with Mrs Chambers.

Almost immediately, the gates swung open automatically. Max eased the car through, and into the grounds. As soon as the car was through, Tonnick noticed the gates closing behind them. The drive led the car past the yew hedge 'screen', and then the splendour of the house was revealed.

It was large, of course, in a faux-classical style, with large portico columns at the entrance. They drove the car under this, similar to meeting the valet parking at some of the more upmarket hotels.

'Just leave it here,' Tonnick said, as he got out. Max got out, too. Ahead of them, the front entrance door opened, and a suited man invited them in, without a word. As they entered, they were met by a young, smartly dressed woman.

'Good day. Mrs Chambers will see you in the morning room. Please follow me.'

She led them down a short corridor, with family portrait photos on the wall, and interspersed with some china and glass display cabinets.

'That's Baccarat,' Max pointed to some fine glass pieces in the well-lit cabinet, 'and that's a piece of Lalique.'

'Is it expensive?' Tonnick was making conversation, but inside he was impressed with the Detective's knowledge.

'It's all pretty expensive,' the woman cut in, 'it's one of Mrs Chambers' hobbies.

'Here we are.' She knocked, waited, and then opened the door. 'Follow me please.

'Mrs Chambers, the detectives are here.'

Jocelyn Chambers looked every inch the grieving widow. Dressed in black, and with some pastoral music playing quietly in the background. She indicated a couch to sit on.

'It's Lyn, please. You have caught me at a bad time, what with Quinton's accident... ' She trailed off, dabbing her eye with a fine lace handkerchief.

'A difficult time, yes, so... sorry to intrude, and of course, you have our deepest sympathies, Lyn.' Tonnick the diplomat preceded the real reason for the visit.

'Nevertheless, we must close off all avenues in the cases. This is why we had to come now. It simply won't wait.'

Lyn Chambers glanced up and looked the detective straight in the eye.

'Cases? What do you mean?'

'Well... there's your husband, obviously.'

She nodded.

'There is another case, seemingly connected. A woman.'

Her curiosity seemed to be aroused but she remained silent. Her face gave little away.

'Yes. You might know her... no... you do know her.'

Tonnick waited for a reaction, but again, nothing came.

'The reason we are following up so quickly is… we believe there might be more to these deaths.'

'Meaning what?'

Max noticed that suddenly, Lyn Chambers was fully focused, and no longer the grieving widow.

'We believe that one possibility is… they were murdered… '

He continued before she could speak. '…so we have to speak to all parties who knew one or both of the deceased.'

'I loved my husband.' Jocelyn Chambers has slipped imperceptibly into defence mode, again, both the detectives noted.

Tonnick pushed. 'Even when you found out about his affair?'?

'Now wait a minute—'

'We have to ask, Lyn, and please don't try to pretend you don't know about any affair. You were aware for a long, long time, right?'

There was a pause before she answered.

'He was such a fool, she was nothing, but she manipulated him. We had everything here. But he wanted to try, you know, something different. She was different. That's it.'

'How did it end?' Max cut in

'When he killed that couple. That was the last straw for me. I gave him the ultimatum. Choose one of us. If you chose her, you will end up with nothing. If you chose me, I will stand by you. I knew he would go to prison. I told him… I will be here when you come out and we can put it all behind us.'

'He chose you.'

'I thought he did, but it seems I was misled.'

Max looked over to Tonnick.

'How did you find out, Lyn?'

'I followed him. One Saturday. He said he was needed at the factory, but he sounded false, so I followed him. He went to that Sunnyhills Estate, and that's when I saw Madeline Torrey once again. In a big executive house. I was shocked and angry.'

Max was writing furiously. 'What happened, then?'

'Nothing there. I waited 'til he got home. Then I had it out with him. He begged for forgiveness, and I was all for giving it. I asked him to tell me everything, to clear the air, y'know, to draw a line.

'So, he did. That's when I had to think long and hard about forgiving him.'

'Go on.' Tonnick knew how to keep the flow going.

'That big house. Who do you think paid for it?' Lyn Chambers' eyes were blazing as she re-lived the moment. She did not wait for an answer. 'HE DID! My husband bought that bitch a house. Not a small house. A massive four-bed house on Sunnyhills. For what?'

She was shouting now.

'That must have been distressing.' The Detective Inspector feigned surprise and compassion, even though he was already fully aware.

'That's not even half of it. That's not the kicker. Do you know what really made me mad? Madeline Torrey is getting paid every month. Via Quinton's company. An administration assistant, I think they called it. She is an 'employee' but she never does any work. She is an official, legal employee but her only 'job' is to entertain my husband.'

Lyn Chambers fell silent. Max was still writing, his head down. Tonnick was watching the woman for any outward signs of guilt. Finally, he spoke.

'So… where were you on the night your husband… died? Sorry to ask but it's the procedure, you understand. Nothing to worry about. We will be speaking to a lot of people.'

Jocelyn Chambers was staring at him, with disbelief.

'You surely don't think… I killed my husband?'

'Lyn, we have to—'

'I think it's Mrs Chambers from now on,' she cut in, 'and to answer your question, I was here, watching TV and waiting for my husband to get back home.'

'Can anyone corroborate that?' Tonnick persisted.

'No. Mia was at a sleep-over with a friend. My son Robert is away at school. I was here alone. The housekeeper and staff had knocked off for the evening, as we had no dinner party planned. The food was already prepped in the kitchen.'

'Where do the staff live?'

'Oh… there's the accommodation on the grounds.'

Tonnick turned to Max.

'Go find that housekeeper. Check the status of all the staff on the night of the death. Take statements from them all.'

Lyn Chambers looked alarmed.

'Wait. What for? They are nothing to do with this. Why do you have to cause me a problem? I don't need my staff speculating that Quinton's death was down to me. If you are going to pursue this, I need to be there to reassure them all.'

'Sorry, Mrs Chambers. That's not how it works. We have no reason to think they will not support your story, do we?'

He emphasised the 'do we?' for effect. Max had already left the room.

'Mrs Chambers… what dealings have you had with your husband's lover?'

'None. No dealings, as you put it.'

'So, you never warned her off? Never threatened her? You only spoke to your husband, even though you knew where she lived?'

'That's correct, Detective.'

'She had carried on the affair. She had benefited financially… still was. And yet… no reaction from you?'

'Still is, you mean. I told you. No. Look… why are you repeating yourself? Yes, she's benefitting nicely. I was very angry about that. It was as if she was laughing at me. I wanted her gone, metaphorically speaking, so Quinton and I could get back to normal. I hated her and I wished she would just disappear.'

Tonnick looked at his notes, then back to her. He wanted to gauge the reaction.

'When I came here today, I said we were investigating two deaths, if you remember.'

She nodded.

'And I said one avenue was possibly a murder investigation, and we were speaking to all the people who knew one or both of the deceased.'

Again, she dipped her head. She was also looking straight at him.

'You fall into the category *both*.'

'What do you mean?' She looked surprised

'Obviously, you knew your late husband, and it turns out, you knew the other deceased too.'

Lyn Chambers stared, open-mouthed.

'Yes… about a month ago, someone died in the bath at her home. On the face of it, an accident involving electrocution. A lady, early forties, name of Susan Bailey.'

Lyn continued to look shocked and surprised but was shaking her head. Tonnick wondered… *because of the information or because of being found out?*

'Turns out, that Susan Bailey was not her only name. She had a new name by the time she moved to the Sunnyhills Estate.'

Tonnick saw Jocelyn Chambers mouthing 'oh no' as she closed her eyes. He continued.

'Yes, her name was Susan Bailey, but before that, she was known as Madeline Torrey. The same Madeline Torrey you also knew. So, you see… ?'

'NO!' Lyn Chambers cried out in anguish. Her head fell into her hands.

At that moment, Lyn's housekeeper burst into the room. Max followed close behind.

'What's going on? Is she all right?'

She could see Jocelyn slumped in the chair.

'The detective is asking me some pretty obnoxious questions. I'm OK. I think these gentlemen are leaving, now. Detective Inspector Tonnick, please make all future requests for information via my lawyer.'

The Housekeeper moved in front of her employer, who was visibly shaken. 'Gentlemen, let me show you out.'

She motioned towards the door. Tonnick stood up, and then reached for his pocket. He passed a business card towards Lyn Chambers, but the housekeeper intercepted it.

'If you think of any other detail which could help this case, anything at all, don't hesitate to contact me.'

With that, he turned and walked towards the door. Max followed, and the housekeeper brought up the rear of the party. Graham Tonnick turned back briefly as he was walking into the hall. As the doors to the morning room were closing, he could see Jocelyn Chambers still sitting in the chair, her head in her hands, the head shaking in what looked like disbelief.

'Wow. She's favourite for it at the moment.' Max was buzzing. 'Especially when I tell you what I found out!'

They were already past the imposing gates and on the main road. Tonnick glanced over.

'Which is what?'

'Well… she lied for a start. There's a lot more to her little tale of being *home alone*.'

'Go on.'

'Right. She was not home alone, because… she was not home. The housekeeper mentioned that she popped out at around seven PM for about ninety minutes. We could probably confirm that anyway from the CCTV. But the interesting thing is… what she asked the cook to do.'

Tonnick's interest was aroused.

'Yes. The cook said she gave him her phone and she instructed him to call a number three or four times. If it answered, he was to hang up without saying anything. The number was her husband's mobile. Cook said that he did the calls and that no one answered. The last call he made was at just after eight PM.'

'So, the mobile we recovered from Chambers body, all those calls from his wife… were, in fact, the cook. She was elsewhere, as yet unknown. She was deliberately hiding her location… any phone company triangulation would see her phone at the house.'

'Right… first thing tomorrow, get us a court order. We need to check that CCTV and formally search the house for clues before she destroys anything.'

***

Liam was heading to a popular coffee shop in town. He had made another call, and the result was as he hoped — another meeting. If it went well, he would suggest a walk around the zoo or the park. That was unless she was not dressed for walking. Then it would be the cinema. Or maybe the cinema anyway. Liam was not used to making this sort of decision, especially when he had an ulterior motive.

He was already thinking about what was to come next month.

SEPTEMBER

Chapter 9

Finally… a new lead. A note that put a whole new aspect on the case. The note was cryptic — it was surely meant to be.

'She's a live wire.

He's an alcoholic wife liar.

Now he's all choked up, and his Jezebel's gone.

Attention! More to come! JASON'

The note had arrived in the post, addressed to 'Detective Inspector Tonnick and team'. It had been posted locally, but exactly where, of course, they didn't know.

In his time as a detective, Graham Tonnick had seen a lot of cases, not all murders but in those murders, there was increasingly some twist — murderers were getting smarter and more creative.

He had also received notes before. Usually, the typed ones or letters that had been cut from newspapers and stuck on a backing sheet. Mainly they were ramblings, but this note was something different. For a start, it was hand-written but there were no finger or palm prints on it, showing that the writer knew how to avoid leaving evidence. It was written with a standard gel pen in black, with thousands of the same pen in use in the city every day. There was some cocky rhyme — the writer had thought about what he was sending. This was not idle doodling — there was a message in the lines of the note, and Tonnick's first impression was, it was not going to be good news. He still could not a hundred per cent put the note with the death of Quinton Chambers. The writer had used a heavy vellum paper, but it was by no means unique and was available all over town.

More than anything, though… the note almost certainly confirmed that they were not dealing with accidental deaths.

Max was already analysing the text, using a photocopy of the note.

''Hard to be a live-wire' — could be an electrician, a party-goer, or maybe a social influencer.' He was writing this up on a section of the whiteboard.

'Or he's referring to Sue Bailey,' Mandi suggested.

'Make a note that there was no forensic evidence on the … note,' Tonnick interjected.

'Could be he's trying to say he's not hiding anything, with that see-through paper? He's being clear, maybe?'

''Maybe… '

'The next part implies that whoever it is has been living a double-life, maybe?' That from Geoff.

'Yes, a 'wife-liar', not good English but what? The person is lying to his wife?'

'So the author, let's call him that, knows that this popular person is deceiving his wife… '

'Alcoholic? That could be Chambers?' Tonnick suggested.

'Yeah… and Chambers definitely lied to his wife.' Max was agreeing. 'And Susan, or is it Madeline… she could definitely be called a Jezebel.'

'Why don't we call him by his name? He's told us… Jason. It's on the note.' Mandi Price spoke to no one in particular.

A few rustlings of paper as some people re-read the note. Detective Inspector Tonnick didn't need to.

'Okay, so what else does this, this… Jason, know?'

'He knows there's more to come, for one thing,' Max jumped in. 'Question is… who is 'all choked up'?'

The D.I. had always had some doubts about the car accident. Did the note mean strangulation or it could be Chambers' sorrow for Madeline dying? Is Susan Bailey the Jezebel? He reached for the phone.

'Hello.'

'Oh hello, Lucy. Is Raymond there? It's Graham Tonnick.'

'Oh… right… perhaps he could call me when he gets back. It's about the Chambers' death.'

In the lab, Lucy Downe had liked being 'in charge' in the absence of her boss. She pushed it further.

'What's the issue, sir? Maybe I can help.'

'OK, can you come up to the incident room? Easier if I show you. OK? Great. See you shortly.'

Tonnick looked around the room as he hung up. Mandi was oblivious but Max and Geoff had big grins.

'Is the grin because you cracked the case, or that a certain lab technician is on her way here?'

Mandi looked at the pair of them and rolled her eyes as the investigators busied themselves with work.

'Something else in the note.' Max was still analysing. 'You think the suspect, this 'Jason' is an attention-seeker? See he says 'attention!' — that could be *pay attention* or him implying that he wants attention.'

'Boss… there's another thing.' Mandi was looking for anything in the evidence. 'Chambers death had an 'A'. A for alcoholic, and previously with Madeline… 'J'… for Jezebel. Maybe our man is spelling it out for us?'

Geoff added the thoughts to the board.

About five minutes later, Lucy entered the incident room and made straight for Tonnick's annexe office.

'Ahh, thanks for coming, Lucy. Right… take another look at this copy of the note.'

 Lucy looked confused.

'Yes, the one you checked for evidence this morning, the one that's still with you in the lab. I'm talking about the contents. One thing is bothering me about Chamber's death.'

'You think it's not a death?' Lucy cut straight to it. Tonnick liked that. Then he realised she was implying that Chambers had not died.

'No… there's no doubt it's a death, but what kind of death? I have to look at all the possibilities and at the

121

moment, we believe it's a murder. What have we listed as the cause?'

'Well… there's the thing,' Lucy jumped in, 'alcohol was involved. He was more than four times over the drink-drive limit. The guy was paralytic. God knows how he got the car started let alone drove it'.

'Oh… so the cause of death is still open?'

'No… the cause is not open. It's narrowed down. He has that huge bump on the head, from going through the windscreen. Then there's the fractured collar bone. The alcohol poisoning. The smashed ribs and punctured lung, and the massive trauma to his throat from, I think, hitting the steering wheel on his way out through the front, but none of those injuries killed him. I think that award goes to the broken neck, though Mr Gunne was doing some other final tests so he has not completely closed the file for now.'

Good man, Raymond, thought the detective. He said to the lab technician, 'OK… Can you arrange one thing for me, Lucy?' Tonnick came to his reason for the meeting 'The note talks about being all choked up so can you confirm whether or not he was strangled?'

Lucy looked sideways at Tonnick because the post-mortem had already been completed and no evidence of strangulation was noted. She remembered that from the report, which Tonnick had already seen, but she said, 'Sure. I'll take a look again and get Mr Gunne up to speed as soon as he returns.'

Lucy turned to go.

'I looked at that note, too. The first line… does not necessarily mean a man. A woman can be a wife-liar too, in one meaning.'

She left his office as Graham Tonnick read the note once more.

'Hi, Luce.' Max was trying to engage her in conversation.

Lucy played along. 'Sorry. Do I know you, mister?'

A snigger from Geoff. Mandi looked up when she heard the phrase 'mister', one she used herself, and rolled her eyes again but Lucy continued.

'Hey, haven't you got a case to solve or something? I just gave your boss a vital piece of info. Could help you along. See yah!'

She winked at Mandi and left, with a backward wave.

'Lucy Lastic.' Geoff was speculating.

'I prefer Sluicy Lucy,' said Max,' Mind you, Luce undies Downe has its attractions.'

Geoff was already wondering out loud what it was about those lab staff names.

'Sluicy Lucy and Ray Gunne, what's next… the new medical examiner… Justin K.C. Krokes?'

He grinned and Max laughed out loud. Even Mandi smiled at that one, as she was getting up.

She walked past the men and up to Tonnick's door.

'Lucy said she had some new clue or evidence, boss?'

Tonnick did not look up. 'Yep. Something about the note's first line was not necessarily a man. Look into it, will you?'

Ten minutes later and the team were still going over the note and the incident details when the phone rang... it was Raymond Gunne. Tonnick hit the speaker button

'Interesting you mentioned strangulation, Graham.'

Gunne was talking like a man who knew something the other person didn't.

'We checked Chambers. He wasn't strangled, sorry.

'But he was asphyxiated. Lungs were full of vomit. He choked to death.'

Tonnick ended the call and glanced at Max.

'Add asphyxiation as the cause of death to Chambers.'

***

Liam was in full preparation mode. Preparing to go out again, but this time for a rendezvous that, if all went to plan, would result in the demise of another of his tormentors. His target this time went back, way back. Back to his schooldays.

Liam thought back to his early years as Nicholas the young, sensitive child, and how he had stood out from the crowd. He was shy and had not mixed in, and children could be cruel. Pick on any differences, and Nicholas Roberts had quite a few differences, back before he became William Granger.

It's amazing how a chance encounter could develop into daily torture, the victim's first reaction confirming to the bullies that here was an easy, timid target, with whom they could have a lot of 'fun'. What started as a single encounter became an almost daily event.

There were a group of three boys, but the ringleader was James Holt, who liked to be called 'Jimmy'. He controlled the other two, Steve Fairley and Simon Stowell and he instigated the bullying, against Nicholas and others, stealing food, stealing money, pushing, dropping the schoolbooks in the mud, and generally throwing their weight around. A daily nightmare for several children at the primary school.

Despite losing his parents as he made the transition, the bullying continued into middle school, only now the demands had become greater. *Bring this amount of money, or else*. Liam winced when he thought of the times he 'borrowed' money from his aunt's purse. Jimmy had developed a taste for thuggery and became a truly menacing character. Everyone was scared of him. Everyone tried to keep out of his way, to stay off the radar. Those caught up provided relief for the others.

Not me, today.

But it was Nicholas, on a lot of days. People sympathised but no one wanted to do anything. He ended up in the puddle, or worse, his head down the toilet, with his books missing and his lunch taken, one or two times a week, when he did not have the money he was told to bring. Sometimes he just hid in the toilet cubicles, which was a brief respite. That was until they discovered him there. Jimmy was informed and came to the toilet block.

His deputies stood guard at the door, while he smacked Nicholas around for a couple of minutes.

'Are you scared? You should be. Do not hide from me. Just do as I tell you, and you won't get hurt. Money. Every week, on the dot. Learn some respect.'

Respect.

The most overused, misinterpreted word going. Respect had to be earned, but there was a group of people, like Jimmy, who wanted to short-cut that. When they said 'respect me', they meant 'fear me'. When you have a knife pointed at your eye, you are scared. It's nothing to do with respect. Thugs try to legitimise their existence by using the word 'respect'. Without the violence and threats, there would be no 'respect'.

Jimmy dropped out of school at age fifteen, and without his tormentor, Nicholas had flourished. He left his sixth-form college with good results and had gone to a city college and trained to become a mechanic. He enjoyed tinkering with engines and once qualified, he applied for jobs.

By now, he was William Granger. With the help of his aunt Rose, before he went to the sixth form college, he had changed his name, changed his appearance and hoped to put the trauma of the last eight years behind him. After sixth form college he went into further education and earned mechanic engineering qualifications. Now he had a new name, and was a new person, seeking his first job. One job was offered at the Wilkins factory; the money was good and it was reasonably close to home, so he took it.

The job started well, and although he was quiet, Liam was respected for his engineering and mechanical knowledge and for what he contributed, but about three years later, it all came crashing down.

He already knew that the owner of the Wilkins factory was none other than Quinton Chambers, the man who had killed his parents in a drunken-driving incident. The man infuriated Liam, and he swore to even things up if he ever got the chance, but that was not all.

Wilkins employed a batch of new workers, and one of them was… Jimmy Holt.

On Liam's side, with his changed appearance and name, and the passage of time, Jimmy did not recognise him, but bullies tend to close in on a man's character, not appearance. Of course, Liam was Nicholas, and despite the outward changes, he could not shake off his inner self. Although he did not link Liam back to Nicholas, Jimmy started to mess with him just as he had done before in school.

Liam had sat in his home and thought about Jimmy on many occasions, but now, with what had already happened this year, he was thinking more intently. In fact, Liam had already decided about Jimmy. Another wrong righted. Another thug off the street. He was doing it for himself, and for all the others affected by Jimmy's behaviour.

Jimmy had to go.

***

Geoff had already arranged to get the search warrant, and they were just waiting for it to be issued. Tonnick was pacing about the office. It was less than twenty-four hours since their last visit to the Chambers' residence but it felt like a week. He imagined Lyn Chambers thoroughly cleaning away and destroying any evidence of her involvement. He tried to imagine what that evidence might be. Then he remembered the ace up their sleeve.

She had lied to them.

She had been somewhere else when her husband had died, and not at home as she had stated. She would again be on the back foot when that little bombshell was dropped. She would be thinking, maybe, *what else do they know?* Maybe that might encourage her to tell all, to 'fess up'. Tonnick looked at his watch again. In all honesty, at the moment, this was their only lead to the two deaths, so he was keen to pursue it, and quickly.

'Where's that damn warrant?' Tonnick's impatience overflowed as he spoke to no one in particular. Geoff and Mandi were out of the station, so there was only Max to reply.

'It'll be here, boss.'

'Yeah, but when? We need to get—'

The phone rang and Tonnick snatched it up.

'OK. Thanks. We're coming there now.'

He put the phone down and set off to the door.

'Come on. Warrant's ready, get the officers in the van. Let's do it.'

For the second time in twenty-four hours, Tonnick pressed the gate bell. Behind him, a van of police officers was waiting for the gate to open. There was only one other gated entrance into the Chambers' property, and Max had instructed two officers to wait there in a squad car.

The same voice as the previous day answered.

'Detective Inspector Tonnick to see Lyn Chambers. A matter of urgency.'

'I don't think Mrs Chambers is here. I will tell her you called.'

'What I have to do does not require Mrs Chambers. Open the gate.'

'Sorry, I am not authorised to let you in.'

'Then fetch the housekeeper. This visit will not wait.' Tonnick glanced up and saw the CCTV camera's red light blinking.

After ten seconds, the familiar voice of the housekeeper came through the gate intercom.

'Mrs Chambers is not here. Please make an appointment through the lawyer, as she instructed you to.'

'Sorry, but this will not wait any longer. I have a warrant. Open the gate or we will open it for you.'

Although he was supposed to state the nature of the warrant, he purposely left that bit off, hoping to get the gates opened.

For fifteen seconds, there was no response or movement.

Then, the gates silently swung open.

As they arrived at the portico entrance, the housekeeper and two heavy-set men were waiting outside the house. Tonnick had not seen them before. Security? Estate workers? He speculated on their presence. The housekeeper stepped forward.

'What is the nature of the warrant?'

Tonnick was standing next to the car as Max walked around.

'Warrant to search the property in connection with an ongoing investigation.'

He handed a copy of the warrant to the woman. She read it, then resignedly shrugged her shoulders.

'Please come to the morning room before you start. Mrs Chambers is expecting you.'

'Oh, so she is here? OK... Max... organise ALL the staff in the house and garden to stop what they are doing and gather in the entrance foyer. The housekeeper, sorry... I did not catch your name?'

'Elizabeth.'

'Elizabeth will assist you, right, Liz?'

The housekeeper nodded.

'Please do it now. I know my way to Mrs Chambers.' He strode off despite protests.

Max took control. 'Right how do we get everyone here? No delays. Or we can send in the officers. On second thoughts, one officer will go to each floor, at this stage, to ensure everyone comes here.'

Graham Tonnick made his way past those same cabinets of collectable Lalique and Baccarat, but his keen eye noticed that one piece was missing.

He knocked on the door to the morning room. An indistinct sound followed, and without waiting, he opened the door and entered.

Jocelyn Chambers might have not moved for twenty-four hours — she was sitting in the same chair and was still wearing sombre clothes, though now the music had stopped.

'What happened to that piece of Lalique?'

Mrs Chambers flinched but said nothing. She motioned for the detective to sit on the same sofa as before.

'So... now you have a warrant. Now you want to disrupt my life even more. Now you want to embarrass me with these outrageous accusations.'

Tonnick was quick to reply, 'No one has accused you of anything... yet. We are here to get to the bottom of this case, and one way or another, we will.'

'My lawyer is on his way. Your warrant had better be one hundred per cent correct.'

Lyn Chambers seemed to be going through the motions.

'Before we start the search, I need to ask you why you lied yesterday.'

Tonnick played his ace and sat back to see what came. Lyn Chambers looked indignant and ready to refute his statement, but then a realisation came over her.

'What do you mean? I did not lie.'

'You did.'

Silence.

'You told me you were home when in fact you were not. Where were you, Mrs Chambers?'

Lyn had her eyes closed.

'Damn you, Quinton! Damn you! Damn, damn, damn!' she shouted, then started to cry into her hands.

Tonnick was unmoved. He had already formed an opinion that Mrs Chambers was able to manipulate situations and emotions to her benefit.

'I say again, where were you?'

'Waterford.'

Tonnick was confused, momentarily, as he tried to think where that was.

'Waterford?'

'Yes, Waterford, detective, not Lalique. It's there… by the window.' She pointed to her left.

Tonnick got up to look. There on the floor were the shattered remains of a glass ornament.

'The last thing my husband bought for me. An anniversary gift. But all the time, he was celebrating another anniversary with… her. You have a good eye for detail, detective. Not many would have noticed it had gone from the cabinet.'

The detective was aware that she was trying to direct the conversation, but he was having none of it. 'Once again. Why did you lie? Where were you?'

Tonnick was focused and was not to be side-tracked.

Lyn sighed. 'I went out. To clear my mind. To think. I needed to be away from the house. From everything. I planned to meet a friend and talk things through.'

The detective reached for his notebook. 'And that friend is?'

'It doesn't matter. We didn't meet.'

'Whether it matters, or not is for me to decide. Name of this friend, please. Now.'

'I did not arrange to meet him. I was going to call once I was out.'

'Really? With what? You left your phone with the cook, remember? C'mon, Mrs Chambers. No more games. Tell the truth. Who is this man you were going to meet?'

'I am waiting for my lawyer.'

'OK, then we will have to formalise this... Davina Jocelyn Chambers... I am arresting you on suspicion of involvement in the deaths of Susan Bailey and your husband, Quinton Chambers... '

He continued the standard police caution but he could see Lyn Chambers had switched off to everything.

At that moment, the door opened and the housekeeper entered, with Max and another officer, plus another well-dressed man.

Before anyone could speak, Tonnick instructed the officer to place Mrs Chambers in the squad car, for transportation to the police station. The well-dressed man sprang forward, introduced himself as Henry Travis, the Chambers' lawyer and began to protest at his turn of events. Tonnick took him to one side.

'Listen, I know you have a job to do… so do I. Mrs Chambers is being obstructive. Therefore, I will be conducting a formal interview at the police station as is my right. You are welcome to join us.'

The lawyer was open-mouthed briefly, then started to protest at the treatment of a person of such social standing. The Detective Inspector silenced him with a hand gesture.

'I recognise the status. Look, I am not hand-cuffing your client. Do you want me to?'

The lawyer shook his head.

'Who can say where murderers come from? Until we can eliminate your client, she remains our number one suspect. Please do not obstruct the process of law.'

With that, he spoke to Max, 'Full search of the property, as per the warrant. You have seen the warrant?' He was looking directly at Travis. 'Any problems with it?'

The lawyer nodded, then shook his head once again.

'Okay… proceed.'

Max went to the foyer and instructed the officers to begin the search, and the house staff to remain where they were.

***

Liam had researched Jimmy.

He knew where the man lived, his habits, his movements, and his daily life. Jimmy was now married but Liam had seen how the bully controlled his wife. She always seemed to be scared, whenever Liam observed her.

There were no children, which was good; although nothing was going to stand in the way of Liam and his mission, the involvement of children might have been hard to reconcile, given his own circumstances.

Every Sunday, Jimmy played football for a local side, then they met after the game for a drink in the clubhouse bar. Liam noted that his wife rarely joined them. Football — shower — put the kitbag in the car boot — drinks in the bar. It was a weekly routine.

Liam liked routines. It made what he was planning easier.

To avoid using the same stores each time, he had located another DIY shop, a bit further from his home and in the opposite direction, and Liam made a plan to visit there later that day, to get the things he needed. He had plenty of Sundays to do what he needed to do — no panic, keep calm, everything was going to plan. Liam took out a sheet of white paper, not his usual vellum, and carefully began to write a short note, using his left hand. Once again, he used a piece of cloth on the paper to avoid touching it and this time he was wearing thin plastic cleaning gloves.

The letter was a suicide note.

Twenty minutes later and Liam sat back in his chair. The note had required more effort than he expected and his back hurt from leaning forward for so long. He read the note again, just ten lines saying he could not go on and that he had done many bad things in his life. Sorry to everyone for the hurt, and for leaving without properly saying goodbye. Liam kept the note generic, and vague.

Keep 'em guessing. He smiled, then folded the note in half, and placed it in his rucksack so he would not forget it.

Moments later, rucksack on his back, Liam set off for a rendezvous with his next target, in the multi-storey car park that Jimmy used for his car while he played football.

***

It had been surprisingly easy to overpower Jimmy. Liam had located his car, and simply let the air out of one of his tyres. Right on cue, Jimmy got back to the car and noticed the flat tyre. He cursed then opened the boot to retrieve the spare from its location under the floor mat. While he was struggling to hold up the mat and release the spare wheel, and with his body bent over the boot lip, Liam silently appeared from behind a pillar and whacked the bully hard on the back of the head. Jimmy collapsed into the boot unconscious and Liam set to work, securing his target ready for the next part of the plan.

Jimmy came to and immediately felt the pressure in his head. He felt 'heavy'. As he focused more it dawned on him that he was upside down. He was leaning against a wall, upside down.

How had he got here? He started to get an uncomfortable feeling.

'Jimmy?'

The unseen voice came from above, from where his feet were pointing.

He started to speak but immediately he was cut off.

'Don't speak. Listen. These are the rules. If you attempt to put your hands on the rope around your feet — I will release the rope. If you try to shout out or attract attention, I will just release the rope. If you try to talk when I do not want you to, I will release the rope.'

Jimmy was listening intently now, his head full of blood, from being upside down.

'Do you understand, Jimmy?'

Liam waited for the response.

'Yes, but I… aarrgh!'

He was cut off mid-sentence and cried out as the rope dropped him about six inches and stopped again.

Once again, the voice above was talking to him.

'You speak only when you are spoken to. I don't need to hear your thoughts, explanations or excuses. Are. We. Clear?'

'Yes.'

'Right… James. Jimmy. Isn't it funny how things turn out? You caused a lot of people a lot of trouble over the years, and now… here we are. Do you believe in karma, Jimmy?'

'What's that?'

'What goes around, comes around.'

There was a silence as Jimmy thought.

'I dunno. Don't think so. Not for me, anyway.'

Liam smiled. He had not thought about how he was going to steer the conversation, such had been his desire to simply get Jimmy into this position.

'Well… you tormented a lot of folks, and now, I am going to torment you. Karma. Maaan… you deserve it.'

'Listen… if this is about those cigarettes… I told them. It was a mistake. I never wanted—'

'Cigarettes? No, no, no. But typical Jimmy, the big I-am when things going well but running for cover when you think it's not. That's the bully in you.'

Jimmy heard the laughter above and began to get angry.

'How's about you release me from this and we sort this out man to man?'

Jimmy was keen to get into his comfort zone. Liam detected the frustration in his voice.

'Remember what I said. Only speak when spoken to. I will not warn you again. I will release you, Jimmy. First, though, I want you to understand why I am here and you are there.'

This was a new strategy for Liam, as he had wanted to remain silent and detached on his previous outings. He looked around quickly. No one else was on this floor of the car park, but he knew there were patrols and CCTV so he had to be quick now. With Madeline and Quinton, they had had an indirect effect on him, but it was different with Jimmy. Yes, this time the interaction between him and Jimmy had been personal. Physical. Mental. He had to face him in a similar way. He focused and took control again.

'Remember your primary school, Jimmy? Remember how you developed a taste for pushing children around? Bullying, they call it, and you were the chief bully, weren't you? You carried it on into secondary school? Remember, Jimmy? Extorting money, stealing food. You were quite the career criminal. The tough guy. Funny how you only picked on those weaker kids, though.'

'They were easy.' Jimmy was squirming on the rope, very uncomfortable now. 'How d'you know so much anyway? Ha! Were you one of them?'

Jimmy was smirking now.

'Yes.'

Jimmy fell silent.

Liam continued, 'Then, you started it up again in Wilkins factory. Same old Jimmy. Same old antics. You thought you were such a big guy. Pushing people around. Pushing me around.'

Jimmy was racking his brain, trying to piece together this latest information — put a name to a voice. Put a face to a name. Liam could see the difficulty.

'Not easy to think with a head full of blood, eh? Let me help you.

'You made my life hell in primary school. Even after I lost my parents, you made my life hell in secondary school. I thought I had escaped you, but then you made my life hell at Wilkins.

'Now it's payback.'

'Who the fuck are you? Wait… junior school… err… Calvin Wright? No… Nicholas… Nicholas Roberts? Or Steven, damn what was the surname?'

'So many, eh Jimmy? You can't even remember who they were, yet you robbed and hurt them.'

'It's Nicholas, right? I remember you in secondary school. You were not so bad actually.'

'Not Nicholas Wright. Roberts. Nicholas Roberts. Get my name correct, at least, since I'm *not so bad*.' Liam was indulging in sarcasm, something Jimmy often did to him.

'Nicholas Roberts. That's what I meant.'

Jimmy was starting to panic, seeing as he was dangling on a rope that was controlled by one of his victims.

'Wait, you never worked at Wilkins. I would have remembered your name.'

Jimmy's head was pounding.

'Oh, but I did, Jimmy. You see... after the incident with my parents, at the end of my secondary school, I changed my name. You would not have known that because you dropped out of school... remember?'

'Let me up, please.'

Jimmy was pleading, just as Nicholas had done in school. Just as Liam has done at Wilkins factory.

'Not so nice, is it?' Liam was enjoying this bit, a moment of indulgence, of payback.

'I'm sorry, Nicholas.' Jimmy was broken and scared. 'I shouldn't have done it. Kids, eh?'

He tried to make light of the past, which infuriated Liam.

'Jimmy, you have not understood anything. Why do you think I went to the trouble of getting you here? To talk? OK, let's talk. Let me ask you something... if you fell, say six metres, what do you think would be the outcome?'

Jimmy was silent. Liam waited.

'I don't know. Broken bones? Broken back? Death?'

'Yes. The likeliest outcome is death. If you land on your head, well that just increases the chance.'

'W… wait.'

Panic had set in. Jimmy was in a world of confusion, partly due to blood overload in his head, fear of what might happen and his lack of control of the situation.

And finally, guilt.

'Relax. You are not at six metres. No. We are on the tenth floor of the Meadow Shopping Centre car park, and the fall is nearer thirty metres. There are no options with that one. If you fall, it's certain death… hundred per cent death.'

'Please Nicholas. Please don't do this.'

Jimmy was pleading. Liam liked it. Payback again.

'Nicholas is long gone, Jimmy. Thanks to you. Thanks to the events of school and home. Nicholas was retired and put to bed.

'I am William Granger.'

A cold realisation came over Jimmy, as he looked back to the Wilkins factory and his relentless pursuit of Liam, and he realised there would be no getting out of this one.

'Oh my god. It was just horseplay, nothing else, William. Sorry, it's Liam, right? Sorry. There was nothing in it.'

'Nicholas Wright, Liam Wright... Jeez Jimmy, can't you get any names right? You have an obsession with right, but you have been so wrong just about all your life. It's not Liam Wright. It's Liam Granger. Remember that, for the time you have left.'

Jimmy could barely focus now. He thought wandered to the bad treatment of his wife. He regretted that, regretted everything. If only he could put it all right.

'That 'innocent' horseplay lost me my self-confidence, lost me my job. I have already dealt with Chambers and his girlfriend. Now I'm dealing with you. Any last words for me to pass on, Jimmy, before I let you go?'

Jimmy heard *let you go* and became hopeful. He was going to be released after all.

'Again, I'm sorry, Liam. My fault. I should have thought about the effects more. I will repent. What happened to Chambers?'

'That's it? You will repent? Oh, Chambers? He got drunk once too often and had a lil' car accident.'

'Did he die?'

'Yes. His girlfriend? Yeah, she died too. Electrocuted.'

There was a silence.

'Okay... I said earlier I would release you, so... goodbye, Jimmy, I don't think we will meet again.'

'No... wait—'

Liam went to where the rope was secured to Jimmy's car and pulled one tail of the rope. It immediately released the knot, under the weight of the body hanging over the side.

Liam heard the scream as Jimmy started his one-way express trip to the ground floor, accelerating all the way, under gravity. He started to pull up the rope, but the thud on the pavement below came well before he had retrieved it all.

He glanced over the side.

Jimmy's body was at grotesque angles and there was a pool of blood under his head. Yes, dead. Gone. He loaded the rope into Jimmy's car boot, re-read the note that he had carefully composed the previous day, before putting it back on the passenger seat, and lastly checked the freshly scratched letter on the fuel filler cap, before putting on his sunglasses, picking up his rucksack and walking down the access staircase to leave the car park.

People were running past him as he reached the ground floor exit door. He followed them to look. Jimmy's head was smashed and broken. The pool of blood was big, bigger than Liam had imagined. He started to turn away.

'Did you see what happened?'

A man's voice spoke behind Liam. A man in uniform. For the briefest of seconds, Liam felt the urge to flee, but then he saw — building security, not police.

'Sorry no, looks like a jumper, maybe suicide?'

The guard was already walking past Liam, who pulled back towards the car-park door he had exited moments before.

A quick look round from under his hoodie, no one looking his way, he walked briskly away from the scene, rucksack over his left shoulder.

Chapter 10

Back at the station, Lyn Chambers sat with her lawyer Henry Travis in the interview room. Opposite them, across the table, D.I. Graham Tonnick was busying himself with papers, and the recording equipment. He switched the recorder on.

'Time is 1242. Present in the room are myself, Detective Inspector Graham Tonnick, Henry Travis, Townsend Solicitors and Davina Jocelyn Chambers. Can I offer either of you any water?'

They declined.

'I would remind you, Mrs Chambers, that you are still under caution. Do you understand?'

The lawyer tried to interject, but Tonnick was having none of it.

'I'm addressing, Mrs Chambers. Do you understand, Mrs Chambers?'

Lyn Chambers nodded.

'Please state it for the record.'

'I understand.'

'Right, Mrs Chambers. Let me explain why you are here today. We are interviewing you under caution in connection with two deaths. We asked you questions as to your whereabouts on the night of the death of your husband, Quinton Chambers, and for some reason, you became evasive, even when we exposed the fact that you had lied to us.'

Tonnick had left of the 'Charles' from her husband's name to gauge the reaction. Lyn Chambers remained impassive. With him dead and gone, there seemed to no longer be the requirement. The detective continued:

'So... we know you were not in the house on that evening, and more, you had deliberately covered your tracks by giving your phone to a staff member, with instructions to call your husband. That takes planning. Forethought. So once again, Mrs Chambers... what were you doing and where did you go?'

'I told you.'

'Tell me again. You see, your initial explanation was less than convincing. If what you claimed was true, why did you go to the trouble with all that the phone subterfuge? What were you really doing?'

The widow looked at the floor, then at her lawyer, then straight ahead, but said nothing.

'All right. We will come back to this, but I want you to cast your mind back to about eight weeks ago, to the tenth of July. Can you tell me what you were doing on that day?'

Henry Travis cut in, 'How can Mrs Chambers possibly remember what she was doing? Can you?'

The detective held his glance at the lawyer for just longer than was necessary.

'Well, I can, but it's not me being questioned. Mrs Chambers has an itinerary. She's busy. She keeps an organiser. Right, Mrs Chambers?'

'Yes.'

'OK.' He pressed the intercom. 'Bring Mrs Chambers' bag to the interview room.'

A few moments later there was a knock on the door and an officer entered with the bag. After he had left, Tonnick gestured for Chambers to look in her organiser.

'It's on my phone, actually.'

She opened the phone and began looking through the diary for the date in question.

'I went to the spa, then shopping.'

'What time was the spa visit?'

'It was at nine-thirty. Ninety minutes.'

'And after, were you shopping with anyone? '

Chambers shook her head. 'No, it was just a mall trip.'

'So, no one to corroborate your story about the mall? What is the name of your spa, please, and which mall did you visit?'

Slowly, she repeated the names of both the spa and the mall.

Tonnick stood and went to the door. He spoke with the officer for a moment, then returned to the table.

'I have instructed the officer to ask my Detective Sergeant to check on the time of the spa visit, and to see if there is CCTV of you arriving at the mall.'

Chambers looked alarmed, but the detective let it pass. He would know soon enough if she was lying.

'Any issues between you and your husband?'

Lyn Chambers stiffened.

'Nothing any married couple doesn't experience. Family. Bad habits. Finances. We are just like any couple, detective.'

'Were.'

'What?'

'You were like any couple but now your husband is dead, so some of those issues might now be gone?' The detective raised his intonation at the end to turn the sentence into a question.

'I'm not sure I understand what you mean—'

'Well, for instance, your late husband had a drinking problem. Even after a terrible car incident, he continued to drink heavily. The autopsy and evidence found at the crash site indicated he'd drunk more than one whole bottle of whiskey. And still hoped to drive home. You did not approve of his drinking, did you?'

Graham Tonnick did not wait for a response.

'And then the situation with Susan Bailey, who you know as Madeline Torrey. His womanising, which you also abhor.'

Lyn Chambers sat open-mouthed, like a rabbit caught in the headlights.

'So we covered 'family' and 'bad habits', that only leaves finances, according to your earlier statement. Can't imagine you had money troubles but ... who knows?'

'He was always criticising me for my shopping, my general spending. Yes... he could afford it, but he said I was out of control, burning through money. Me... his wife, and yet the money spent on his mistress... ' Her voice trailed off.

Neither Tonnick nor Travis could relate to lavish personal spending, but there again, neither of them was married to a wealthy industrialist and factory owner.

'OK, so, finances aside, you didn't like his drinking and your husband died in a drunken stupor, and his other woman, his infidelity, a threat to family life, just happens to be Madeline Torrey who is also now dead.'

He paused.

'Two people who had hurt and humiliated you. Both now dead, and you don't have an alibi for either of them.'

Lyn Chambers had her head in her hands and was sobbing.

'I think my client needs a break, detective.'

Tonnick considered the request briefly.

'OK. Five minutes. Do you need the washroom? The officer will accompany you, if so. I will organise some refreshments now, but we need to finish this interview.'

He made the required timestamp and reason on the tape, then stopped the machine. He rang out for some water and coffee.

'I was preparing to leave him!'

Lyn Chambers almost shouted it out as Tonnick turned back from the telephone. She had stood up but was being restrained by the lawyer.

'It's OK. Let her go. She can't get out of the room. What's that?'

He turned to start the tape.

'No. wait. Not on the tape. Not yet. Oh. I'm so confused. Why has this happened?'

Tonnick turned to face her.

She continued, 'That night. The night he died. I went to meet a man who had done a valuation on some of our assets. He had compiled a report for me. I did not want anyone to know.'

'So, you are telling me you were planning to divorce your husband?'

She looked down, as if ashamed. 'Yes.'

'You know about this?'

Tonnick turned to the lawyer. He was met with a shrug of the shoulders and a shake of the head.

'He doesn't know, he's mainly property. I did not want to tell you this before. I don't know what instructions my husband gave him in the event of a situation such as this.'

Again, the palms raised, facing away and a shrug from the lawyer. Tonnick pressed for answers.

'What instructions did he give you?'

'None, detective. I don't think Quinton expected this outcome.'

'Detective Inspector, I did not kill my husband. Nor that Madeline, though I wished her dead, that's for sure.'

The refreshments arrived, and after a moment's silence, Tonnick re-started the tape.

He immediately asked Lyn Chambers to repeat what she had told him off-tape, which she did.

'OK, we need to corroborate your statement. I need the details of the person, this man you say you got an asset valuation from. So... name and contact number, please.'

After a slight delay, just enough for Tonnick to think she was going to refuse, she again reached for her phone and went to her 'contacts' list.

'Here you are, detective.' She passed the phone to him. He noted the details, then looked up, paper in hand.

'Your husband... who are his enemies? Who would want to harm him? Who could have killed him?'

Lyn Chambers was quiet, as she thought. No doubt, Quinton had some 'enemies' as the detective had phrased it, but murder? She went through his friends in her head. No one jumped out at her as a possible.

She finally replied, 'If there was someone like you say, then I have not met them.'

There was a brief silence then the lawyer jumped in. 'My client has answered your questions, Detective Inspector. Is she being charged with anything?'

'Not at the moment.'

'Right. She explained her whereabouts when her husband died. She has explained her location on July the tenth. She has revealed her plans for divorce. If you disagree, then speak up, otherwise, I think this interview is over.'

He stared momentarily at Tonnick, before getting up, and urging Lyn Chambers to do the same.

The detective remained sat, then spoke, 'Please sit down... we are not finished.'

The lawyer paused, and Lyn Chambers sat back down.

'We will follow up on your statement. You remain a person of interest until and if we can clear you. Do not leave town.

'The interview is terminated, time 1410.'

He switched off the tape.

***

Liam was back in his house, after a roundabout route involving buses and taxis and finally walking for over a mile. He smiled, happy in his success.

Three down.

Three wrongs righted, and best of all, no connection to him. He was confident that no one had seen or followed him. He was getting away with it. This time, he had nothing to dispose of, so he went up for a bath, after first putting his clothes into the washing machine. He had a date with a certain young lady and nothing was going to spoil that.

***

Tonnick was back in the office, reviewing what had happened earlier. Geoff had gone to the spa and was expected back imminently. The call to the asset-valuer, who Lyn Chambers had said she was meeting, was unanswered but Tonnick was not concerned... he had the statement on tape. He would call again in a while.

Just then, the phone rang. It was the desk sergeant.

'You might be interested in this one, Sir. A suicide over in the Meadows car park. Yes, the multi-storey, that's right. Only thing is, the jumper worked at the Wilkins factory and I know you are on a case involving that place.'

Tonnick stiffened at the news. *What now*?

'Thanks. I'm on my way.'

About twenty minutes later, he pulled up at the car park and walked to the police officer handling the scene.

'Jumper. Name of James Holt. His car is on the tenth floor. He—'

The officer was cut off as Lucy came out of the access stairs door.

'It is another one. At least, it's got the key elements. The letter scratched inside the circle. I recovered the victim's payslip from the car. He worked at Wilkins so there's another connection. Also... I don't think he jumped. There's a note too but the writing looks like it was written with a pen in the mouth or with the wrong hand, you know what I mean?'

Tonnick nodded.

Lucy continued:

'Yeah, it doesn't look real. This one smells of murder made to look like suicide. Even without the connections to the other two deaths. There's a big coil of rope in the car boot, too. I will be testing to see if it played a part.'

'Anything else?'

Tonnick was making to go upstairs.

'Nope. That's it.'

'Pity the CCTV did not capture anything.'

D.I. Tonnick was looking at the sign by the door stating *CCTV recording in operation*

'We're just checking that now. It's not a manned system, just passive recording and the cameras go out quite often. The video feed goes into a small handyman's office here in the building.'

Tonnick started on his way to the tenth floor. He just got through the access door onto the level when his phone rang.

'Well, what do you know? We have our Jason on film!'

Tonnick stopped dead. 'What?'

'Building CCTV captured everything. The management company guy here says the whole event is captured. The officer is recovering the recording as we speak!'

***

They were all gathered back at the station. The office administrator was setting up the large TV screen and linking it to the PC to play the CCTV recording from the car park.

'Right, what have we got?'

Tonnick was impatient and speaking out to Max and the others. The situation, coupled with the links to the previous deaths, had become more serious now, and Raymond Gunne was also present.

'Some links,' Max replied. 'The letter, of course, an 'S' in the usual circle, to go with the 'A' last time. The deceased worked at Wilkins, Chamber's factory. On top of everything, we have a video of the whole event. The crime scene was made to look like a suicide, i.e. no foul play, same as was presented with the other deaths. There was a note on the car seat to support that, but... then there was the rope in the boot. Mr Gunne, can you fill us in on that you found?'

Raymond Gunne stood up and moved to the centre of the room.

'Well, it was not a suicide, we know that, even without that video. That rope we found in the boot was used on the victim. He was strung up, upside down, judging by the rope marks on his ankles. They are deep, suggesting he was in that position for quite some time. There was rope burn too as the suspect did not simply tie his ankles but looped the rope so he could release the victim, James Holt and pull the rope back up. The video only confirms everything I detailed based on the physical evidence.'

Gunne and Tonnick had watched the CCTV recording already.

'The crime scene itself. Just over thirty-two metres between the car location and the pavement? A fall from that height will result in death, especially if he hit the floor headfirst, which it seems pretty obvious, he did.'

He let that sink in for a moment.

'Play the tape.' Tonnick broke the silence.

They all turned to look at the screen.

'Right so there's the suspect. You see he's going to let the victim's tyre down. That's how he distracted James.'

They watched in silence. Mandi was scribbling notes.

'Now he moves behind that pillar to wait.'

'He must know about the cameras... that's why he's dressed so eh, boss?'

'Definitely. Our man is fully aware. Are we going to say this is our Jason? You notice he's got that oversized hoodie and a cap to shade over his eyes, and a bandana but round his nose and mouth. Baggy clothes so we cannot properly gauge his size. Right... here comes Holt now — apparently he was playing football or something?'

Max confirmed with a nod.

'OK, so he comes back to the car from the football and sees the tyre. You can almost hear him cursing — see his reaction?'

'And playing right into Jason's hands. He's distracted from his surroundings,' Mandi chipped in.

'Exactly. See now the boot open and this is where our man makes his move. James Holt is leaning into the boot and... boom! See... he's out cold.' There was a collective intake of breath at the violence. 'The suspect now looking round... ' Tonnick was giving a running commentary, '...and immediately produces the rope from his hiding place behind that pillar, to secure the victim.'

Moments later and the CCTV footage now only had the suspect in view.

'So we know… one. Jason came by transport. He could not have walked any distance without arousing suspicion with that rope and two… We know he knows knots and rope craft. You have to be confident to string a guy up and push him over the side like that.'

'See how he secured it to the car? That must have been sussed out before if that was going to be relied on. We should check other days on the CCTV.'

Tonnick looked up at Mandi who nodded and added another note.

'He's strong, too. Maybe works out? We can't really tell through the clothing but James Holt was not a lightweight, yet he was picked up, placed on the parapet, and lowered over until the slack tightened against whatever he secured the rope to on the car.'

'What's he doing now?' Max was peering.

'If I had to guess I would say our Jason there is scratching that letter on the filler cap. His calling card.' Gunne had seen the handiwork first hand earlier.

'Notice at no time does he give us any shot of his face, his eyes, anything. He's a pro. He knows he's giving us exactly… nothing. Oh and now… there goes the note, into the car.'

They watched Jason pull back out of the driver's side and return to the parapet.

The recording seemed to almost freeze, with only slight movements from Jason above. He was leaning over the parapet slightly, and they surmised he was talking to the victim. This went on for about nine minutes. Then abruptly, Jason straightened up, turned to the car and pulled on the rope tail. He released it and immediately started pulling the rope up. He did not stop 'til all the rope was on the tenth floor. He glanced over the parapet one more time, but then untied the rope from the car and placed it all inside the car boot.

Then without another look, he collected a rucksack from behind the pillar and walked off towards the staircase. The door closed behind him and the recording finished.

The team sat back.

'We know what happened. We have the timings. We know he did it. We just do not know who he is. Mandi… follow up on the previous CCTV recordings. Max, can you check into any CCTV away from the car park? Which way did he go? Can we identify his vehicle? Where was that rope purchased? Oh… it looks like he did bring the rope in that rucksack? So maybe, no car. We have leads. Come on everybody. Time is pressing. I want Jason caught!'

***

There's been another one! The words were still ringing in his ears. The immediate effect, the meaning beneath that single, short message was not lost on him, right there and then. Now on his way to the Chambers' residence, Detective Inspector Tonnick thought about what he was going to say.

Too soon, he entered the residence and walked down the same short corridor, very much on, not off, the beaten track.

He noticed in passing that the broken ornament had not been replaced. He remembered Lyn Chambers' words — it was *Waterford, detective, not Lalique*.

Tonnick was ushered into the morning room and waved towards the same sofa he always sat on during these visits. He sat back and filled his cheeks with air then puffed the air out, sounding a bit like a steam locomotive. He was looking at Lyn Chambers, sitting in her favourite chair in that morning room.

She seemed detached from this event. She was looking out of the window, watching the gardener cutting the grass.

Tonnick broke the silence.

'Mrs Chambers… I need to talk with you. I have information which I think will be good news to you.'

The widow turned slightly, and glanced at the Tonnick, *making himself comfortable in my morning room*, she thought.

'Then you better tell me, Detective Inspector.'

'There's been another one.' Tonnick parroted the message he'd received earlier.

'Meaning what?' Lyn Chambers played dumb.

'Another death. Looks like a murder, and the links are there.'

Tonnick was measured in what he could tell her.

'What does that mean?'

Lyn Chambers was in no mood for riddles.

'Sorry, I'm not at liberty to give you any more details, but I can tell you one thing it does mean. At the time it happened, we knew where you were. In fact, you were… with us.'

Her eyes opened wide.

'So, Lyn, it seems you are not the killer.'

***

The team were busy with the latest information. The links were now solid, as was the fact that these were murders, not accidents.

Max had already gone to the factory offices to find out more about James Holt's background. Once in the meeting room again, with June Davies, he learnt of Jimmy's bullying antics, the incessant horseplay and the effect it had on shop floor morale. During the interview, she revealed that it sometimes got really bad, with workers missing work, and complaining to management. When asked to elaborate, she repeated how Liam Granger ended up getting dismissed and she said at the time that she thought Quinton Chambers had gone too far the wrong way — picking on the victim and leaving the perpetrator unpunished.

Max checked when that was, then again wrote it all down, including William Granger's details.

Geoff had researched Jimmy's schooling, and while looking into his secondary school, he learnt that the youth had dropped out of education at fifteen, after several incidents involving extortion and violence. There his trail went cold.

Mandi had been tasked with the car park CCTV. She had previously found out that Jimmy only played football one day a week so had concentrated on that sequence of recordings only. The car park management company said they only kept thirty days' recordings before they were overwritten with the newest days. Therefore Mandi only had three other recordings to look at. It took time because she had to go through all the video feeds until she found Jimmy's car each time, and then go through the camera recording that captured the vehicle. It was on the earliest recording that she found what she was looking for. There was Jason on the recording, walking around the car. Bending to look more closely at something, then walking away again. The cameras tracked him until he was outside the building then he was lost.

Later, Max checked external CCTV on the day and tracked Jason on foot for about 500m, but then he ducked into an alleyway and that was the last of him. Max thought he had got changed and emerged incognito from the other end of the alley.

Once again, he was clean and clear… away from them.

Then, the familiar vellum note arrived in the post.
The Sadist Jimmy Holt, a bully by any other name. Fell ten floors off the 'park and his injuries did a lot more than maim.

I decided to call a halt, to his victims I really was kind.
So c'mon Gray'n'Co, you're really lagging behind.
JASON

Tonnick read it twice, then looked at the team. *Are we lagging behind?* Without speaking, he handed it to Max to include on the case board, then went back to his office.

***

The team had analysed the last note from Jason. Everyone felt their cheeks flushing when they read Jason mocking them personally, including the detective by name. One of the descriptions given for Holt had been 'sadist' — he enjoyed seeing people suffer, so that tied up with the note and confirmed that Jason was aware of this. Mandi was writing up 'Sadist' on the board. 'S' for sadist, to go with 'A' for alcoholic and 'J' for Jezebel. It seemed that part of her observation, at least was proving correct, with the clue in each of the notes.

'Who are these 'victims'?' Mandi was curious. 'We must assume that Jason is one? But... who else? It might be an opening... '

'True. We need more background on Holt. Max, look into that please. We need to stop lagging behind and get in front.' Tonnick was annoyed with the note's implication.

About a week had passed since Jimmy's death, and Liam was already thinking about number four. He was at home, just had a late lunch, and was idly watching TV. As

162

before, the loose ends from the car park incident had been tidied up. The rucksack, gloves, face-covering and hoodie were all burnt in the brazier on the same evening.

He had taken to getting up late, for no other reason than he could. The trust fund money came regularly every month and was more than enough to maintain his lifestyle. Admittedly, that lifestyle was not much. Stay-at-home, meet friends very occasionally, the trips out with the new girlfriend, though this was more a cynical move to get information than any real long-term relationship.

Oh… and the odd murder, now and again.

Liam thought about what he had already done, and what was still to pass. Until now, he had remained detached from the reality of murder, but now, today… suddenly it weighed heavily on his shoulders. The enormity of his actions. Life-changing for the families of his targets. Life-ending for the targets.

He was no case-hardened criminal. He was an ordinary man, burdened by past injustices and wanting to put everything right. Revenge? Evening the odds? Eye for an eye? No matter how Liam cached it, it was murder and he was a murderer. Maybe now was the time to stop? He had achieved a lot of what he wanted.

But that was the crux of it… a lot, but not all.

He sighed and went back to the television, but now he was confused and troubled. Was what he was doing right? In everyone else's eyes, the answer to that had to be a resounding, 'no'.

On the TV, a movie was just starting, one that Liam had not seen before, and so he decided to settle down and watch it and try to take his mind off his mixed-up thoughts.

Within twenty minutes, Liam was asleep on the sofa.

It was mid-afternoon when a phone rang. He awoke with a start, for a moment unaware of his surroundings, and where he was. This phone rarely rang because it was not in the name of William Granger.

This phone was registered to Nicholas Roberts. His Aunt had bought it for him when he was thirteen. Not that Nicholas was ringing too many people, but she liked to be able to get hold of him. She told him it could help in an emergency. He had kept it ever since, as a 'just-in-case' option, and along with countless other people, he liked the idea of being a man with two mobiles. He had forgotten, but it was the number he had given when he got his job at Wilkins factory.

The caller was not a number he recognised, he almost answered it but decided not to and it rang off. Liam got up for a glass of water, then went to the dining table and started checking the ads in the paper for jobs. He had not worked since losing his job at the factory. Before he could concentrate on the vacancies, the phone rang again.

He answered.

'Mr Granger? This is Police Sergeant Anderson. We got your number from the Wilkins factory. We need to have a chat.'

Liam was frozen with fear, just staring at the phone.

How. The. Hell?

He was sure he'd been very careful. No, they could not have worked it out. They couldn't. He was panicking now. Could he escape? Might be best to run for it. Get away, regroup. Make a plan from there. He pondered 'regrouping' when it was just him. A group of one? No matter. Keep this guy talking while I grab some stuff?

'You are at home now, right?' The sergeant snapped him out of his flight plans.

'Yeah. What's this about?' William tried to sound relaxed but he was anything but.

'Let us in and I will explain.' William was hyperventilating. Jeez. No chance to flee. They are right here at the house. 'Us'? Means… more than one? *Oh my God. They've come to arrest me.*

On autopilot, Liam found himself walking to the front door, and opening it. Coming up the path were two police officers. He stared at them, frozen to the spot.

'Mr Granger? Good afternoon. Sergeant Anderson. We spoke before, on the phone. May we come in?'

Liam turned and walked back to his seat. The officers looked at each other and followed, awkwardly.

Jeez… Just get it over with.

Liam was churning inside, thinking to himself, *how does this work?* He was expecting the words, 'William Granger. You're under arrest… ' to be uttered any second now. He had his eyes closed.

'You are aware of the recent incidents in the area?'

Inwardly, he was thinking, *what the fuck is this? Toying with me? Effin' sadists.* Liam felt small and trapped, the same as when he was huddled in the corner at school, with Jimmy and his henchmen towering over him.

Outwardly, he managed to say, 'If you mean the death of Mr Chambers and one of his workforce, yes.'

'OK good. Without telling you too much because of the ongoing investigation, the victims all have an association with the Wilkins factory.' The officer was looking at William with alarm. 'Hey, are you OK, sir?'

'Yeah, sorry. I have not been sleeping well.'

Liam had worked out that they were not here to arrest him. Not today, anyway. But then he glanced around the room and saw his computer station with the printer and on top of it... the pack of heavy vellum paper. He froze. Did they see it? It would only take a sharp observation, and knowledge of the case, and he was finished. He broke his gaze and looked at the two officers. Now he was keen to make and keep eye contact.

'So how does this affect me? I don't work at the factory.'

'No, but you did. One possible line of enquiry is that someone has a grudge against the factory owner and his business and is targeting employees or those who were connected to it.'

The second officer was now looking around the room.

'Really?'

Liam spoke louder than normal, hoping to focus the attention back to him. He opened his eyes wide. *If only you knew how right you are*! That was quite funny. They were on the right lines but had no idea that at this very moment, they were in the same room as 'Jason'… as long as they didn't make the connection between the case and the vellum paper, that is.

'Yes, and we are doing the rounds for employees and ex-employees who were not at the factory. They were all told in a mass meeting at work. It's a long shot but we are warning you to stay vigilant until this murderer is caught. Contact the police if you see anything suspicious. Anything at all.'

Liam was inwardly smiling, his smug self-confidence returning. 'OK. Sure. I can do that.'

'Great. So… if you do see anything suspicious can you give me a call?'

Anderson handed over a card with the contact number, as he stood up.

'Sure.' Liam also stood to show them out.

It was only after they had gone that Liam allow himself a laugh out loud, a laugh of relief more than anything.

OCTOBER

Chapter 11

William Granger was sitting in his kitchen, looking back over the events of the last three months. As he sipped his coffee, he thought how pleased he was with how everything had gone. He was on target on all fronts. The first three events had gone flawlessly. There was no link back to him, nothing to make him have concern that the police were onto him.

Additionally, he was developing a relationship with the young lady from the detective's team. They had done the initial, slightly awkward coffee in town, and the park walk, but by the time they did the zoo, an air of relaxation had set in. The cinema visit had also been fantastic, like a proper boyfriend/girlfriend. It had developed as he planned.

That was going nicely, but the hoped-for flow of information through her was in reality just a very small trickle. Liam had not pushed it. He had already realised that he had to be careful asking questions about the case. His girlfriend was sharp. It would not do if she became aware of his obvious requests for information which could be highlighted if he asked too frequently. However, he had to measure that against the whole purpose of the relationship which was to get that inside information.

Most of the info had come when he said something like 'Haven't you caught the suspect yet?'. This usually elicited a response that they did not have any actual suspect but they knew some stuff like he was strong and he was literate, because of his witty notes. Neither 'Jason', 'William Granger' or 'Nicholas Roberts', were ever mentioned, nor any information snippet which could be connected to them. It seemed from that, at least that he was not going to be picked up any time soon.

Liam was, in any case, concentrating on the next target.

This person had been around, right back when Chambers' affair with Madeline was carrying on, and had even been directly involved with that relationship. The target was a long-standing resident of the area and had also known his mum and dad. They had been friends.

In Liam's eyes, Edward had facilitated the affair and in the process cheated his parents. He had helped the lovers to cover it up. He had prolonged it. Who knows, without him, the relationship might have faded away and Chambers might not even have been driving at speed to meet up with Madeline on that evening.

And his parents might have still been alive.

Every time Liam thought of this, his eyes welled up.

No… if he was doing this, and he was… Edward had to go.

***

'Anything?' Tonnick was asking in hope. A new lead. A new note. Anything. He was acutely aware of three deaths, all seemingly attributed to this one man, this… Jason. It was an observation amplified at his last meeting 'upstairs' with his own boss. *One man is doing this, Graham. It doesn't look good for the department if we are not making progress. What do we tell the press?*

At least the Detective Chief Inspector was happy with his methods. Tonnick thought briefly of those countless TV detectives, fighting the criminals, fighting the boss and fighting their demons within. He was relieved that he had his boss's support… for now anyway, but to keep it, he had to deliver results.

Therein lay the problem. There wasn't much 'results' material to go on. Jason seemed to melt away incognito as soon as the murder happened. Tonnick's team had noted the three murders had happened on consecutive months so they looked at the pattern. Was Jason away for much of the month? The deaths had all occurred at around the same time each month. Then there was the Wilkin's factory link. This needed further investigation. What if it was a current employee doing it? Or an ex-employee? Tonnick wanted to see progress. His reputation depended on it. He strode purposefully out of his office.

'Geoff. Find out how many people have left Wilkins in the last, say, one year. We can follow up on them just in case there is a disgruntled ex-employee. We need to get back in the game. At the moment, this Jason seems to be holding all the cards.'

'We could speak to June Davis, again. Also, have there been any blow-ups with people still working at Wilkins?'

Geoff said what Tonnick had been thinking earlier.

'We could. In fact... forget it. I will do it. I want to see the factory environment. See if it's toxic, or what. What's the culture like. You can get a lot of information from observation.'

Geoff turned but smiled as he did so. Tonnick had told them all that a thousand times: Look at what they are not showing you, look at what they are not telling you. There, you will often find an answer.

Geoff was working on another case now anyway and left to follow it up. No one else was in the office. Tonnick gathered his mobile and notebook and walked down to the carpool.

***

Liam was in a taxi, heading to a meeting. He had driven his car to another residential area near the park and was picked up there. No sense in showing anyone where he actually lived. The taxi was a regular — Liam had his number and lately, had always called him first.

171

'What's on today then, guv'nor?' The driver was making conversation.

'Oh… err… meeting with a lady.'

'Very nice. If I had a penny for every drunk lady I took home over the years, I could retire!'

Liam smiled.

'Luckily, we don't get drunk. Things can happen!'

'Yeah true. I have had to stop more than once on the way while the lady was err… ill at the roadside.'

'So, you work days and nights?' Liam was double-checking what he thought he already knew.

'Yeah. Have to. I need the money. Starting nights next Tuesday for a week. OK, here we are, Mike. Hope you have a great time.'

Liam stepped out of the taxi after paying.

'Keep the change, Eddy. I'll be in touch again soon.'

'Fair play. See you later.'

The taxi pulled off slowly, his light going back on. Liam watched him go. He had used Mike Kallin — the same false name that he used with his new girlfriend and that was working very nicely. Next Tuesday was in four days. *Yeah, Eddy. I will see you soon. Mr Edward Eddy 'Farepay' Fairley. That is a cast-iron guarantee.* He crossed over to the other side of the road and walked towards the shops.

Eddy had been doing a lot of thinking lately. He could not ignore the murder victims because… he knew all three of them. They had all gone back a very long way together. When Susan Bailey's original name was revealed as

Madeline Torrey sometime after the death, he was shocked but then almost immediately he came to hear about Quinton Chambers' demise.

Then, he was spooked.

Two people, close to him, who he had given rides to, who he had covered for while they carried on, were dead. Eddy was under no illusion. Somebody had planned it and killed them. Then there was Jimmy Holt. His son Steve had been in Jimmy's gang at school. They had grown up together. Jimmy had been to his house many times. Now he was dead, too. Three were dead and he had a connection to them all. It was all a bit too close to home.

He knew it. The killer probably knew it. How long before the police started to put it all together? he wondered. How long before he was the prime suspect for those deaths? Eddy had been in trouble with the law several times in his life. Burglary and GBH in his younger days. He had had two spells inside, one for thirty days, one for six months. His wife had persuaded him to go straight, and he started driving the taxi. He had been doing it ever since.

He looked up at the faded photo of his wife, above the car mirror. She was gone too, now. Taken by cancer five years ago. Eddy didn't have a lot left. His son had moved out and was working a long way away. The more he thought, the more convinced he became that the police would be coming for him. It looked like the killer was setting him up.

Oh, God. I didn't do it. Please leave me alone! He spoke softly to himself. He was so caught up in the emotion of the moment that he drove past the outstretched hand of a customer on the pavement. He saw the person in his rear-view mirror and spun the taxi around, doing a loop to pull up at the roadside.

'I thought you didn't see me.'

The girl was loaded down with shopping. She looked normal and Eddy managed a smile.

'Never miss a stranded lady.'

'Well, thanks. I need to go to Sunnyhills Estate.'

Eddy's face clouded as he set the meter and pulled off. Two friends died there. He had been avoiding it. *C'mon… face the demons, Eddy.* He was talking in his head. *They died, not you. You are alive. The deaths were nothing to do with you.*

He smiled again. 'We're on our way!'

***

Detective Inspector Tonnick pulled up at the security hut at the entrance to Wilkins factory. He signed the log and was directed to the visitor's car park, near reception. He had already called ahead to make sure the HR manager was available. As he swung into a space and switched off the engine, she appeared on the office steps.

He got out and walked towards her.

'Hello, Detective Inspector. We will have to get you people an office here.'

'Hopefully, we will be out of your hair soon. It's always the details we are chasing. New leads or new aspects to follow up. We will not crack the case if we don't.'

She led him straight to the meeting room, waving away the receptionist who was pushing forward the visitor's book.

'OK Detective. What's the new angle?'

They sat down at the boardroom table.

'Who's running the company now?'

'A management consultant firm. It's temporary. Mrs Chambers took some advice and we appointed them. We will be permanently replacing the position in due course.' She looked alarmed. 'There's no issue with that, is there?'

Tonnick ignored her and continued, 'Tell me, how many are working here?'

'About half of them.' She laughed a little nervously. Tonnick merely registered the humour. 'No, sorry. Not the time for jokes. Two hundred and sixty-two now.'

'Right, and what sort of churn do you get?'

'Oh, it's low, a few a year.'

Tonnick was writing it all down. 'OK, can you tell me how many have left in the last twelve, no, make it fifteen months?'

'I need to check. Just give me a minute.' She got up and went to the door.

Tonnick called after her, 'I will need the names and details.'

She waved her hand in acknowledgement.

Almost as soon as the meeting room door closed, it re-opened and the receptionist came in.

'Can I get you a tea or coffee? Water?'

'A coffee, please. Milk, no sugar.'

June Davis was longer than a minute. The receptionist came back carrying a tray with the coffee, plus a cup of tea, a plate with biscuits and two glasses of water. Tonnick looked to the door, then took a biscuit and the coffee. The HR manager re-entered the room a minute later.

'Ahh good… Coffee arrived. Do help yourself.'

She reached for the tea.

'Right… in the last fifteen months, seven people have left the factory.'

Tonnick sat forward and picked up his pen. June stopped him.

'I have printed it out for you Detective Inspector.' She handed him a sheet of A4.

Tonnick took a sip of his coffee as he scan-read the list. Two ladies, five gentlemen. His eyes popped out of his head when he saw the name of one of the men who had left.

Jason Brown.

He held back from saying anything because the police had not yet released that name officially.

'Yes, and the background is there for each one,' June continued. 'One lady retired and the other left to have a baby. Two men retired, one was dismissed for timekeeping issues and one was dismissed for stealing. The last man found a better-paying job.'

'Any of them bitter? Possibly seeking revenge?' He was looking at the two dismissals.

'The guy who was sacked for stealing, Tommy Pearson on your sheet there, became angry when he was caught. Shop floor talk was that he said he would get his own back. Funny really... ' get his own back '...when he was stealing someone else's stuff. He was a friend of Jimmy, but they fell out after we apprehended him. The man who got the better job was always complaining about money when he was here. Had a run-in with Mr Chambers on at least one occasion that's in his record.'

'What about the other dismissal?'

'That was a bit unfortunate. William had some personal issues and I felt that Quinton was harsh with how he dealt with him, but to his credit, he left quietly and was no trouble at all.'

'Did he know Jimmy, too?'

'Detective... everyone knew Jimmy. He was that kind of guy.'

'OK, what about current employees? Is anyone feeling hard done by for anything? Any grudges?'

June Davis thought for a moment.

'There's one guy Nate... Nathan Hill, who missed promotion. Two times, in fact. Said he felt undervalued. Others were getting ahead, and he wasn't. He could not stand Jimmy either.'

Tonnick looked up.

'Jimmy was a bit of a bully if the truth be known but Nathan is way over six foot tall and built of muscle. I think he works out two or three times a week. Anyway, Jimmy never did anything to him. He couldn't. That did not stop Nate from despising him.'

'Where is Nathan Hill now?'

'Oh, he's here, working. He's still in the same position but I have already indicated that from the HR viewpoint, he's ready to move up.'

'Does he know that?'

'No… we've not told him yet.'

'So… he still thinks no one is interested in him?'

June nodded, resignedly.

'OK. Anyone else?'

The HR manager shook her head. 'No, that's it.'

'OK… Mr Hill's details too, please.'

June Davis excused herself and returned five minutes later with another sheet of paper.

'Right, Ms Davis, I think that's all for now.'

They said their goodbyes and Tonnick headed back to the station.

***

It was a few days later, at ten PM and Liam had called Eddy again for a ride. He was checking that Eddy was on his night shifts. Eddy had agreed to the pick-up in about thirty minutes.

Of course, Liam was not at home. He had left his car in a multi-storey carpark about one kilometre away and had walked back to the park he was familiar with.

Although busy during the day, the park got quiet in the evening, with just the occasional dog-walker or jogger. It was a backwater, and ideal for Liam's plan.

The wait for the taxi gave Liam some time to scope it all out. Where was best to park the taxi? The best route to leave the area without being seen, the nearest houses? The park was surrounded on three sides by residential buildings, all older and four storeys. This was an expensive neighbourhood. He already knew the park layout and there was a direct route straight through it to the main road that made up the fourth side. He noted one or two vacant parking spaces, and although there were streetlights, the houses all had thick curtains. He checked his watch — the taxi would be coming any minute now. He walked back to the edge of the road to wait.

The taxi appeared virtually bang on the time stated. Liam wondered whether Eddy had waited around the corner somewhere. As the taxi pulled round to where he was waiting, Liam turned to the house behind and waved up to a window as if saying goodbye to someone, then opened the taxi door and got in.

'Hi Mike, you know people around here? Posh neighbourhood, isn't it?'

'I guess… yeah… some friends just moved in so I came to see the place.'

'Where to?'

'Oh… take me to that Indian restaurant on King Street. I forget the name. It's on the corner.'

It was also near the car park and Liam's car but he did not mention that.

'Delhi Palace? That one?'

'Yeah, that's it. Thanks.'

The taxi sped off. Liam was checking the taxi interior, for what he was planning. It was an older vehicle and did not have the divider separating the driver from the passengers. The hand brake was an old-fashioned lever, not a button. Seat-back adjustment, ignition, everything else was just as Liam expected. But most of all, he noted that there was no cabin camera.

He saw that Eddy was not his usual talkative self. When he asked, Eddy just replied that he was tired from the night shifts as he did not sleep well in the day.

They travelled through the traffic in silence and ten minutes later arrived outside the restaurant.

As usual, Liam leant forward, handed a single bill and said, 'Keep the change, Eddy.'

'Oh… fair play, Mike, thanks.'

Once out, Liam quickly walked away towards the restaurant entrance and Eddy sped away. He stopped, waited a moment, and then crossed the road to the car park. There would be plenty of time for dinner out after he had completed his next mission.

Eddy was back at the tea-stop. He was due a break and was grabbing a sandwich.

'Hey! Fairpay! How are you coping with nights?'

He looked up. A group of drivers were getting drinks.

'I'm not! Hate it! Got to do it, though.'

He went back to his sandwich.

'Have the police been in touch, yet Mr 'Farepay' Fairley?'

Eddy froze. His chickens were coming home to roost.

'Yeah... it's only a matter of time, eh? All those rides you gave to Quinton Chambers and Madeline Torrey. You must be on their radar. Didn't they tip you, then?'

'Now look... ' Eddy pushed his chair out from the table.

'...and he knew Jimmy Holt. Don't forget that!'

Eddy turned to the group, who were all laughing.

'Just kidding around, Eddy.' He laughed too. 'Mind you, police might not see it that way.'

Eddy finished his sandwich and took a last mouthful of tea as he stood up.

'I have been thinking the same thing. Bloody nightmare.'

A moment later and he was in the taxi and pulling away.

In the corner, one of the other drivers watched him go and then reached for his phone.

***

Graham Tonnick was making his way to work the next morning. He'd done the train, got the coffee and was now walking up the steps into the station. Today he was following up on those names he got from June Davies.

He had already eliminated one of them the previous day. He had had high hopes for Jason Brown, but despite those hopes, the man who left for a better-paying job had been on vacation when James Holt died and was at a family dinner on the night of Chambers' death. It had taken a while but Tonnick had gathered enough statements and corroborating evidence to satisfy himself that this was not the Jason they were looking for. He smiled. He had been willing this to be the perpetrator but it was not to be. There were still those other names.

He entered his office and was just switching on the computer when he got a call.

'Another lead for you in the Quinton Chambers case.'

Tonnick grabbed a pen. 'Go on.'

'Someone called it in last night. Taxi driver. Name of Edward Fairley. He knew all three of the deceased. The caller says he became agitated when one of the other drivers mentioned it. Told them he feared the knock on the door.'

'That's interesting. Thanks.'

He grabbed a sheet of paper and wrote all the names down the left side including the new taxi driver lead. Next, why they were on the list. Next, which of the deceased they knew. Then any individual note.

Jason Brown — eliminated with alibis.

William Granger — sacked — knew Chambers and Holt — no indication of revenge.

Edward Fairley — the taxi driver — knew Chambers, Torrey and Holt — concerned when this was pointed out, fears police visit.

Nathan Hill — passed for promotion — knew Chambers and Holt — argued with Chambers. Hated Holt, was strong, went to the gym. Could easily lift Holt over the car park wall.

Tommy Pearson — sacked theft — knew Chambers and Holt — threatened revenge, fell out with Holt after being caught (some link between them and theft?).

Mandi Price walked past his door just as he finished writing out the table.

He called out to her. 'Hi Mandi, look at this for a moment, please. Anything jump out at you?'

After a moment. 'Jason Brown had the right name, but you say you eliminated him?'

Tonnick nodded.

'OK, only Edward Fairley knew all three. Hill and Pearson had a possible motive on Holt. Hill was strong, so moving bodies about would have been easy. Granger, Hill and Pearson all had possible motives on Chambers. Not sure if Fairley had any motive on any of them, despite knowing them all?'

Tonnick considered the assessment. 'Pretty good sum up. Now the million-dollar question. If you had to pick the most likely suspect, who would it be?'

'Based on this? Well... Nathan Hill fits the best, but we don't know enough about Edward Fairley. There could be some deep, dark secret.'

'Agreed. Let's either eliminate Fairley or move him up the suspect list. Can you follow up? He's a taxi driver so should not be too hard to find.'

'I'm on it. Can I just finish what I'm doing on my other case?'

Tonnick gave the thumbs up.

Chapter 12

Today was the day. Liam was focused. By the end of this evening, Eddy would be history. Another police statistic. Another Jason crime.

His method this time was simple. He did not need anything from the DIY store and no clothes to burn afterwards. Just his thin gloves to prevent any fingerprints. It was just after his lunch and Liam settled on his sofa to watch some TV and hopefully drift off to sleep. He would be out late tonight.

When he awoke, it had gone six-thirty PM. He got up to put the kettle on and splashed water on his face. Things always go better with coffee... who had told him that? He agreed anyway. It was almost like he could not function properly until he had the caffeine fix.

He did not want to be cooking a big meal with what he had to do later, so he turned to many a student's favourite comfort food — corn flakes and ice-cold milk. He sat, eating the cereal and watching the TV. He was trying to take his mind off what was going to happen later. With every door he closed while righting the wrongs, Liam felt the extra weight that had been put in an imaginary bag on his back. Weighing him down, pushing him down. He could not take that bag off.

He got up and paced about. He was waiting for something.

Waiting to go out and kill someone.

His focus had slipped. For the first time, a fear came over him. Once again, he thought about the reality, the immense criminality of what he had already done. In his head, the seeds of doubt were sown. Should he quit now? Quit while he was ahead. He might get caught if he carried on. He might fail to carry out the act, leave a witness, or get overpowered and detained. Surely he had done enough? The main protagonists had been dealt with. It was only minor players left.

But then he thought… why leave anyone? Why should those others get off? Liam started to get angry with himself. Anger was the best cure for fear. *This has to be completed, stop wimping out. They are all guilty. No one is going to be spared.* He drained his coffee, now almost cold.

This one should be easy. Straightforward.

It was time to get ready.

***

Eddy was getting ready also. Ready for his night shift. For him, getting ready meant taking a shower to wake himself up, a mug of hot tea with plenty of sugar and some digestive biscuits. Suitably wakened, he turned his thoughts to his meal, his packed lunch for halfway through the night shift. There were some slices of cooked beef in the fridge. Eddy thought of beef and horseradish on buttered white bread. Yes, that's it, plus a KitKat, an apple and a coke. Perfect.

The biscuits and tea he had earlier had only been a 'wake up'. Eddy now busied himself with the obligatory fry-up for his real breakfast. He was leaving earlier than usual today because he needed shopping. This was his second night of eight. He had slept well in the day and was ready to work, unlike the first night. He didn't like nights but the money was better, with quite a few drunken tips coming his way. *Maybe another five years of this taxi game*, he thought. *Maybe then I can retire*. Despite his earlier run-ins with the police, he had kept out of trouble and had managed to save a lot of his earnings. His pension plan was looking healthy and with luck, he would be able to retire before sixty-five.

He grabbed his jacket and his bag with the lunch, plus his private, and the Company mobile phones, and the key to his own car. Five minutes later and he was on his way to the supermarket for his shopping, and after that, he would be heading to the taxi company offices and the start of his shift.

***

Mandi was in the city and stopping taxis to find out how to contact Edward Fairley. She gathered he was known as

'Eddy' or 'Farepay', and that he worked for Universal Taxis. Someone said he might be on nights. No one had his number, or at least… no one was sharing his number. She got the Universal Taxis address and made her way there.

'Hi, I'm looking for Eddy Fairley. How do I get hold of him?'

'Who's asking?'

She showed her warrant card. 'I really need to speak to him.'

'He's not here. Not 'til later anyway. He's working nights so right now, I guess, he's sleeping.'

'OK, what time does he start work?'

A quick glance at the roster. 'He's on from ten PM.'

Mandi checked her watch. 'OK, that's a way off. I will come back at ten.'

As soon as she left, the controller was on the phone.

'Eddy. Hi. Listen… the law was here. Looking for you. I stalled them but she's coming back at ten tonight. Yes… I know. No dunno what she wants. Well… you could come straight into the garage, not the office and take the cab out immediately. I can delay her and I will try to find out what she wants.'

Eddy was at traffic lights as the call ended and sat back in his seat, thinking. So… maybe he was a suspect for the murders and yet… he had not done anything. What else could the law want? It had to be in connection with the deaths.

A car horn blast behind snapped him out of his mental turmoil. He pulled away, raising his hand to the car behind. The supermarket was just ahead and he turned in. He needed time to think but wait… he had been thinking. The killer had set him up. He was sure of that. He knew he would not be able to avoid the police forever. So… what to do?

Eddy pushed his trolley blindly round the aisles, lost in thought. He put items in, noticing that people seemed to be staring at him. Guilty in the eyes of everyone? What did they all know? He became paranoid… the police were waiting for him around every aisle. Waiting to grab him for crimes he did not commit.

He pushed his trolley to the in-house coffee shop and bakery. *Time to pull myself together*. He ordered a tea and a Danish. *Just sit quietly and decide the best action*. He sipped the tea and started to calm down. He had done nothing wrong. He smiled for the first time since the call and took a bite of the Danish.

He was not involved in the murders.

***

Liam was in his SUV, heading to the car park in the city that he had used before. He was running through all aspects of what he was going to do later. He knew the walk back from the park took about fifteen minutes if he did not draw attention to himself by running. He did not need to cover up for the event. The only witness was going to be

189

the target. There were no cameras in the car and no cameras in the park. He could not see any cameras on the houses that surrounded the park, but Liam was not going to take any chances. Maybe they were looking down at the entrances. He would still wear the baseball cap which should take care of overhead eyes. It was going to be dark anyway, but still... infra-red capability. Liam's face clouded over as he played it through. *Lucky I brought the bandana.*

He arrived at the car park entrance at about nine-thirty PM, drove up to the third floor where he found a space near the door. Just need to wait until ten, ten-fifteen, then call Eddy.

He pulled his bag from the back seat and checked the contents. The Gaffa tape, two plastic bags, some large zip ties, an indelible marker pen, his bandana and the thin latex gloves. No weapons this time. No need for what he had planned. He switched off the engine and reclined the seat. The waiting game had begun.

***

Eddy was back in his car, the shopping all stowed in the back. He was making his way to the Universal Taxis garage. He pulled in at nine forty-five. Sat in the car and looked around. No police. No strangers. He was not going to clock in, just in case and instead, grabbed his lunch bag and walked to the supervisor's cabin. No one was there so he grabbed his keys from the safe and walked briskly towards his taxi.

No one challenged him, no one called out and no one intercepted. He made it to the anonymity of the cab and got in, switched on his work phone and started the engine. One minute later and he was on the city streets and almost immediately got a fare. Maybe there is no issue. Maybe they made a mistake. He dropped off his first customer, who paid and walked away. He had only driven a hundred yards when a second passenger flagged him down. Wow! Two fares and it's only just ten PM. This is going to be an epic night, he thought. He forgot all about the police and dropped his second customer at the destination. A third customer was waiting for the taxi to clear. He smiled. If only they were all like this. The taxi moved off and was about a kilometre into the trip when the phone rang.

Eddy jumped back to reality again and his heart missed a beat but then he saw the number and relaxed. It was Mike, no problem.

'Hi, Mike... how's it going? You need a ride?'

'Yeah, Eddy. When you are free can you pick me up at Mountain Mall? Yeah... went to see the skiers, but now I'm due with my friends for a party. Fifteen minutes? OK, don't be late!'

Eddy dropped his passenger off and set off for the mall. The phone rang again. This time it was work.

'Eddy where are you? That police lady is back here and looking for you. You did not clock in. I'm not amused.'

'Sorry boss, I was up and out early and forgot. I have just dropped my third fare! It's going to be a good night, I think.'

'Never mind that. How long before you can get back? I need you here now. No more fares, OK?'

'OK.'

He cut the call and turned the cab back towards the garage. He had driven about five hundred yards when he remembered Liam.

Damn! But he's a regular and I can't let him down. Another fifteen minutes is not going to hurt anyone.

He turned the taxi once again and headed for Mountain Mall.

Liam had walked to the mall, his bag inside a large plastic carrier bag. The baseball cap was on and covering his face. He waited by the entrance, like some shopper looking for a lift home. Eddy pulled up five minutes later.

'Need a ride, Mike?'

'Yeah, thanks.' Liam got in and settled back, his bag between his legs.

'You want those posh houses by the park, is it?'

'Yep, that's it.'

Liam was already opening his bag inside the carrier.

'Did you get me anything nice?'

Eddy was more talkative this time around.

'I might have something in the bag for you, Eddy. Let me see.'

He rummaged around in his bag and found the packet of mints he had placed there earlier.

'There you go.' He handed them over.

'Thanks.'

Liam was already checking the other things he had in the bag for the driver.

He took out the thick plastic bags and the Gaffa tape, it's tail already loose from the roll. Next, he pulled out the two large zip-ties and placed them on his knee.

The taxi turned slowly into the park road.

'Drive on round the end.'

Eddy cruised forward and made the turn. They were at the bottom of the park and it was quiet.

'Here is fine, thanks.'

Liam had the money already. Eddy pulled up and stopped. He went to pass the cash forward as usual but deliberately dropped it into Eddy's footwell.

'No problem.' Eddy reached forward to pick it up.

As he did so, Liam slipped the first large zip tie over Eddy's head and pulled it tight.

There was a gurgle of surprise and panic from the driver as his hands went to his neck. Liam lifted the seat-back adjustment and pushed it as far forward as it would go at the same time pulling the handbrake on. Eddy was now pushed forward and could not straighten up. His hands were clawing at the zip-tie, his foot pressing the accelerator. The engine revved loudly.

Liam leaned forward and switched off the car engine and then he put the first plastic bag over Eddy's head. The second zip tie was added and pulled tight. He felt Eddy's fists trying to hit him, trying to defend himself, but he was restricted by the seat belt and the seat itself, pushed forward. Liam added the second bag. Eddy was fighting for breath, his hands pulling feebly at the plastic bag. Liam was already winding the Gaffa tape around the plastic, sealing it off from the air. He could hear the irregular gasps as Eddy slowly choked.

Liam looked out of the taxi window. A man was walking a dog on the opposite side of the road. He would surely see the commotion if Liam did not do something. Reaching forward each side of the driver's seat, he grabbed Eddy's flailing arms and pulled them back. The life was almost out of him but he still struggled against this new restraint. The struggles were weak. Then they stopped altogether and he was still. Liam watched the dog walker pass by, unaware of what just happened inside the taxi.

A phone rang. Eddy's phone. Liam glanced at it. 'Control'. *Hmmm, you won't be controlling this driver any more*. Liam waited another couple of minutes, to be certain, then pulled Eddy's seat back into the upright position and released the seatbelt. He looked around again. Nothing. No one was outside checking the taxi. Rich people don't meet outside. All in your posh cells, Liam thought. Oblivious to what just happened, the street was silent.

He moved the passenger seat and pulled Eddy into the back and sat him up. Then Liam removed the Gaffa tape and zip ties and finally pulled the plastic bags off the dead taxi driver. Eddy looked like he was sleeping. Liam gathered all his stuff up into his bag, then reached forward and took Eddy's phone, and the mints. He took the battery out of the phone and everything went into Liam's bag.

Leave nothing.

Well... almost nothing. Liam leant forward once more and resting his hand on a bit of the plastic bag, with his indelible marker, he drew a circle, then another, smaller circle, inside it, on the windscreen. The pen and the ripped plastic bag went back into his bag with all the other stuff. He switched off the taxi's two-way radio.

Checking around once more, he opened the door and stepped out into the cool night air. He then pulled Eddy over onto the seat and lay him down. He lifted the driver's feet onto the seat. Anyone glancing in would just see a sleeping taxi driver. His final act before leaving the scene was to reach into his bag and pull out a folded piece of paper, which he placed on the passenger seat. He closed the door quietly and then locked the car, throwing the keys into the park bushes.

Then he put on the bandana over his face so that only his eyes peeped out from under the cap, picked up the carrier containing his bag, and set off through the park, to the main road. It was a leisurely stroll back to his car. Once again, he had pulled it off.

At Universal Taxis, Mandi was getting impatient. It was thirty minutes since she arrived and still no Edward Fairley. She looked at the controller again. He shrugged his shoulders and picked up the telephone. After another few seconds, he walked over to her, a troubled look on his face.

'Well, now I cannot reach him. It's going straight to voicemail.'

Mandi looked back. 'Where was his last customer?'

'I will have to check. Wait please.'

'Don't you have tracking on your taxis?' Mandi was thinking ahead.

'On the newer ones, yes, but Eddy's taxi is old. Due for a change, actually so, no.'

You mean, you have no way of knowing where he is?'

'As I said, the older taxis keep in touch with the radio and the phone.'

'So... ask the supervisor. When did Edward... Eddy last call in? Did he give a location?'

A few minutes later, 'Said he had dropped off his third customer on the High Street near to that Bistro Wine Bar, and he was about to go to Mountain Mall for a regular.'

Mandi knew both the wine bar and the mall. In the traffic, there were about ten minutes between them.

'But we don't know the regular customer or where they were going? We don't even know if they were picked up.'

'That's possible because I called him at around that time and told him to not do any more fares and come straight here. He may not have even gone to the mall.'

'Okay, we can check the CCTV outside the building.'

Mandi was getting the beginnings of a bad feeling about the situation. How could a guy disappear? And his phone... coincidentally on the blink or switched off? Mandi was not a fan of coincidences.

'I could put out a general message to all my drivers to be on the lookout because he's disappeared and we are concerned.'

'Do it.' Mandi needed all the help she could get.

The controller relayed the request and within a minute some messages returned.

'Base… his phone is out of action or switched off. I just tried it.'

'Base… some police were sniffing after him. Maybe they got him?'

'Base. Have you got his personal mobile number? I don't, but he had two phones. Maybe try that one?'

Mandi was interested in the last one.

'Give me that mobile number. If it's still switched on, we can trace it using the cell network.'

'Wait… we are still looking for it. He did not divulge it officially.'

After another fifteen minutes, the supervisor came to the office with the mobile number.

'Got it from one of his driver friends. It rings; we tried it.'

Mandi took the number and immediately called the station.

'Trace and pinpoint this phone number as a matter of urgency.' She spoke to the unseen responder, 'Call me straight back with the answer.'

A silence fell over the room as they waited for the call-back. Mandi was now thinking the worst. Driver disappears. Cannot be contacted. The phone is off or broken. He has a connection to the other deaths. The killer has not killed this month, assuming he's doing it monthly.

A phone broke the silence.

The controller grabbed it.

Mandi leaned in expectantly, but he waved her away. His hand over the mouthpiece, he said, 'Member of the public, not him,' but moments later, he looked shaken.

'Yes, yes that's ours. The address please.' He was gesturing fanatically, even though Mandi was only two meters away. 'And he's… asleep? OK great! We will come now. Thank you so much for calling.

'It's Eddy. His taxi has been found, and he's in it. Asleep, apparently. I have the address.'

'Give me the address.'

'C'mon… we're going there.'

'Give me the address… I have to tell my boss.'

The controller handed it over and Mandi called Tonnick with the latest information.

'OK, thanks, Mandi. I don't believe he's sleeping, do you? No… I think it's going to be bad news but let's see. I will meet you there. Make sure they bring the spare keys. Keep an open mind, but having said that, I'll wager a dinner on me that Jason is involved.'

He rang off.

'OK let's go.'

Tonnick got there first and immediately approached Eddy's taxi. Engine off. Doors locked. A man was on the back seat asleep? On his shift? The start of his shift? No. No chance. The detective rocked the car, but there was no response from the occupant. Tapping on the window got nothing either. As he walked to the front of the car, he could see some markings on the windscreen. He peered closer, then stepped back and turned away.

At that moment, he knew Edward Fairley was dead.

Mandi pulled up just then with the controller. He had brought the spare key for the taxi.

Tonnick took it and asked him to stay back. To Mandi, he only said. 'It's another one. Call the lab.'

Before she could call out, Mandi's phone rang — the station relaying the location of the phone. It was her location.

'What does he mean, another one?' The controller was curious.

Mandi said nothing but called the lab. Raymond Gunne answered.

'Mr Gunne. Mandi here. Yes, here with D.I. Tonnick. We have another one. In town. Taxi driver. He asked me to call you right away.'

She passed the address, then ended the call.

Tonnick had unlocked the car and opened the rear door, being careful to shield the view from the onlookers who had gathered on the opposite side of the road.

He checked for a pulse, then looked into the car. He could now see the 'O' in the circle clearly. As he straightened up, he noticed a piece of folded paper on the passenger seat.

Heavy vellum paper.

The detective pulled himself out of the taxi and locked the car door again. He walked away from the crime scene.

'Mr Gunne is coming.' Mandi was waiting at the police tape. 'Any update?'

'Same as before. The symbol. The note, but this time it's at the crime scene. The body, of course.'

Tonnick had updated the taxi company controller, and they were all talking together when Raymond Gunne arrived.

'Good evening all. Is he over there? Let me make a start.'

He took the keys and walked to the taxi.

***

Liam had got home without any incident. He had decided to walk a circuitous route rather than going direct to the car park. Along the way, he had slipped into a side alley, and taken his bag out of the carrier. The carrier was folded and put into the bag, and he emerged a few moments later, with the bag on his back and the cap inside out on his head. He continued towards his car, now approaching its location from the opposite side to the park and the taxi.

He reached his vehicle without any incident. He got in and sat there for a while. A huge sense of relief washed over him. Yes. Number four. Completed. A car was pulling out just to his left so he quickly started up and reversed out of the space. He caught up with the exiting car one floor down, and left the car park in the same direction, looking as if they were in convoy somewhere. Two blocks further and he peeled away at the traffic lights, turning back towards his home.

Twenty-five minutes later and he was parked one street away from his house and had walked up to his front door.

The street was silent as he went in, closing the door on the world outside.

NOVEMBER

Chapter 13

Tonnick was reading the note found on the taxi passenger seat.

Bloody taxis. All the same. Always L8.
Observe fair play?
He didn't! Fair game, his fate.
JASON

The note at least confirmed that it was him. It had not been released that the murder victim's nickname was 'Farepay'. Edward 'Farepay' Fairley. *Fair game*? What had he not observed or not done to make him *fair game*? 'Fate' made it sound like it was on the cards for a long time? The whole team were getting jaded by the notes, which closed one question and seemed to open many more.

Tonnick was secretly pleased he know what 'L8' was, even if he had been 'late to the party.' Late. He had used it himself in texts to his fiancé. He allowed himself a smile inwardly, for the briefest of moments, then focused back on the case.

The cause of death was asphyxiation. The lab had suggested that he had had a bag over his head and it was taped up. He had a heart condition which may have contributed, but Eddy did not just die. He was killed. There was the 'O' for Observer, again stated in the note. Tonnick, Max and Mandi settled down to try to make some sense of it all. An Alcoholic, a Sadist, a Jezebel and now this, an Observer. It seemed the perpetrator was accurately summing the victim up in a single word.

Another piece of the 'JASON' jigsaw. Where did this fit?

Much later, and work was finally over. Mandi Price skipped out of the station. There was a broad smile on her face. She was off to meet someone.

It was early days in the relationship, but she had a good feeling. This might end up being her last hunt for 'the one'. She looked ahead to marriage, kids and the whole 'life together' thing. Two of her close friends had already tied the knot, with Mandi a smiling participant at the weddings. She thought, how beautiful they looked, resplendent in their wedding gowns.

Mandi smiled even more — despite her modern name, she wanted a traditional wedding day, too. No short-skirt ensembles and the groom in an orange tux with a sponsor's name on the back! No, no... it would be grey morning suits for the guys; they could have a paisley waistcoat, she decided. Four bridesmaids in pastel purple. She did not even have four names, yet. Finally, for Mandi, a traditional, full, white wedding dress with a train and veil.

She put wedding plans to the back of her mind, with a mischievous smile — *don't want to scare him off* — and took a taxi which was an extravagance. Normally it was the tube, but today she was feeling good. She had contributed. The boss was happy, she thought. He had even said 'well done'. Yes... today had been a good day, and now, drinks in one of her favourite bars with her new man.

The taxi pulled up at the Bistro Wine bar. She had been going there even when she was just too young to drink legally. Sneaking in with her giggling friends and plucking up the courage to order *Martinis* and *Cuba Libres*. There was a good vibe, happy people of all ages, socialising over wine and canapes, even good meals — it was a real bistro, after all. They did very good coffee too which she had sampled on more than one occasion.

On the opposite side of the street, Liam Granger was watching her from the shadows. This detective had joined the team around the time he had started his quest with Madeline. The others he was familiar with. He needed to find out more and was in the ideal situation to do it. He stepped out from the shadows and crossed the road. Mandi was waiting with her back to him, by the entrance, looking at her phone. He approached silently. She was so intent on the phone she did not hear him even when he was right behind her. She pressed 'call' and raised the phone to her ear as she turned around.

Liam's phone started to ring, even as she turned. She shrieked.

'Sorry,' he said, raising his right hand in front of the startled girl. 'Dunno if you were early or I was late… ?'

She had a hand on her heart but was laughing as he put the raised hand on her shoulder.

'You were late. Where did you come from anyway? I did not see you when I arrived and that was only a minute ago.'

Always the detective, Liam thought. He waved vaguely behind him.

'I just crossed over from there. I saw you arrive.' A pause. 'Shall we go in?'

***

Graham Tonnick was still pondering the latest death. He was late. He should have left forty-five minutes ago but he was trying to link the other deaths in the case. There was no doubt in his mind that this was a single case with multiple murders. One person was doing it. Jason. They knew it from the calling card, the scratched letter in the circle, and from the notes. He was trying to avoid the term 'serial killer' and all the images that conjured up. Smart criminal, running rings around the force, killing at will, no one safe, pressure from the bosses, pressure from the public and the media whipping it all up to sell more copies.

That same press was due an update and the DCI told him that, this time, he should lead it. It was tomorrow. Tonnick was not looking forward to it. He did not even know how they came to know about 'Jason'. Someone talked. He envisioned 'Jason Strikes Again' as one of the headlines.

He felt that some progress had been made with Jason. The crimes were linked, and centred on the factory and seemingly, Chambers. Except they had no link to Edward Fairley, yet. Also, they needed to find out more about Madeline. Mentioned as the lover of Quinton Chambers and that she was a teacher, but they did not know much else about the woman. He made one of his mental notes to explore her further.

Tonnick's phone rang… a call he had been expecting, and dreading.

Gemma.

He sighed and brought the phone to his ear.

'Hi, Gem.'

'What's the plan, Graham? We are supposed to be out in ten minutes. Where are you?'

'Something came up. I'm just leaving now.'

'Oh my god! You are going to be another forty-five minutes! I will have to ring them and say we will be late.'

Tonnick hated *we will be late*. He hated being late for anything.

'OK tell them, I will get a rush on… see you in the taxi.'

He cut the call and reached for his case and jacket.

Gemma was slightly annoyed. It was her roommate's pre-wedding party, and they were honoured to be invited, and Graham could not attach any importance to that, could not make some effort, just for once? Is that the sign of

206

things to come? She knew Graham was dedicated and police work had always come first. His career reputation was founded on not being distracted. But… just one time? He did not even ring me.

She sighed. To be fair, even though they were still not living together fully, he had been getting home at a regular time up until now, so she couldn't be too hard on him. Gemma sat back in her chair. It was going to be at least forty-five minutes before he pulled up outside in the taxi. She grabbed her mobile and called her friend.

***

Liam and Mandi were having a great time in the Bistro Wine Bar. This evening, they had gone for food and they were tucking into some delicious choices from the menu.

Liam was conscious that, soon, he would be going away. Away from the area and the events, as he called the killings, and away from Mandi. Just one more 'event' and then a break. From everything.

He was still working on the 'going away' bit but next month, he would be gone, with or without a job to go to. It had been playing on his mind, and he did not quite know how to bring it up. He was looking for a way to raise the issue softly, and he hoped that this evening was going to be the right time.

'The boss has us on background checking now.'

Mandi was unusually talkative, and without any prompting from him, either.

'Oh really?' Liam picked up on it. 'Background on the victims, surely as you have no suspects, yet.'

'We had a suspect,' she continued, 'they had the ultimate alibi though, for one of the incidents. Us. They were with us at the time the victim was falling from the car park.'

Liam remembered the sound of the body hitting the ground from ten floors up. He remembered the pool of blood. He winced.

'Now… we are checking on people with a grudge at the factory, employees and ex-employees.'

Liam was suddenly focused and attentive.

'Ahh, good move. Big factory. Probably a few who didn't like the boss!'

He was laughing as he said it, trying to make light of the suggestion.

'Detective Inspector Tonnick is sure it will be factory-connected. The third victim was also connected to it.'

Liam just managed to stop himself saying *yeah… that Jimmy Holt was a serious head case, bully and troublemaker*. Wow! That would have given the game away. How could he know Holt? He was not connected to the factory. Well… Liam was, but Mike Kallin was not and tonight, he was not Liam Granger.

He excused himself and got up for the restroom. The place was very busy tonight and he had to slowly force his way through.

'Oi! Liam!' the voice came from the left, towards the toilets.

He looked around, trying to recognise anyone.

'It's me! Jeez, Liam, you forgot me already, mate?'

In front of him was an ex-colleague from the factory, Gary Poole. They were only nodding acquaintances and Liam barely knew him. The first thing Liam noticed was that Gary had shed a lot of weight. That and that he had grown a thin beard; Liam assumed it was an unsuccessful attempt to hide the sores and spots across his face and neck.

Liam looked over his shoulder to make sure Mandi had not seen this interaction. That could have blown his cover.

'Oh err… Gary. How are you doing? You lost some weight, eh? Excuse me… I was on my way to the toilets.'

'Police been round yet, Liam?'

'Police? For what?'

'You can expect them. They are coming to see all the ex-employees. We had the pep talk in the factory last week, that's for employees but the ex-employees… '

'…oh right… yeah. They came last week.'

'Oh right… and what? Nothing?'

Liam shook his head.

'Good for you because… you know you're a prime suspect?'

'Eh?'

'Well… I think you hated Chambers for sacking you, can't blame you for that… but I have a theory… I know you hated him for something much worse, right?'

'I don't follow?'

'Sure you do… Liam… or is it… Nicholas?'

Liam froze.

'Yeah… didn't Chambers kill your folks when you were little? A car accident when he was pissed up? Maybe you didn't know, but I used to be in the archivist club in this city. In my spare time, I read up on this stuff. When Chambers died I did a little research, him being my boss n' all. It intrigued me about his car crash and the Roberts family, and especially about the 'son, Nicholas… ' and I dug deep. There I found the name-change documents. Nicholas is you, isn't it, Liam?'

'Impressive, Gary, I thought no one could find that. Yeah, I changed my name, but a long time ago. To make a clean break and start fresh, nothing more.'

He looked at Gary more closely now and noted the waxy complexion.

'Hopefully, I can do that without you blabbing to anyone, eh?'

'Did you do it? Did you kill Chambers? Those others?'

Gary was looking straight at Liam and just blurted it out, loudly. One or two people turned to look who was talking.

'What? No, of course not!'

Liam noticed that Gary's arms were shaking slightly.

'Relax… your secret is safe with me. I didn't like Chambers either. Or Jimmy.'

Gary was looking at Liam like they were pals. Liam played along.

'Yeah... they were terrible. So... you sharing this theory with others, mate?'

'No. No... No need, right? I got to go... but I will be in touch. Bye.'

Liam was suddenly alone, standing in the crowd. How long had he been standing there talking? Quickly, he pushed his way through the crowd and into the gents. Once inside, he realised he had not refuted Gary's claim to keep his secret safe. Damn! That was like... admitting it.

Five minutes later and he was back at the table. Mandi had ordered some more drinks. She never commented on how long he'd been so he assumed nothing was untoward. They started chatting again, but Liam could not get Gary out of his head. *What was he wanting to contact me for? He hasn't even got my number — has he?*

Later, Liam and Mandi were back at her apartment. It had been a pleasant evening and this was the first time it had 'gone further'. Liam had forgotten his unwelcome encounter in the bar, and was in Mandi's bathroom, having a wash. She had an early start in the morning so he also had to be up and out — she was not yet ready to leave him alone in her home. Still, everything on this relationship mission was developing as he had hoped, including tonight with her telling him that very important snippet. He towelled himself dry and smiled. Information was finally coming, and he was in control of everything.

The next morning, Liam was finishing the last of his coffee and toast, as Mandi was grabbing her work bag. He was dressed but only half-awake — he had got used to getting up late, and Mandi's early morning start was a shock to the system. He put his mug in the sink and followed her to the door. In her work clothes, she was a different person. Professional, sharp, focused. Liam was a little intimidated by this situation — the police detective off to the police station to investigate murders carried out by... well... by him.

They got out of the house and into the weak, early morning sun. For once, the weather was kind for late autumn. They said goodbyes and each walked to their cars which were parked in different streets.

Liam went straight home.

Once back in his comfort zone, he ran a bath, made another coffee and grabbed his notebook and pen, plus the tablet he had been using during his internet job searches. He finally settled into the hot bath, with water up to his chest, took a mouthful of his coffee, and switched on the tablet.

A few jobs caught his eye and he noted the details and links for each one in his notebook. The coffee was going down very nicely when he saw an advert which he thought could have been written just for him. *Wanted: Engineer for immediate start. Overseas appointment. Engineering background. Qualifications and references are required. Single status position. Email us for more information*. Liam noted it all down, then googled the company who posted the advert. It was a cruise line business, predominantly based in the Caribbean.

Liam lay back in the bath, dreaming of sunny days working around the islands. Was the job land-based? Or maybe even… ship-based! Liam warmed to the job even more. At that moment, his phone rang — his seldom-used 'Nicholas' phone. It was downstairs on the kitchen side, and he was not getting out of this relaxing bath just to speak to some telemarketer. He let it ring off.

It wasn't until much later, when he was back down in the kitchen and preparing a late lunch, that he remembered the earlier call and checked the phone. It was not a number he recognised. Maybe a wrong number?

He forgot it and started to make chilli, one of his favourite easy-prep meals. He decided to make enough for four portions and freeze it. Economies of scale. He smiled. It was not like he needed to save money. His bank balance had been steadily growing from the trust money paid in each month, and his lack of expenditure. While he waited for lunch, Liam looked back at the cruise ship vacancy and applied using the email address given and sending his resume.

It was the afternoon and Liam was full of Chilli-con-Carne and watching an old movie. He was on his third glass of wine was feeling pretty contented. He had just put his feet up when the phone rang again. Really? Every time I'm set to relax… He smiled. Maybe it's Mandi?

It wasn't. It was the unknown number again. Liam waiting until the tenth ring. He had made a mental deal with himself. Answer it on ten.

There was no voice at the other end, so Liam also stayed silent. After ten seconds, a voice spoke.

'You there, Liam?'

'Who's this?'

'Who d'you think? I said I would be in touch.'

Liam looked up at the ceiling and sighed. Gary Poole.

'What's up, Gary?'

'Oh … nothing. I wanted to meet up. I need to tell you something.'

'Why not now? Here on the phone.'

Liam was in no mood for games. Gary was no friend and he didn't want to waste time.

'Nah. This needs face to face. Come to Backstreet Bar tonight. Seven-thirty. It's in your interest, so don't be late. Cheers!'

The call cut before Liam could respond.

He thought back to the previous night's conversation. So this Gary knew about the name change, and he seemed to be saying he had a reason to think Liam might be involved in the murders. Liam started to get an uneasy feeling. Now, he was not in control. This… this Gary had driven his tank right onto Liam's lawn. What did he know? Who else knew it? Liam was not a fool, and he pondered the most important question.

What did Gary want?

***

Detective Inspector Tonnick was reviewing the information the team had gathered on those factory people, both current and past, who may hold a grudge. There was not much for most of them, except for William Granger and Nate. He had learnt more of the bullying dished out by Jimmy Holt, and how it had ended up getting William dismissed. He also knew of Quinton Chamber's role in it all, turning a blind eye, so there were two strong connections — nothing to Madeline though. Nor the cab driver.

He knew that Nate also hated Jimmy and he hated Chambers. The team had followed up on Nathan, as requested by Tonnick, and discovered that the man had no solid independent alibi for the dates of the Torrey or Holt deaths, but he did for the Chambers death.

Nathan was otherwise clean — no brushes with the law. He had a history. A complete one whereas William Granger did not. What was his early life?

'I think we need to have a meeting with Mr William Granger. Some missing stuff in his record here. Max, can you go and see him? If we need to, we can bring him in for something more formal.'

'Will do, boss. Later today, if I can. I need to close a couple of things on my new case.'

Tonnick kept forgetting that his team did not standstill. Other work was coming in.

'OK. When you can. It won't hurt for a couple of days.'

Chapter 14

Reluctantly, and with a little trepidation, Liam was getting ready to go to the Backstreet Bar for his rendezvous with Gary. He had decided to get there early and wait. He wanted to check out Gary's arrival, and especially he wanted to gather any information. He was feeling at a disadvantage. Gary seemed to know quite a bit about him. He knew nothing about Gary Poole.

It was just past six-fifteen and Liam pulled the SUV out from its parking spot and headed to the bar. The trip was only twenty-five minutes but Liam wanted to be there, parked and in a position to observe. He arrived at the bar and found a space in a side street. Then he jumped out, walked back to the junction and waited. The time dragged and Liam thought someone might report him for hanging around the parked cars.

At just after seven twenty-five, a small and very old Ford pulled slowly past the bar, the occupant seeking a parking space. The driver was Gary Poole. Liam noted the make, model, colour and number plate of the car, then watched to see where he would go. The car stopped and he saw Gary reach for his phone. In a flash, Liam pulled his own phone out of his pocket and muted the ringtone. Even as he did it, a call came in.

It was Gary. Liam answered from his vantage point behind a parked car.

'Hi. Are you here yet? I just arrived.'

'I'm just getting there, now. See you inside.'

'OK don't be late. I can't stay too long.'

The call cut. Liam did not like Poole's confidence and continued to watch as Gary found a parking space, thankfully not on the same side street as him. He walked briskly down to the bar and went in.

As soon as he disappeared, Liam sprinted up the street to where Poole's car was parked. He looked around the vehicle for any additional information. Nothing was showing in the car, but on the window was a parking pass, and it gave the building name. Jackpot. Liam intended to follow Gary after this bar visit, but it was always easier if the destination was already known. Liam did one final scan of the car and headed back to the bar entrance.

Gary Poole was standing at the bar and already had a drink. He did not offer one to Liam.

'Times are hard for me, Liam. You got out at the right time, and now you got the trust money your days of worrying are over.'

He saw Liam's look of surprise.

'Oh yeah… the trust fund detail was all in that court archive I found. Me? I am not so lucky, stuck at the factory.'

Liam let it pass, even though he was intrigued by how to find out such information. He entered the conversation under force. He did not want to be there

'It's work, right?'

'Work! Hah! Yeah, but there's no money in the storekeeping job, Liam. You engineers were getting well-paid but that's a world away from me.'

Gary Poole was wide-eyed and staring at nothing in particular.

'Sorry to hear that. Maybe things will change now that Chambers is not in control?'

'Oh but a Chambers is still in control. Lyn Chambers is taking over, with a management team to help her, didn't you know?'

'No. I didn't.'

'Tough times. Not sure how I can carry on. I am looking at other options now.'

Poole was speaking like a machine gun, so fast that Liam could barely understand him.

'So why not leave? Find something better.'

'I'm not qualified, Liam. This is the best I can get.'

He reached for his cigarettes and took one out. Tapping it on the bar, then he put it back in the packet. He started looking around the bar furtively.

'So... what do you want to tell me that couldn't be said over the phone?'

'Not so much tell but ask you something.'

Liam noticed that the earlier confidence had gone. Gary was nervous, now.

'Ask what?'

'OK… err… remember what I mentioned the last time we met? What I found out? About you.'

Gary was rubbing his face with his hand and staring at the floor.

'Go on… '

'So… money is not a problem for you, right? I figured you might want to help me out a little bit.'

Liam could tell that Gary was reciting a well-prepared script. Now, he had taken the cigarette out again and put it in his mouth.

'Nothing too much. Just, y'know… support me while I get myself sorted out.' Poole was sniffing and wiping his nose with his finger a lot, Liam noticed.

'What?'

'It could be bad if my theory came to the attention of that detective… Tonnick, isn't it?'

Finally… there it was. Blackmail. Liam did not react outwardly, but inside he was seething.

'I see… so what were you thinking of, Gary? What sort of help?'

Poole took a swig of his drink; his throat was dry. 'Oh I don't know… maybe a couple a month.' He sniffed again and coughed, and his arms were shaking. 'Thousand. Two thousand a month'.

'For how long?'

'Just 'til I get myself sorted out.'

'I don't carry that sort of cash around with me.'

Liam was buying time. Gary Poole breathed out slowly. It had worked. His hand shook as he lit the cigarette.

'OK. We can arrange another meeting. Tomorrow.'

'OK. And this theory of yours? Put to bed now?'

'Yes.'

'Oi mate! You can't smoke that in here!' The bartender had been tipped-off by another customer

'Sorry, yeah.' Gary stubbed it out on the packet.

'Who else knows about this?'

'No one… just me and you.'

'OK. Keep it that way, mate.'

Liam was careful with his choice of words. He wanted to make Poole think that he was OK with it all.

'Will do, Liam. Thanks, mate. Right. I have to go now. We can meet tomorrow, OK?'

'Sure.'

Gary Poole swigged the last of his drink, then made for the door. Liam gave him thirty seconds, then left too. He saw Poole walking up towards his car. Liam ran to his SUV, pulled out of his space and down to the junction, lights off. From this position, he could see Poole's car.

A moment later, it pulled out and set off up the road. Liam switched on the lights and followed at a safe distance.

They crossed town to a more down-market part of the city that Liam was unfamiliar with. He became aware that his car stuck out in this area. Everything was run down and shabby, and his gleaming SUV would be just begging to be stolen if he left it anywhere. He grimaced but tonight... needs must.

He wanted Poole's apartment number.

The beat-up Ford turned a corner into some parking in front of a low-rise tenement building. Liam swiftly pulled up, switched off and got out. There was only minimal lighting in the parking area, and Liam blended into the shadows as he watched Poole exit his car and make his way towards the entrance. He followed towards that same entrance. When he got there, he saw no lift.

Perfect.

Poole had to take the stairs so Liam could easily follow. He got to the stairwell and heard the sound of footsteps above him, maybe two floors up. Silently, Liam climbed those same stairs, listening for a door being opened.

When he heard the door, it was directly above him. He quickly climbed the flight of stairs and caught the door before it closed again. He opened it quietly and peered inside. Poole had turned left and was shuffling slowly along the corridor. Liam counted the doors he walked past until he stopped and fumbled for a key. As he turned the key in the lock and slowly pushed the door open, Liam stepped into the corridor and moved silently towards the closing door. It closed as he got there, but now he had Poole's apartment number. He had everything he needed. Liam walked quickly back to the stairs and descended again. His car was a minute away. Thankfully it was still there and there was no damage. He wrote down the apartment address and drove home.

Back in his own house, Liam was deciding what to do about Gary Poole. This unexpected development in his mission had thrown his plans into the air. He already had a target for November, but now this. As he thought about it, Liam started to form a plan. This might be a blessing in disguise. As far as he knew, Poole was unconnected to any of the others. He would be stopping this month, come what may.

No problem. He could resume next year.

But Liam also realised, he was not getting away with everything as easily as he had thought. He reviewed the previous events. It was clear he had been complacent. He had made the mistake of believing he was invincible. The friend of Madeline Torrey could have come to the house sooner, he could have been spotted in Quinton's car, or bashing him from the shadows near the bar, he could have been seen dropping Jimmy, or the CCTV might have captured him, that dog-walker passing Eddy's car might have seen the whole event, or he might have been identified on house security cameras.

Liam realised it was not skill… it was luck. Luck that he had not been caught or identified. Now, someone else knew enough to incriminate him and he was being blackmailed. Maybe there were others. He better sharpen up and he better deal with this latest development quickly.

* * *

Early the following morning, he was parked round at Poole's building, watching. At eleven, Poole emerged, looking rough. He was still wearing the same clothes as the previous day, and he was unwashed. Instead of taking his car, Poole started walking in the opposite direction, his shambling, shuffling walk the same as yesterday, only quicker. Today he walked with purpose. Liam was dressed down, one of his familiar hoodies and old baseball cap, and some non-descript black jeans. Only his SUV stood out. He got out and soon caught up behind Poole, but he had to be careful. The other man was constantly looking around for something or someone.

Liam suspected he knew what Poole's problem was. Paranoia was one classic sign of a drug user. Put that together with what he had already observed and he was sure Gary Poole was tied up with drugs. Then it hit him. Pool wanted his two thousand a month to score. He was an addict.

Up ahead, Poole had stopped and was talking to a furtive adolescent a block down. After ten seconds, Poole passed over something, money Liam assumed, and the boy disappeared, only to reappear a minute later with two carrier bags. No words were exchanged. Poole took the bags and turned to walk back. Liam turned and sprinted back towards his car, hoping that Poole had not seen him. As before, Poole shuffled back up the stairs with Liam following behind and re-entered his apartment.

Liam gave him thirty minutes then knocked on the door. It took an age but eventually, the door slowly opened. As Liam went to enter and say *hello*, all he saw was the back of Gary Poole, walking towards the living room. Liam slipped into the kitchen and looked around. It was as he expected. Unwashed crockery, spilt food, a filthy microwave and an overflowing bin. He was amazed that Gary managed to turn up for work every day. He slowly approached the living room door and looked in. Gary Poole was sitting on the floor, resting his head on the sofa behind him. His eyes were closed. *He was expecting someone else.*

Liam looked around. One of the carrier bags was on the floor, tipped out, showing a lot of different types of packages. Next to three piles of cash, one of the smaller packages was open on the table, clearly a substance that Poole had used. There was an open vodka bottle, now over half-empty, and an overturned glass on the floor next to him. He was not moving now, and emboldened, Liam entered the room and picked up the syringe from Poole's lap. So… he's selling and using.

Liam thought for a moment. The situation was perfect, if only he knew what to do. He had never used drugs in his life. He flipped out his phone and typed in 'drug use methods'.

If it was crystal meth, which believed it was, then it should dissolve in water. He scraped a generous amount of the powdery crystals into a beaker on the table, then reached for a squeezable dropper bottle. He pinched the bottle and a small amount of fluid squirted out and into the beaker. Liam realised that he was doing what Gary Poole had probably done a little while earlier. The powder started to dissolve as he added a little more water. Liam added more powder. He wanted the mixture to be as concentrated as possible.

Gary had remained motionless the entire time.

When the mixture had entirely dissolved, Liam took the syringe, carefully filled it up and approached the prone man. Would he move? Would Liam have time to inject the drug before Gary struggled or shifted?

He moved closer, the needle now a couple of inches from Poole's arm. With one swift movement, he pushed the needle into Gary Poole's arm and immediately depressed the plunger. Gary's eyes shot wide open, scanning the room, looking confused. The empty syringe now out of his arm.

Gary tried to speak, 'What are you doing? Liam? What's going on? Did you bring my cash?

Liam said nothing as he concentrated on re-filling the syringe again.

'Liam… what are you doing?'

'I'm helping you, mate.'

He scooped up one of the piles of cash from the table.

'I got your money here.'

He dropped the cash into Poole's lap and picked up the syringe. While the addict was distracted, he again injected him with the concentrated drug mixture.

'Ow! Liam. St… stop. It's too much. Thanks, for the money, I mean. Oh, my head. I drank too much, I think. All last night, waiting for this delivery from my bosses.'

Liam was not listening. He concentrated on filling the syringe for the third time.

'What is this drug, mate?'

'Crystal. The best. You want to buy some? I have a little bit spare, but most of this is sold already.'

'Let me try it.'

Liam picked up the syringe and pretended to roll up his sleeve. Gary had his eyes closed again. It was so easy to inject him once more.

'Ow… Liam! Please stop. I need some water. Help me, please, I'm very hot and thirsty.'

Liam looked at him, just lying there and thought about finishing him off. He went to the filthy kitchen, found a cup and some water from the fridge. He poured some out, then came back and spooned some more crystal powder into the cup. He quietly stirred it until it was dissolved, then offered the cup to Poole.

'Gary. Water. Here… get it down you. You look hot, mate. This will cool you down.'

Gary Poole's hand was flailing about, desperately trying to make contact with the water. His breathing was much faster now, like he had been running for an hour. He was sweating. Liam grabbed his hand then put the cup handle in it. Poole snatched at the cup, brought it to his lips and gulped the contents down.

'God that tastes awful. So bitter. Was that the water in the fridge?'

'Yup.'

Liam was quiet and just waited. Gary Poole had deteriorated considerably. Whether it was due to excessive alcohol the previous night, or the overdose now, he was suffering.

'I'm so hot, Liam. Really hot. Can I get more water? Jeez, my heart is racing. I think something is wrong… '

Liam repeated the water and meth mix, then sat still and quiet, watching.

'Liam… you there, mate? Help me, please. I think I am sick. Too much ice and booze. This is serious… better call for help.'

His words were fast, same as before but now they were slurred. Liam just sat there.

Gary Poole was overdosing on the massive amounts of drugs that Liam had given him, coupled with his heavy night on the booze. He kept rubbing his face and clutching at his chest, grimacing as his heart started palpitating.

'Liam… Liam… where are you?'

His eyes were open but he could not see Liam, sitting behind him.

'I think I'm dying, mate. I need an ambulance. Quickly.'

'You are dying. Hopefully, it will be quickly.'

'What?' Gary understood the reply, even through his pain and fear.

'You think I want to help you? You fuckin' drug dealer. Spreading this filth through the community and trying to blackmail me to pay for even more of this shit. How many lives have you ruined, I wonder? Well, the last life to be ruined will be … yours.'

Poole was crying. He could not move. His throat was dry again, he was incredibly hot, and his heart was fit to explode. He looked around for his tormentor.

'Please. Liam. Please. I'm sorry. You don't have to pay me. I made a mistake.'

'You made a mistake trying to blackmail me, that's for sure. And sorry? Hah… sorry it's ending badly, not sorry you spread this crap all over the place. Sell your soul for money, right? Hang the consequences, you don't care. You are disgusting.'

'Wait. I… '

Gary had a massive convulsion, throwing his chest upwards from his position on the floor. He held it for a couple of seconds, then slumped back and slid down the front of the sofa. He was still.

Not breathing.

Liam continued to sit there, letting ten minutes pass… to be sure.

He slowly got up and pushed Poole with his foot. The body rolled over, and the head hit the hard floor with a thud before again becoming motionless.

Liam looked around the squalor of the room. The drug equipment, the money, the drugs themselves and everything in a dirty environment. He looked again at Gary

Poole, lying dead on the floor. This is how so many addicts end up if they overdose, he thought. Not a clean hospital bed surrounded by nurses, or at home with family. The end comes in this sort of environment and usually, alone.

Liam went to the kitchen and found a knife. He came back to the living room and walked over to Poole, then bent down and with the knife, he cut a neat letter 'N' inside a circle, on the wooden coffee table. He had to move the money to get proper access, and he idly counted it out… six thousand, five hundred in total.

For a moment he thought of pocketing it, but… he did not need the money and up until now, he had very definitely never taken anything from the death scenes. He placed it neatly back on the coffee table, but then he had an idea. Once again, he scooped up all the cash and put it into one of Gary's carrier bags. His final act was to place the familiar vellum note:

He tried to extort.
Of course, he fell short.
My secrets are safe and
The narcotic dealer has gone to his grave.
He dealt in the drugs.
We know it's for mugs.
This one you'll agree.
Without him we have a safer so-ci-et-y.
JASON

With one last look around, he carefully opened the door and looked both ways before stepping out into the empty corridor and taking a breath of the fresh air.

As soon as he got home, he replied to the overseas job email, giving them the information they requested and making it clear he was available with minimal notice. Then he went to make a late lunch.

Barely twenty minutes later, the laptop pinged, announcing a new email. It was from the Cruise Company.

Liam read with increasing excitement: Please provide copies of your qualifications and passport and state the date you would like to start. Please provide a contact mail for your reference.

He photographed his certificates, then stopped. A reference? That could be awkward. Who? Certainly not Chambers — he was dead. Ahh, wait… June Davis. She had seemed sympathetic. Liam thought again though. He did not want anyone to know where he was going. He decided to miss-spell her email address and see what happened.

They wanted him. Liam knew that by the speed of the next email. Barely five minutes had passed when the laptop pinged again.

Dear William, the email began. Liam read on. *Delighted to offer you employment…* The email laid out the offer and asked that if he was happy he was to print, sign and send back a copy. Liam emailed back to say he accepted and would print the contract straight away.

Another part of the plan was sorted out. Liam was driving back from the copy shop, with three copies of the contract. I'm one step ahead of you again, Detective.

It was now evening and Liam was in a very good mood. The last email from his new employer contained details of a flight, booked for him to the Caribbean in just over a week. He had a lot to do in the time, including buying a suitcase and some new clothes for the trip but right now, he sat back in his favourite chair, with a glass of red and a big smile on his face.

WINTER

Chapter 15

He had only just digested Jason's last note concerning the fifth murder when another one arrived. Tonnick read the new note and re-read it. There were only six words. Jason was succinct.

Bye. I see you... Soon
JASON

'Bye? Bye, what? Goodbye? Forever? For a while? Leaving the city? Or a misspelling of 'buy' See you around? Could Jason be leaving and coming back, or coming to see me personally?'

Max cut in, 'I see you... If you take the phonetics... that's I C U... ICU in the hospital... Intensive Care Unit. You think Jason has a medical condition?'

'And he's had to go to intensive care?' one of the other team members chimed in.

'Maybe he was injured after one of the incidents? Makes sense... they weren't all straightforward.' Detective Inspector Tonnick was on the wavelength now.

'But why would he give us a clue? A clue that might help us catch him?'

Mandi's voice cut through the wave of excitement. 'He's been smart so far — no clues. This would be out of character for him.'

'What character?' Max was agitated. 'We don't know his character. We only know he kills people… '

'…and he's smart,' Mandi persisted.

Tonnick stared briefly at Mandi.

Ignoring the outburst, Tonnick mulled over the note and the suggestions. It didn't add up. She was right — why WOULD he help us?

'One of you… review all the notes and all the clues that he's sent us and that we have gathered. In order, with the death details in each case. I know we've been through them but look again. Any clues following over between the letters? Letter patterns. Letters spelling words over the murder notes? Double meanings? Date patterns?' He looked at Mandi. 'Perhaps you could take that on?'

'Sure, boss.' Mandi looked up. To her colleagues, she muttered, 'Maybe the new girl can crack the case!'

'That's the whole point,' Tonnick cut in abruptly. 'You are fresh. Maybe you see things differently to us old-timers.' Mandi looked over. He was again staring straight at her. Just then, the phone rang.

'Boss, there's been another one.' Max had just finished speaking with the desk sergeant.

The words that Detective Graham Tonnick did not want to hear. With his heart sinking, wearily he turned to the team.

'Damn! What's the matter with us? This guy, this Jason. He's running rings around us.'

The team all felt it. From such a small beginning, it had grown into a monster, consuming them. Tonnick pulled himself together.

'OK… sorry. Hang on. We don't know it is Jason until we check it. Look, let's someone go see. Max? This one's for you. Where is it, anyway? Who found the body? C'mon, and everybody? Really cross-check everything. One small detail that we missed. It has to be there.'

Max left to go to the scene. Tonnick was delegating and trying to use his role as an overseer. Strategy. Analysis away from the field. He was again reviewing what they knew and how the whole case had gone. How did they know it was 'another one' by Jason? Seems the whole station was 'chasing ghosts', and just like the PC Technician with the unknown server fault, right now he couldn't do anything about it.

They had joined the dots for the first three murders, hampered by the name change of that teacher, and had learnt of the death of the parents of one boy, now a man, but had not been able to catch up with him.

It had initially looked like the wife of Quinton Chambers had been involved, either directly or maybe through persons unknown, trying to get their hands on the factory, perhaps? She had admitted finding out about the money her husband had given Madeline Torrey. That and the expensive house on the Sunhills Estate. Tonnick was sure that pointed to motive. It must have hurt seeing your husband's mistress living it up in a house she did not have to work for. However, she was with the police when Jimmy Holt died.

Although she had a cast-iron alibi for murder three, that murder was also connected to murders one and two, so... did she have accomplices?

The team were still sitting in the main room thirty minutes later, going over the previous incidents and what they knew. The whiteboard was covered with names, dates, arrows. Some members of the team were doodling into notebooks, idly writing down details, trying to make any consolidating connection.

The phone rang. It was Max, who had gone to the latest murder, with an update.

'So, he's in the living room and it's a bombsite, boss,' Max was saying. His voice reverberated around the squad room, as it had been put onto speaker.

'There's blood everywhere. Looks like a fight. There's a note: *'Chew on that one, detectives'*. Looks like the victim has been gagged, but after the violence. He's been bludgeoned to death. The room has been turned over, as has the bedroom.'

'What else does the note say?' Tonnick was quick to ask.

'Nothing. That's it.'

Tonnick looked around the room. He could see concern and understanding from Mandi as a result of his question, so he asked one more.

'So you say there was a fight? The victim is bludgeoned to death? Like… that's it, just straightforward deadly assault?'

'Yes,' came the reply, 'Boss, I got to say something here.'

Tonnick was scribbling on his pad. 'Go on, Max.'

'Based on this… this scene, I don't think this one is Jason.'

Detective Inspector Tonnick looked at the team, then held up his notepad to the room

On it was written: 'It's not him.'

'Jason is subtle,' Tonnick was explaining. 'He leaves ambiguous messages. His modus operandi is to conceal the act of murder. Remember, we have not released that information, so only Jason and this team know it. This latest incident… the perpetrator would not have known about those little details. A little detail, but an all-important one. This is detective work. The killer's note was not signed 'JASON', and this murder was a straightforward assault and possibly robbery — a pretty horrific one, don't get me wrong.' Tonnick was speaking to the team in the office. 'But there was no disguising it.'

The latest death was on the front cover of the media and it was also the lead story in the local news the following morning. There were more than a couple of suggestions that serial-killer Jason was involved, though with little fact being released, the stories were a triumph of sensationalism over substance with a lot of impertinent speculation. It was well-known that fear-mongering sells newspapers. Tonnick thought back to his recent press briefing, and how he'd had to defend his team, as the media tried to sensationalise the 'spate' of murders.

The team had already discounted this latest event, even more so when it came to light that there had been a robbery at the incident address — Jason never stole anything. The murderer tried to imply it was Jason to conceal what he was really doing. They were once again focusing on the murders that they knew were the work of one man.

Later that day, one of the front desk officers came to the team room with a letter.

'Hand-delivered about five minutes ago,' was all he could say, 'a cyclist dropped it off.'

Tonnick looked at the officer, took the letter which weighed virtually nothing and opened it.

The team saw the familiar paper, heavy vellum, and stiffened. Everyone leaned forward.

That 1 U C, it was not me.
A copycat, simple as that.
U got 2 remember…
I don't do December.
JASON

Tonnick was straight on the phone to the desk. He wanted to know everything about the delivery.

'A cyclist? Yes. Wearing a helmet and cycling shorts. What else? Sunglasses? OK. Did you get a good look at his face? Ahh. Any detail you can remember? Wait? The CCTV! I want a copy of the recording covering that delivery, OK? Great thanks.'

He cut the call.

'A cyclist, white male, estimate the age to be between eighteen and twenty-five, wearing a black bike helmet, gold lenses in the sunglasses, Day-Glo green bike top, one of those skin-tight ones, black cycling shorts. Black cycling shoes — he can't remember any branding.'

'Put the word out... we need to try to trace this guy. It's probably not Jason but he will have seen him... go!'

Mandi tore off five sheets of A5 paper and started with Madeline Torrey. She wrote the victim's name at the top of the first sheet in capital letters and added the date of the murder below that (and underneath that, in brackets, she added the month as a word in capital letters). Then there was the letter inside the circle that they found on the bath panel. This was added large and in the middle of the sheet of paper, and 'Bath 'was written below in brackets

Next came the cause of death — electrocution.

Mandi thought — what else to add?

She remembered. There was no note for this first incident but Madeline was implied in the note for the second murder.

Mandi added the word 'Jezebel' and made a reference to the second note they received. She thought again and copied out the note's contents on the next line below. She

238

made a mental note to state which month the note from Jason had been received.

What else?

She glanced down at the case notes and picked up the file for Eddy Fairley. Taking the second sheet of paper, she repeated the information for him on the sheet, and the word 'Observer'. She had no connections but as a taxi driver, he may have known some or even all of them.

She went back to the first sheet and added that Madeline knew Chambers. She smiled as she thought, Chambers probably 'knew' Madeline in every sense of the word. She laid the two sheets side by side and tried to see any pattern, any commonality, but apart from the familiarity, there was nothing.

She picked up James Holt's notes next. As with the other two, she filled out the sheet of A5. Something was bothering her now. The information she had written, plus the history of the whole case, was going around in her brain. There was something but it was not coming out. She thought deeply, looking at the three sheets, closing her eyes and trying to coax the information out of her head.

After a minute, Mandi grimaced, opened her eyes and continued. She added the horseplay at the factory to the note. She then added Chambers as the name of someone that Holt was associated with, and for the first time, she also wrote down the name of Liam Granger as a victim of bullying.

She quickly grabbed the next case notes, which were for Chambers. She smiled as she looked at his name —

Quinton Charles Chambers. It was written like that on the case notes. *How pretentious!* She smiled again, as she only copied 'Quinton Chambers' on another A5 sheet and then added all the details, same as on the other sheets. She added asphyxiation and car as the cause and location.

At the bottom, she added Torrey, Holt and again William Granger plus a note about June Davies thinking Holt was getting off lightly.

One more to go — Gary Poole. She started writing up the detail on her last sheet of A5 but then went back to Chambers and added the note they received in the post, again linking it to Madeline Torrey. Then she realised she had left the note they found at the scene off Eddy Fairley's sheet. She corrected this, and then returned to Poole, adding the Chambers connection.

Now, with all the sheets completed, she spread them out, looking for anything linking them, apart from some of the victims knowing some of the others.

Days. What about the day of the incident? She thought. This might narrow the search down if they were all, say, Tuesday. Madeline's was a Monday but James Holt was killed on a Sunday so that theory was out of the window. She added the other days to the other sheets.

Mandi was staring at the sheets, willing something to leap out. Observer. Drug dealer, no wait… Narcotics was the word used. She corrected the sheet. Poole and Torrey were at home when they were murdered but they were the only two that were. Similarly, Chambers and Fairley died in their vehicles. Fairley and Chambers were secured for

240

some of the time. Wait... so was Holt. Sadist. Jezebel. Alcoholic. Those one-word sum-ups seemed to be pretty spot-on.

Mandi noticed that the sheets were laid out but not in chronological order. She moved them around until they were. The first thing she noticed could not be missed — it was leaping off the sheets. The letters in circles in the middle of the pages, when in the correct order spelt a word. A name.

J.A.S.O.N.

Jason. Mandi noticed the one-word description's capital letters also spelt out a word. Jezebel, Alcoholic, Sadist, Observer, Narcotics Dealer. Again it was 'JASON'.

Was it deliberate? Making words fit his name? It was a possibility. Then she noticed the pattern in the days of the week. Madeline was on a Monday, Quinton on Friday, James Holt on Sunday and so on, no two murders were on the same day. Five murders on five different days of the week. July was Monday, August was Friday. Mandi tried hard to find any link, any pattern across the five sheets of A5.

She was idly scanning all the information on all the sheets when it hit her. That realisation that she had made a case-changing discovery. *OMG, how could we have missed it?* There is a word there in front of us all the time! She looked again, just to be sure, but there it was, shouting out from the papers. She scooped up the A5 sheets and walked towards Detective Inspector Tonnick's Office door.

Mandi felt trepidation and elation at the same time. She had done as asked, she had found something. At the same time she knew… her boss was probably not going to be happy.

'Come, come,' Tonnick called in response to her knock. 'You have something?'

Mandi entered slowly, walking over to the desk. She nodded.

'OK, let's have it.'

Tonnick was not expecting anything new but was impatient all the same. Mandi took a deep breath.

'His name is not Jason.

'You asked me to find a link,' she continued, 'something we had missed before. Any pattern or play on words… '

'Yes, yes,' Tonnick was slightly impatient, 'what you got?'

'…Words or letters I think you said… '

Before he could answer, she stepped to the side of the desk and laid the sheets of paper out in chronological order.

'…and remember *I don't do December,* he told us.'

There was a silence as Tonnick scanned the sheets. After a few seconds, he looked up inquisitively.

'What am I looking at?'

Mandy leaned forward with the red marker pen she had brought with her and underlined the months she had written at the top. For effect, she circled the first letter of each, but Tonnick had already seen for himself.

In sequence, the months were July, August, September, October and November. Tonnick sat back in his chair and let out a long sigh. He had already grasped the meaning of the highlighted letters.

They too spelt... JASON

'His name's not Jason — that's the months.' Mandi was summarising her research. 'The letter in the circle at each crime scene simply added a date-stamp to the incident. He further emphasised that with the one-word sum up of each victim. That was carefully thought out. 'J' for Madeline, the Jezebel, another 'J', in the month of July. Everything reinforces those months of each murder. He even signs 'JASON', not Jason. We just assumed it was his name. We have just 'joined the dots' he helpfully provided us with those one-word descriptors, to distract us. He's actually clever because those single words really do sum up each victim.' He knew what he was doing all along.

Tonnick looked at the evidence for a good while, trying to discount the theory, but no matter how he tried, he came to the same conclusion.

'So... we don't even know the suspect's actual name? Damn! Wait. What happens if there's another murder? How does that work, with 'D' for December?'

'I'm willing to bet there will be no more murders, not this year, at least.'

Mandi seemed pretty sure of herself, Tonnick noted but then he remembered what she reminded him earlier.

I don't do December.

Looks like the girl was right about everything. He looked up.

'Good work, Mandy... thanks.'

'Thanks sir, not Amanda, and it's spelt with an 'i', sir. Thanks.'

Tonnick seriously tried to spell the name as 'Mindy' and make it sound correct. Being old school, the name ended in a 'y', always had, always will.

Then he once again looked at the bigger picture. The case. If it is months, and if he 'doesn't do December'... Does that mean... its over?

Despite a rapid reaction to the cyclist delivery, sometime later, the first report came through.

'No sign of him. Disappeared. The street cameras had a cyclist matching the description but he shot into the side street feeding that multi-storey carpark. Never came out. We went, but... no bike, nothing. He must have left in a car. He did not exit through the shops, well, not with the bike, anyway.'

***

That part at least was correct. Liam had taken the bike to the top floor, then lifted it on top of the lift motor-house where it sat, out of sight. His bag had contained a change of clothes which he hurriedly put on, then walked back down using the car ramps rather than the stairs, so that he looked like another driver. He exited into the big food store on the ground floor — it was very busy, of course, and made his way to the drinks' aisle. One bottle of water later and he was at the check-out paying cash, and then leaving through the front door. *The best you will find, if you're lucky, is an abandoned bike and no evidence to collect*, he thought to himself, as he walked back home.

***

A week later and Liam was already on his way out of the country. He had boarded the plane flying him to Antigua, and now the aircraft was rising steadily towards thirty-seven thousand feet. Ahead of him lay a three-month contract aboard a winter cruise ship. He felt very pleased with himself. The offer of work was like a dream. He had found it, had applied and had been accepted. The timing was perfect, too. He had always intended to take a break after November. Get away, relax, and focus on something else. Refresh and recharge, away from the cold of winter. He thought again of Detective Inspector Tonnick and the team, the bewilderment that they were no nearer to catching him.

His final act before leaving was to drop off a large donation to the drug rehabilitation charity in the city. The cash was in a sealed envelope and he was gone before the staff could rush out and thank him.

He pictured Tonnick on those cold winter mornings, travelling by train to the office. The detective's breath causing frosty mist every time he exhaled, and which caught in the early morning sun, its weak rays matching the detective's wan complexion and red-eyed appearance. The coffee he bought each morning from the stand feeling even hotter than usual, and his hands warming on the small breakfast parcel he had collected. Winter was no fun first thing in the morning, and this was before the snow was on the ground.

***

Liam thought about the cruise ship moving between the Caribbean islands, the warm sun shining down on the vessel, the passengers without a care in the world. He imagined his off-hours, basking in that same sunlight, maybe even a quick shore-leave to visit some of these islands. Yes... things had worked out very nicely.

Of course, there had been the issue with Mandi.

He had had to drop the bombshell he was going to be working away. Liam had been oh-so-careful in what he had told her about himself, where he worked, what he did, and so on and simply referred to himself as an *engineer*. Despite being a detective, Mandi's knowledge of her boyfriend was actually quite limited. There's that saying... 'blinded by love'. Liam smiled. It was certainly true in her case. He told her it was a short-notice two-week assignment to limit any protests and promised to keep in touch over Skype.

But now he was on his way. His suitcase packed with essentials for the contract, his work boots and his qualifications safely stowed, his laptop in the cabin stowage and enough cash to tide him over until his first payday, not that he needed the money.

He had checked out the entertainment system and now the cabin staff were moving down the aisle, taking the food and drink orders. The ticket had been provided by the cruise company, economy of course but to Liam, economy was not at all bad. He had himself a window seat, not because he had requested it — it had been allocated.

Liam had read somewhere about people demanding the 'window seat' on a flight and kicking up when told they would have to pay. What the hell was the big deal? Liam wondered. So you sit in the window seat and look out at... the airport and runway. Similar views as from inside the terminal building. Then the plane lifts off and for six or seven minutes, you can see the ground disappearing under you as the plane climbs and then... nothing. For several hours. Again... what's the big deal? You are trapped if you need the toilet, and everyone does need the toilet if the flight is several hours. You can't just get up and walk around, which you could if sat in the aisle seat. In fact, in his row, the aisle seat was empty. Liam decided to swap into it when he went to the bathroom.

For now, though, he selected a movie and once he had worked out how to use the headphones, settled back to watch it.

***

Back at the station, Tonnick was preoccupied with where Jason had gone, if he had indeed concluded his activities. *Bye, I see you*, or 'bye I'll see you', implied he would be back. Back when, though? And back from where? Abroad? Out of town? Or sitting under our noses the whole time, here in the city?

Again, he pondered on just how little they knew, even after five murders. They were not yet all linked. That guy Gary, and the taxi driver, Eddy? On the face of it, they were not connected. Yet, the first two deaths were linked. Linked back to the Wilkins factory, yes, but somewhere else, too? It had already been established that there was a link between Chambers and Torrey which went back over fifteen years. What about the others? Do they go back too?

They had already tried to make a connection in the hospitals, thanks to those I.C.U phonetics, but it was a dead end. No one had come in around the time of each murder, especially that last one with any suspicious injuries. The team had questioned staff at the Accident and Emergency departments of all the city hospitals.

For the first time, Graham Tonnick thought about the cost of this investigation so far. He shuddered. The buck stopped with him; he had to justify the 'spends'. He was not looking forward to facing his boss, as the team had so little to show for the outlay for investigating five deaths.

Again, he looked at the wall, showing the victims photos and details. One photo stood out because there was hardly any writing underneath it.

Susan Bailey. Or... Madeline Torrey as she was.

What did our Madeline do when she was that teacher before she became Susan and worked over in the Druton company's accounts department? We know her liaisons with Chambers, but what else? What was her background?

He looked into the main room. Only Geoff was in the corner on the terminal, uploading some statistics for his weekly report.

'Geoff. Got a little job for you.'

The detective looked up.

'Why don't we have the full rundown on Madeline Torrey? The board looks pretty empty here. Like she had no life other than Chambers. Where did she live? What did she do? Who did she know?'

'I think Max has that.' Geoff looked back to his screen. He picked up his mobile. 'Wait. I'll give him a call.

'Max? Yes... yes, listen. The boss is asking for that background detail for Madeline Torrey. You do? Yeah, I thought you did. Yes... he's asking so... nothing that helps, eh? OK... you are? OK. I'll let him know'.

The call ended. Tonnick had gone back into his office. Geoff stuck his head round the door.

'He's on his way back, boss. He's got all the notes and he will update the record, but he said there's nothing of value in it.'

About an hour later, Max had finished updating the wall. Tonnick walked past as he was putting his notes away.

'Nothing interesting, sadly. Sorry it was not there before.'

'So... she was a teacher way back then, that much we knew.'

'Yes. Gave it up shortly after the Chambers incident and never came back to the profession.'

'Did she teach the Roberts' boy? Nicholas, wasn't it?

He looked up and along the wall for confirmation.

'Yes, he was at the same school. She taught him.' Max remembered double-checking that detail.

'Do we know where the Roberts boy is now? Also... I wonder if James Holt was at the same school... in the same class... '

Tonnick was thinking out loud.

They had linked Madeline Torrey and Quinton Chambers but so far, not Jimmy Holt. And then there was Eddy Fairley. And Gary Poole.

'I will check that and let you know, boss.'

'I want a bit more background on Holt. The bullying in the factory. That man, what's his name? William something... William Granger... lost his job. I don't think Holt was a suicide. Jason was involved, we know that so, what's the link'?

250

'And we still have not spoken to Granger,' Max cut in.

Graham Tonnick had to check himself. They were all working on new cases. Jason was on the backburner. He looked at Max, who stared back. Nothing needed to be said. Max smiled slightly and nodded.

He understood The Detective Inspector's frustration.

Tonnick had gone to Liam's address, which they had got from June Davis. The SUV was not parked anywhere nearby. No lights were on and no sounds came from within.

He knocked on the front door.

Silence. He knocked again, more persistently, but again there was no response. He took out his business card, wrote a short note to get in touch, and posted it through the door. He peered through the windows. A neat and tidy house. No body was on the floor, not in the living room, anyway.

Let's see how long before you call me. The detective smiled as he walked back to the pool car.

***

It was the following day when Tonnick got his first break in the Jason case.

Geoff had been out gathering information for his new case, Tonnick thought when suddenly, he burst into the team room, spied Tonnick in his office and came straight over.

He knocked, then entered.

Tonnick looked at Geoff, who was out of breath. He had spared no time in getting back from the playground case, including, by the looks of it, running from his vehicle to the office.

'Geoff... catch your breath. Calm down. I'm here... tell me.'

Geoff took a couple of long breaths, then looked over to the Tonnick's chair.

'I've linked the murders. All of them.' He looked triumphant.

Tonnick sat up. He could only be referring to the Jason case.

'OK. Slowly. I'm looking forward to this.'

'OK... we have... Madeline Torrey, Quinton Chambers, James Holt, Gary Poole, and Eddy Fairley.'

Tonnick nodded, patiently.

'Right, Torrey and Chambers were having an affair, which we already knew. We also knew that Madeline was a teacher at the local school. What we didn't know was that this school was also attended by... Jimmy Holt. In fact, Madeline was his teacher. He was a handful, a bit of a thug by all accounts.'

Tonnick was listening intently, making the connections in his head.

'There's more, though. Again, we know Jimmy Holt then got a job later at... the Wilkins factory. I checked with June Davis. He was a handful there too, she said. She was aware of his run-ins with other employees, but Chambers did not want to rock the boat on the factory floor.'

'What about the taxi driver? Where does he fit into all this?'

'Ahh yes, the taxi driver. Eddy Fairley used to transport Madeline back from functions when she could not drive, and he had ferried Chambers and Madeline to intimate dinners on more than one occasion. And here's the thing: Eddy also knew Holt. His boy was pals with Holt in school. Apparently, it was a sort of gang. One can only imagine what such a gang might get up to in school, eh?'

Tonnick nodded again.

'The last guy, Gary Poole — he was harder to link, but here it is… he's an acquaintance of Eddie Fairley and Quinton Chambers. And wait for it… he also worked at the Wilkins factory.'

Tonnick was wide-eyed and shook his head slowly.

'Yes, I know, it's a bit tenuous. Again, June Davis confirmed that Chambers used to be friends with Gary Poole outside work. I got the taxi link from one of Eddy's fellow drivers, who also told me about Holt and Eddy's boy, Steve. He said Poole was a regular fare. He also said that Eddy was fully aware of the affair between Chambers and Torrey. He was part of the subterfuge, he felt. It did not bother him as long as he was getting the taxi fare and a nice tip from Chambers.'

'This is good work, Geoff.'

Tonnick was happy with anything that could move this case closer to closure.

'Wait — there's more, boss. In school, the Roberts boy was bullied by Holt. It went on into secondary school, before and after his parents were killed. So Nicholas Roberts has a link to Chambers, Torrey and Holt. He would be mid-twenties now. If he was aware of Eddie Fairley's involvement, then him too. Four of them.

'Perhaps he did. That Granger man was the one who got dismissed. Could there be a connection? Check it out.'

'Will do.

'Boss… sorry, I was supposed to be working on my other case but I thought this was important. I can… '

'Don't worry. This is all good and you did the right thing. Get it all up on the board.'

'Err… boss. The board… '

'Sorry, update the paper record of the case.'

Tonnick remembered the board had long since been wiped clean, ready for new cases, but not before the information and photos had been transferred to a paper copy, which was now on one of the corridor walls.

Geoff left the office to update the case record.

Good information but what do we do with it? That's the question. *We have linked the deaths. Now link someone through the links.* That was one way forward. We had not considered that before, but now we could. Tonnick banged the desk with his hands, a feeling of progress running through him.

We need to find and interview Nicholas Roberts and William Granger.

Chapter 16

Liam had been on the cruise liner job for almost one month. One month away from his home and all the drama that was there. He had quickly settled into the job, which was, if he was honest, easy. He was one of a small group of engineers who, in addition to checking the smooth running of the ship's drivetrain, carried out day to day maintenance around the vessel.

He had been ashore five times during the cruises, to experience the Caribbean lifestyle, and was more than happy with his current situation. He had even stopped thinking about what he had done the previous year.

Being observant, he saw the poverty of the nationals on some of the islands that the cruise ship visited, the shacks and shanties they lived in, the groups of young children in brightly coloured clothing, staring aimlessly, or playing together, the younger ones happy and oblivious to their predicament, the older ones quieter and just staring.

He saw how the cruise ship guests chose to ignore this, glossing over this reality, taking their photos along the beaches, in the gardens and of the old houses, or some of the carefully selected locations on the island bus tours — nothing would be acknowledged that might spoil their holiday. The tourist areas were well-policed, to make the rich visitors feel safe. Smiling faces from the locals in the shops, bars and markets. Despite their poverty, many of the locals spoke three or four languages — a necessity if they were to offer services and interaction with those visitors. Even those same visitors did not speak four languages.

Visitors and natives, together on the same island, but a world apart in every other way

***

It was the start of the New Year. Christmas celebrations were already well out of the way, and the offices were getting back to the world of work, after too much 'celebrating' over the festive period. A period of excess if we are honest, thought Tonnick, as he stirred the coffee he had just made.

He had not been out to usher in the 'new year' for years. He couldn't remember when he last did. This year he had been with Gemma's elderly parents, after he and Gemma had eaten out in their favourite restaurant. All very quiet, and like so many other families, it just consisted of waiting. Waiting for the clock to strike midnight, before wishing everyone good luck and asking if they had any new year's resolutions. Graham's this year was to get married, but he kept it to himself when asked. By ten past twelve, they were all making their way to bed.

But now, a couple of days later, and back at the police station, the absence of any new deaths that might be considered to be Jason's work only put the detective on edge. Detective Inspector Tonnick once again reviewed the case in his head. He told us 'Bye'. He told us we could see him again, but no specifics or dates. So he will be back, but we don't know when. He's away somewhere, but we don't know where.

Tonnick had followed up three times to William Granger's house, and it was on the third visit that a neighbour informed him that William Granger was away with work. He did not know where but William had told him it would be several weeks.

The police work did not halt simply because Jason had disappeared, and so, in the absence of new leads or follow-ups, everyone was working on new cases. The 'Jason case' was not the only one in the station, but even though he too was now working on new cases, in the back of his mind was the nagging doubt that the team, and he, had missed one vital piece of evidence, evidence that could turn the case.

***

It was halfway through February and the ship was underway heading to the next cruise location. Liam was just finishing his shift and looking forward to a night of good sleep, when one of the Deck Stewards entered the locker room.

'Boss wants to see you, Liam.' He added, 'What have you done!'

He was smiling genuinely, so Liam knew he was making light of the request.

'Probably *'employee of the month','* he replied, '…again.'

They both laughed and Liam gathered up his phone and tools and set off to the Chief Engineer's office.

Liam arrived at the door to the office, knocked twice… and waited.

'Come.'

Liam turned the handle, opened the door and entered the small room. Small was an understatement. With the desk and chair, and a chest of drawers already inside, there was barely enough room for two simple chairs against the back wall.

The Chief Engineer motioned Liam to sit on one of them.

Liam sat down on one of the chairs and rested his tool bag and phone on the other one. He looked up expectantly.

'So, Mr Granger. I'm hearing good things about you. Looks like you settled in well.'

Liam smiled. It was good to be recognised. This was the sort of environment he would like to work in permanently. And… why not? He was not tied to his hometown. Well… apart from his mission to right those wrongs, and the murders, of course. Still… this was the future. He looked straight at his boss.

'Thanks. I appreciate the approval.'

'Which is going to make what I say next all the harder.'

The Chief was not smiling. Liam heard the words and his face clouded somewhat, with confusion.

'What's that?'

'I'm sorry… there's no easy way to tell you this… so, I'm afraid to say, your job will be coming to an end. You will be finishing, and not just you. Most of us. For a month, at least. There's a problem with the electrics. A serious problem. Some of the wiring is too old for comfort and is presenting a fire risk. There's been one incident on board, you probably know?'

He did not wait for an answer.

'The Company will not take any chances with passenger safety. They knew there was a much smaller issue before the season started but were advised that it was OK to carry on. It's got much worse and it isn't OK. The ship will return to port for investigation, and some other delayed refurbishment work in addition to sorting out the wiring. Obviously, the company will not keep us on salary just sitting in the dock.'

The smile had been wiped from Liam's face.

'Wait. What about the mechanical side? There's work to do, and this stop is the ideal time to get it all completed.'

'You are right, but that has already been considered. There's not that much to do and they don't need the whole maintenance crew. You were the last in, so, unfortunately, you will be the first out, so to speak. They have already decided who the maintenance team will be. Sorry, Liam.'

Liam looked at the floor in front of his feet. His hands were two tight fists. He exhaled deeply, in resignation to the situation.

'When do I leave?'

'When we get to the end of this cruise. The next passengers have been transferred to other ships or refunded. So maybe… six days' time.'

'OK. Thanks for telling me.'

He stood and made to leave.

'If there are any changes, I'll let you know.'

Liam gave the thumbs up over his shoulder as he left the cramped office and into the corridor, closing the door carefully behind him.

Once out, he left out an 'aaarrrrggghhh!' in frustration.

In the office, his boss looked up, listened, and then went back to drawing up Liam's termination paperwork.

***

Graham Tonnick felt… cheated.

It was now the latter part of February and the Jason case was on the back burner. There had been nothing new on the case he had previously been handling for eight months. Five months of the active case and then… no more murders, no leads, no evidence and not one break to help him close it. He was still trying to think how anyone could do what the perpetrator had done, then simply disappear.

Like… he had closed the door on those activities and had returned to normality, whatever that was.

And that was the point.

The detective and his team had no idea who Jason was, where he lived, what he did. It was a big, fat blank. He again thought about the last note. And the note before. He did not 'do' December and he would be seeing us at some point in the future. J A S O N D did not have the same 'ring to it'. He was certain now that Mandy, or was it Mindy? Tonnick was still struggling with the spelling she gave him. Anyway… the 'new girl' had been correct. Jason was not his name, just part of his MO along with those 'calling card' letters scrawled at the scene. He had been true to his word in the note. There has been nothing in December or January, or February, so far. The obvious next question, the one pre-occupying Tonnick, was… when would we be seeing Jason again?

Because, if all his notes were true, and there was now no reason to think they were anything but true, Jason would be back. The detective looked troubled, like he was thinking ahead with foreboding.

At that moment, his mobile rang. He glanced down. Gemma's smiling face stared back at him. He snapped out of his concerns and picked up the phone, fearful of missing the call.

'Hi.' She sounded upbeat.

'Hi. How are you?'

'Yeah… OK, thanks. Just wanted to say… I can get that time off in March or early April. Can you?'

The idea of a holiday and getting the time off had been a long-running joke between them. First, he could not, then he could but she couldn't. Then he could and she could, yes... but then she has something urgent and had to postpone. Now here they were in late February and again, she could. But could he?

'Let me check and get back to you!'

He was laughing because it was the same response from each of them, every time. She laughed too.

'I need a break, Gray.'

His mind wandered to the tropical paradise he had daydreamed about.

'Mmmm. Me too. Can you get two weeks?'

'Yes. A little more if necessary.'

She was making it irresistible. His boss had already told him he should take a break, after the last year, so he was sure it was, at last, going to be all right.

'Let me go check now... give me ten minutes.'

'OK bye. Love you.'

'Love you.'

The call cut. Tonnick jumped straight up and headed up the stairs to the offices on the upper floor.

***

Liam had headed down the stairs and to his bunk and was lying down but he could not sleep despite being tired. His mind was racing and the whole situation was sharply in focus now. No more kidding himself that nothing had happened back home. No more dreaming about cruise ship mechanics jobs and never having to face the music. He could quite easily be heading home in a week, far earlier than he had planned. He considered all the options, but first, he jumped up, moved to the galley kitchen and made himself a coffee. Liam always thought better, clearer, with a shot of caffeine inside him.

He sat at the small table in the crew mess-room and doodled on his notepad. *1. Home*, followed by *2. Job doesn't finish*. After some thought: *3. Stay here. Holiday. 4. Find another job*. That one was more in hope than anything. He had been lucky with this job. Good luck was unlikely to strike twice. Then he went back to '3.' and added: *'on the island obviously. Not the ship.'*

Then he started to fill in his thoughts. Against '1.' he put: *a. back to the house, b. somewhere a long way out of town*. Liam thought about doing a home road trip. He could hire a camper van and be 'lost on the roads' for weeks. He warmed to this idea.

He stared at '*2. Job doesn't finish*' for a moment, then added: *but it's going to. We KNOW it is*.

Now he was looking at 4.; '*Where and what*' was added to the notepad.

That left '3.' He thought about that one. He could stay in the Caribbean. No reason not to. He had money… a lot of money. But visiting islands for twenty-four hours is vastly different to living on one island for weeks. There again, he could hop islands if he got bored or didn't like one place. Yes… it's possible. Probably the best option, in fact. Liam resolved to get some sleep, then research some other islands with a view to staying on in the Caribbean.

He washed up his mug, picked up his notepad and headed back to his bunk for some rest.

***

It was just a day later and the vacation plans were being finalised. Tonnick had got the required leave in early March. They had looked at the brochures and done some research online. Two weeks somewhere, probably The Maldives, as Tonnick had favoured the location from the start.

'Gray… just looking at all the options. What about one of those tropical Caribbean islands?'

Gemma was not as convinced as Graham Tonnick about the Maldives.

'Show me. We are open to anywhere, so go on… sell it to me!'

Tonnick was smiling, the smile of a husband-to-be, not a detective.

'I like the idea of seeing some of the island life. Somewhere like Antigua or St. Lucia. The Maldives looks amazing but… they are all resort islands. There's no 'real life' there, just the hotel complex. It's lavish and luxurious but it's still just a hotel.' She added, 'They are very nice hotels, though, Gray.'

'A very exclusive and relaxing hotel experience,' Graham cut in. 'OK let's research hotels on those two islands. Why not? Could be fun.'

***

It was four days later on the cruise liner, and the atmosphere aboard was low. Low morale and a bit of despondency plus uncertainty, and of course, disappointment. Everyone was now aware of the situation and that most of the crew would be leaving in two days. The lucky few staying had been moved to accommodation on the ship that was away from the rest of the crew, to avoid any flare-ups on the ship, which was still full of paying guests.

Liam had looked at islands and the more he looked the more he thought he could stay in the region. No need to go home to a cold, wet winter. He smiled. He had looked online for rental properties and had found one on Antigua, where the cruise liner was now returning. It was a little out of town, looking out to sea and the price was good. The island was big enough to keep him entertained for a good amount of time. He looked at the beaches and had already checked out some of the activity around English Harbour. He imagined exploring Nelson's Dockyard and taking a beer at the Lookout Bar while watching the sun go down from Shirley Heights. He read they had a weekly BBQ party and he started to salivate thinking about that — he had gotten over the shock of his job ending and was now more positive but… he had not eaten since yesterday.

It was time for food.

***

Graham had Gemma were leaving the travel agents with a bunch of paperwork — all related to the vacation that was now booked. Being last minute, they had got a great deal and it was not long until they would be travelling.

Graham had warmed to the Caribbean, for the reasons given by Gemma. They had checked out the hotels and resorts and looked at what there was to do. The Maldives had that exclusivity which Graham still preferred, and the idea of a beach villa with an open-air shower appealed, as did the 'no shoes, no news' philosophy. But in the end, he let Gemma decide. We are a team. She has a say, she can make decisions for us.

Now, it was all booked and paid for. The only thing left was to wait for the travel day. Graham was smiling from ear to ear.

***

'Liam! Got a minute?' the staff administrator called from the engine room door. Liam looked up. More bad news? He was resigned to leaving and didn't need anything to rock the boat again.

'Coming.'

Once again, he found himself knocking on that small office door and hearing the same 'come' from within.

He had not washed up; as he only had two days to go before the ship docked for the last time, he had a 'couldn't care less' attitude. He stared at his knees.

'Fancy a job in the Maldives?'

Liam looked up.

'The company has a cruise liner out there. Nothing fancy like this. Small, too. But they think they are going to need someone. Someone like you.'

The Chief was smiling as if he had cured all the problems in one go.

Liam remained unmoved.

'Tell me about it, then.'

It was less money, still doing island hopping but in the Indian Ocean. A small boat with only eighty guests, but all paying big bucks. The islands were not inhabited by any locals, though. It was all hotel and resort complexes. Not really Liam's thing.

'I don't know… '

'What?' The Chief was shocked at this response. 'I got you work on another boat, in an amazing part of the world, why would you not—'

'No thanks. It's not for me. Thanks for thinking of me, though, I appreciate it.'

Liam had made up his mind and cut in to save any further conversation.

'I'm very surprised, Liam. OK. I will pass it on.'

Liam left to go back to the engine room.

Graham Tonnick allowed himself one small indulgence while at work. He created one of those paper calendar things, same as some office receptionists might do, where he could cross off the days until he was flying out. He kept it tucked away in his desk drawer. Already, he had chalked off three days. He couldn't wait until March. The detective was getting excited.

Mandi was on a short break at the moment — there was some personal issue that she had to go back to the family home for. It was something to do with a sick relative but the detective did not pry too much. He had granted her three days and said to call him directly if she needed more. Max had also asked for about a week off. Most of the team had not had a proper break for nearly a year due to last year's caseload, but Max had had four days at Christmas so Tonnick resolved to check if Geoff wanted any time off. Geoff would be covering Tonnick's role while he was away, so it made sense to give him a break beforehand.

As was his routine, Tonnick checked his emails, then looked in the 'in-tray' and lastly, he spoke with the lab. It could just be thorough policing, checking for updates and any new information, but really, the only information Tonnick wanted was that connected with Jason.

There was none, same as the previous day, in fact, same as the last week.

Tonnick busied himself with his current case, a factory break-in, and after thirty minutes of shuffling the paperwork connected with the case, he left the office to drive over to the scene. The factory boss had been away but was returning this morning. Tonnick needed to get in front of him without delay. There was a suspicion that this break-in, and the small fire that occurred at the same time, were connected with an insurance scam. The insurance company had already voiced concerns, as all the items that had been stolen, and the one area of the factory that was fire-damaged all had a high value. They were looking at paying out a considerable sum. Tonnick's research had shown this company were struggling in the market, and there had already been some redundancies. That was all common knowledge but the detective needed to flesh it out with the owner.

Tonnick thought back to the Wilkins factory. No fire there, and the works were flat out with a bulging order book. A real tale of two factories. Again, he found himself dwelling on the Jason case.

He really must stop doing that.

***

The cruise ship had docked at the Heritage and Redcliffe Quay in St. John's and disembarkation was well underway. Happy groups of people saying their goodbyes, some last-minute group photos and the exchange of contact details with newfound friends. The buses were already waiting at the exit gate to take the holidaymakers to the airport, the plane and back to reality.

Liam was already in reality.

He was not going home. The company had got his ticket but he said he was staying on the island for a while before returning. He had told a couple of his engineer mates that he had rented a house on the island and was taking a holiday. Liam had, wisely, never told a soul about his trust-fund income. He had what the rest of the team did not — the ability to choose what to do next. He had also saved most of his salary while on board, so the one thing he was not short of was cash.

He was scheduled to leave the ship in two days' time but had requested an immediate finish, and this had been granted. Now, walking down the gangplank, Liam was looking forward to the break. No routine. No getting up early. He smiled. It was just like being home again, except... no ice and cold. He was pleased to discover that he could stay for up to six months with no visa. No traceable document to show where he was. He looked up at the blue sky and sunshine, but his face darkened momentarily as he thought of home again and what was still to come.

But that was for later. He pushed the thoughts out of his mind and went to find a taxi to take him the nineteen kilometres to the letting agent' office.

Thirty minutes later and he was with the agent, in English Harbour. It was just a formality really. Sign the agreement and collect the keys. The agent was happy with any tenant paying in cash. She agreed to run him over to the house, which was a little way beyond Nelson's Dockyard.

Another thirty minutes later, and Liam was sitting on the porch of his rented house, looking out to sea. There was a small welcome pack of food — water, milk, coffee, sugar, bread, butter and jam, and some vegetables. Not a whole lot but enough until a visit to the supermarket could be made. Liam had called a car rental shop to see about hiring something to get around the island on. He settled on a small-engined saloon and the shop agreed to drop it off at his accommodation later that day.

So now, with a coffee and some toast in hand, Liam looked out to sea, relaxed and planned for a lengthy, incognito vacation.

***

It was the first week of March and Graham and Gemma were only a few days away from their long-awaited holiday. Gemma had moved in with Graham in readiness for the break, though she had made it clear she was not making the move permanent — yet.

Like the detective she was engaged to, Gemma was thorough. All the arrangements had been made by her, and not just the flights and holiday accommodation. The transport to the airport, the money changed into locally-acceptable currency so they were not without cash when they got there. The sun-cream. The sunglasses. She smiled when she thought about that. She was ready, but her fiancé's preparations had been far from complete, until she mentioned it. He had no sunglasses and he had got a suitcase but when she saw it and looked at him, he agreed to get a new one. His original looked like something from the seventies. Battered, worn out and with no top handle or wheels.

Now, equipped with a new case, new Oakley sunshades and an updated selection of clothes, he was ready, and she finally relaxed. They were all set for the off, and the 'off' was the coming Tuesday.

***

Graham Tonnick was in the office with his team, and it was his last day before jetting off on holiday. He had already pulled together most of the end-of-the-month documentation and reporting. He briefed Geoff separately on what needed to be completed, and who to send everything to.

Now, he spoke to the team about the current cases. He was updated and told Geoff to include the latest update into the reporting. He was generally satisfied with the progress, and particularly the factory fire, which had now been established as being set deliberately. The owner was now co-operating with his officers and with Raymond in the lab. Just a few loose ends, mainly who actually set the fire, but he fully expected the case to be closed before he returned from his break.

As he drew the meeting to a close, he realised he was going to get away with no mention of the 'JASON' case before he went. He tidied his papers and thanked those who wished him a great holiday. Even his boss had come down from the upper floor. He said he was here to wish him a great break, but of course, it was mainly to touch base with Geoff and reassure him to call if anything cropped up that he was not sure about while Graham Tonnick was away.

People were drifting away, getting back to the day's work, when Max spoke up, 'Do you want us to text you if there are any developments in the other case?'

Graham froze. *The other case*. Everyone knew which case Max was referring to.

He had hoped to forget that case, to get away and forget work. Forget that case, the one that was currently beating them all, but his boss was standing in the office doorway. It seems like the whole room had fallen silent; everyone keen to see what he would say.

Tonnick looked around at everyone.

'You betcha!' He forced the smile and laugh, and everyone joined in.

***

Liam had done a fair bit of travelling around in the car in the first few days of his new adventure, but today he was relaxing on Mayo Bay beach. He had left the car up on North Shore Road and was now under the shade of one of the coconut trees that stretched out along the narrow strip of sand. He had already done two bouts of snorkelling, but now, the sun was too fierce and he could feel his back burning. No need to overdo it — there's plenty of time to get a great tan, he told himself.

He lay back and looked up at the radiating pattern of the tree's leaves, the dappled sunlight dancing on his skin. Could he ever get bored of this? Probably, but then again, he would not be doing it day in day out. There were plenty of other things to do on Antiqua.

He felt himself drifting into that trance-like state of mind, at peace and about to fall asleep. In his shaded spot, the sun was just warm enough but not too warm. The gentle breeze brought the fresh air and the smell of the sea. Distant happy laughter caressed his ears until he was gone. Deep in sleep. Without a care in the world.

Well... for now, anyway.

SPRING

Chapter 17

'C'mon. The taxi is here!' Gemma was excitedly calling.

Graham Tonnick had a last look around his apartment. His police equipment was locked away. He double-checked the windows were also locked, and all the lights were off, well, apart from two security lights on timers, to give anyone passing the impression that there was someone home. Gemma had already unplugged the TV and the kettle. There was nothing much in the freezer and the fridge all but empty, so no disaster to come home to. He walked to the door and put the key into the lock, picked up his cabin bag, another new purchase and left the hall, closing the door behind him.

'And... did we forget anything?' Gemma was walking towards him.

Graham looked bemused, assuming it was a game.

'...like... your shiny new suitcase?'

In his efforts at thoroughly checking his apartment, he had walked right past the suitcase, which was in the middle of the floor. It was amazing he had not tripped over it. He nodded, then opened the door again and retrieved the case.

Again, he double-locked the door, then turned and pulled his new suitcase like some errant child. Gemma laughed.

'You really need this… no wait… we really need this break. Come on, Mr Tonnick. Time to go on our holidays!'

Gemma was irrepressible. Tonnick was smiling, too. She was right. It was, without doubt, time to get away from everything for a couple of weeks.

***

Liam had enjoyed a fairly heavy night in a couple of the bars. He had walked home… or did he get a lift? He honestly could not remember, and crashed out, sleeping it off until almost lunchtime the next day. Now he stirred. Rubbed his face, as if dry washing it, then his temples, remembering the previous night's partying. He grimaced. Now came the headache. He reached for the water by his bed and took a long drink, something he should have done the night before.

One trip to the bathroom later, and Liam was in his small kitchen, making a coffee. Outside, it was windy and a little overcast, but not stormy. Liam fully expected it to clear later. He sipped the hot brew before going outside to his garden table. It was then that he remembered he had left his rental car in the town. Liam let out a long sigh. He had to go and rescue it straight away before it 'walked off'. He popped a couple of paracetamols, finished most of his coffee, and then went to the bathroom for a quick shower.

Armed with a bottle of fresh, cold water and a baseball cap to keep the sun off his face, Liam set off to walk back into town, but he had not gone more than two hundred meters when a car approached from behind him and honked the horn. Without looking, Liam stepped to the side to let it pass, but it slowed and came to a stop next to him. Inside were two girls from a group he had been chatting with the previous evening. He smiled and said *good morning*, and automatically, the passenger glanced at the car clock, then laughed and said 'No… Good afternoon!' Liam smiled back.

'We thought it was you walking along. Where are you headed?'

'I'm just walking back to town to get my car. I was too drunk to drive it last night!'

They laughed, remembering how wasted they had all been.

'Yeah… you were certainly sticking them away!'

The driver leant over to join the conversation.

'It's a long way on foot… .'

Liam laughed again. 'Yeah, and no taxis when you want one!'

'Well… I could be a taxi if the price was right.' The driver was flirting a little.

'And what might that price be? I'm not a rich guy… ' Liam played along.

'Oh. Jump in. We will drop you at your car. Just buy us a beer next time!'

Liam climbed into the back and they set off. They had to pull in to let a large black sedan pass them, but just five minutes later and they pulled up where Liam had left the car. Thankfully, it was still there.

'Did you get lunch yet? I'm starving.'

Liam was offering but the girls had already eaten, and in any case, they had other plans and asked for a raincheck.

They said their goodbyes and Liam was left at the roadside, next to his rental car. He glanced up at the line of bars, and a lunch menu caught his eye across the road. He was very hungry, having only drunk one coffee and half a bottle of water. He ambled across and went in.

About an hour later, Liam was in the car and aimlessly driving through the town, when he remembered he needed some supplies and headed for the supermarket.

Back at his rental accommodation, the black sedan had pulled up for the fourth time, and two men were walking up the path towards his front door.

***

They had been flying for over ten hours now, the longest time that Graham Tonnick had ever been on a plane. He was restless and felt cooped up, a common experience on long-haul flights. Gemma and he had chatted happily for the first twenty minutes of the flight, then the cabin crew came round to offer refreshments and give out the meal options and before he knew it, the first meal had arrived.

They chatted through the novelty of the aeroplane food and the coffee afterwards, then once the trays had been cleared away, they settled down to watch a movie on the in-flight entertainment system. With one movie completed and after a bathroom break, they started watching movie number two, to pass the time. However, halfway through this second movie, Gemma had fallen asleep, leaving Tonnick to finish watching that movie on his own.

Now, with a belly full of food, drink and movies, Tonnick's mind wandered back to home, his job... and the Jason case.

Once a detective, always a detective.

He began to think about how Jason could simply disappear so completely. It was like he... had left the area completely. Or perhaps he'd gone on vacation. Tonnick sat up. That's it. He has, maybe. Maybe he had left the country. His note said he would be back, in effect but again, back from where? He did not 'do December', or January or February it seemed. That implied being away at distance, possibly. Three months and counting. That's not a vacation. Maybe he's working? If only we knew his real name, we could start to crossmatch people and travel and jobs. Tonnick looked down. Damn! We still just don't know enough.

At that point, the plane started to buck about — a shock to the system when you have flown in a smooth line for hours and then encounter turbulence. Within seconds, the seatbelt sign came on and the tannoy re-iterated the captain's requirement to buckle up. Tonnick reached over to put the belt onto the sleeping Gemma, but she woke as he was tightening it. She stretched and smiled, then uttered the popular question of travellers the world over.

'Are we there, yet?'

'Yes!' Tonnick replied, 'Come on! Last one in the sea buys the dinner!'

'You go first.' Gemma was wide awake now. 'It's thirty-seven thousand feet down to the water and a bit cold just outside the plane!'

Tonnick remembered seeing the 'outside temperature' on the data screen of the entertainment system. Minus fifty-four Degrees Celsius. Very cold!

'Maybe I will get another drink first.'

'You won't. We are all confined to seats due to turbulence, remember?'

He sat back, too. 'OK… nothing to do but sit here, then.'

He reached over and squeezed her hand.

'Can't wait now. I am so looking forward to warm water, sunny days and relaxation!'

She smiled, nodding in agreement, as the plane sped towards their holiday destination.

***

Liam had returned to his rented home and carried in his shopping. He had one package held high, and so did not see the note left on the small windowsill beside the front door. He stowed the purchases in the fridge and pantry, then pulled himself a beer from the fridge, but after thinking about the previous night, he put it back and flipped the kettle on for another coffee.

Alcohol-free day today, he decided.

He looked out to sea. As he had predicted, the low cloud had burnt off and it was another sunny afternoon. He made the coffee, grabbed a couple of cinnamon biscuits and sat down in the armchair. He had a call to make. A call that someone back home was excitedly awaiting. He picked up his phone and dialled the number. The international call took a few moments to connect, but finally, it was ringing.

'Hello?'

He smiled. There was no mistaking that voice — one he heard at least once a week.

'Hello, Mandi.'

***

'We have about forty minutes to go,' Gemma was whispering to Graham who had himself dozed off. 'Grab a bathroom break and freshen up.'

Tonnick stretched in his seat, then unbuckled the belt and stood up.

'I need to stretch my legs anyway. I'm getting a coffee — you want anything?'

'Just some cold water, thanks.'

The detective inched his way down the narrow aisle, careful not to kick those passengers sitting in the outer seats, who had left one leg out in the aisle. It was a bit of an obstacle course with pillows and blankets in the aisle as well, but he finally made it to the toilets. As he expected, there was a queue.

About fifteen minutes later, he shuffled carefully back to his seat and passed Gemma two cartons of chilled water. He put his coffee down on Gemma's tray table, together with two cinnamon biscuits. Gemma declined his offer of one of the biscuits, so he sat for a while enjoying the refreshment while she packed her phone, magazine and wet wipes into her bag.

About thirty minutes later came the cabin message they were waiting for:

'Ladies and gentlemen, as we start our descent, please make sure your seat backs and tray tables are in their full upright position. Make sure your seat belt is securely fastened and all carry-on luggage is stowed underneath the seat in front of you or in the overhead bins. Thank you.'

They looked at each other and smiled. Their holiday proper was just minutes away.

***

Liam looked out of his window, watching the gulls hanging on the light breeze, effortlessly wheeling left and right. Behind them, another object was flying towards him. Liam noted that this object needed a lot more effort to even stay airborne, the same as every aeroplane. The plane continued to approach the island, and Liam assumed it was a holiday flight *en route* to the capital.

Part of the reason Liam's rental house was good value was that it was on the flight path. By now, Liam had gotten used to the planes, and there were not so many each day. It did not bother him. He watched the plane, much closer now, fly over him, and noted it was a flight from his country. Then he went to run a hot bath to relax in and try to sweat out his hangover.

***

'Cabin crew — please take your seats for landing.'

The flight attendant hung the intercom phone up and looked down the cabin.

The captain was on final approach. The passengers were largely silent now, all belted in and upright, staring ahead and waiting for the skid and bounce as the plane touched down. Gemma and Graham were also sat back in their seats, holding hands and smiling. They could see the ground rising to meet them; everything speeding up as they neared the runway.

A few minutes later, and loud thump as the plane touched down and immediately started the slow-down process, the spoilers extending out of the wings and the engine roar increasing as the thrust reversers were activated. This only lasted a few moments and the plane decelerated quickly. The engine noise fell back to a tick-over and the final slow-down was all via the wheel brakes.

They seemed to take forever to taxi to the parking place, under the control of the Marshaller.

At last, the plane came to a halt, and the engines started to wind down. Despite clear instruction from the cabin crew, some people jumped up and immediately started opening the overhead bins and pulling down their cabin bags. The majority remained seated until given the instruction to release their seatbelt by the stewardess. Soon, however, orderly but slightly impatient lines of travellers had formed in the aisles, waiting to exit the plane.

Finally, the door swung open and the passengers were ushered out of the plane and down the mobile staircase. There was no waiting bus. The airport staff directed the passengers towards the arrivals' hall, a short walk from the plane. Gemma and Graham joined the passengers walking towards the low-rise building. They looked at each other as the heat and humidity hit them, their shirts damp in a matter of seconds.

***

Liam was relaxing and he was tired — the fresh air and stress-free lifestyle meant that he was sleeping better than he could remember, as good as when he was at the weekend cabin with his parents. The sun had set and he was ready to turn in when there was a loud knock on the front door.

Liam was startled. No one was ever 'just passing' so the caller, whoever it was, had come for him specifically. He panicked. Surely no one had come from back home? He remembered the plane coming in to land earlier in the day. *Oh My God. Surely not…*

Quietly, he moved to the kitchen door at the back of the house and silently opened it. He slipped out and snuck into the darkness of the garden, to see what would happen, and not a moment too soon. An unseen individual had come into the back garden and was now looking through the kitchen window. He appeared to be in uniform. The visitor tapped on the window and waited. After a few seconds, he knocked again, louder this time.

'Anything?'

The voice came round the corner of the house. A second visitor.

'No, but he's around. The car's here and the lights are on.'

'Let's sit and wait.'

The pair moved back around the house and out of sight.

Liam's brain was racing. Who? Hell… how? How had they traced him? He listened but there was no sound. He crept out from his hiding place and edged around the other side of the house. He peeked around the corner. A car was outside his gate, engine and lights off, but he could make out the two visitors.

After twenty minutes, one of the visitors got out of the car and walked towards Liam. For a moment, Liam panicked until he remembered the path skirted the circular lawn in front of the door. The intruder passed him and a moment later they all heard a firm knock on the door. This was repeated half a minute later, followed by actually calling out Liam's name. Another minute passed, then again, the unidentified person walked past Liam and got back into the car.

Liam waited. There was silence from the car. He was holding his breath, hoping they would leave. For another minute, which to Liam felt like an eternity, nothing happened, but then the silence of the night was broken by the car engine starting, and then the car moved off.

Liam did not know what to do. He was scared to enter the house in case they came back with reinforcements and broke in. He would be recognised if he went into the town in his car for sure, so that was out. There was no way he could get off the island, an island that suddenly felt very small to Liam. Maybe he could drive the other way... and sleep on the beach. This idea made sense. He could hide the car, and rest under the palm trees. No one about and no evidence of him being there. Liam made up his mind.

He went inside, grabbed his car-keys and jacket, plus some water, and got in the car. It was silent outside and no streetlights, just the moonlight to illuminate the road. Quickly, started the car, but kept the lights off. His eyes had become accustomed to the moonlight and he could see where he was going.

Liam drove out of his parking spot as quietly as he could and set off up the coast, away from the town. He passed two beaches but at the third one, he saw a small shelter set back from the road, where he might conceal the car. Liam pulled up behind the shelter and switched off the engine. Then he walked across the road to the beach. He looked back. The car could not be seen. He walked down onto the sand and made for a group of palm trees, which were strangely still and quiet.

Liam looked down at his watch… it was after ten PM, now. He walked up to the trees and cleared a small area of leaves and debris. Then he rolled his jacket into a pillow, put the water bottles on the sand next to him, and lay down. All was still and quiet. Liam lay for a while, thinking about what to do next. The next day, he meant. He could not go home, early morning he would go into the town, and stash the car, then disappear into the coffee shops for the day. He dozed and finally fell asleep.

***

Gemma and Graham moved forward, past immigration and on towards the baggage collection point. Her case was one of the first out, they smiled, but that turned to frustration as Graham's suitcase failed to materialise.

They waited.

'It's got to come out soon.'

Gemma tried to sound positive but did not feel it, especially when Graham answered.

'Maybe it's not on the plane, or they lost it?'

'Oh, Gray. Don't say that. It will come… look! Here it is!'

Graham's new suitcase appeared in the baggage hall, and he moved to pick it up.

'OK… where now?'

'Out and to the left. Someone from the resort is there to meet us.' Gemma was fully organised.

They walked out briskly and immediately saw the resort representative.

***

Liam awoke with a start. He was momentarily disorientated but quickly focused on his situation. It was just after three-thirty AM. He looked around from his low-level resting place. No one on the beach and no cars on the road.

Perfect.

He got up, stretched and walked towards the car, still hidden behind the shelter, carrying his jacket. Moments later and he was heading back to the house for a wash and change.

After his shower, he indulged in coffee and toast and savoured the moment, clean and fresh, and with his first caffeine hit of the day. One hour after getting back to the house, he put the mug and plate in the sink and walked towards the front door, keys in hand. He swung the door open and physically fell back in shock.

Two uniformed men were standing on his front doormat.

'Good morning, William. We have been looking for you. May we come in?'

Liam was picking himself up. He motioned to the sitting room. The men entered and closed the door. There was an awkward silence as the three of them stood in the sitting room, looking at each other.

Liam had got over his shock, now that he had had a chance to look at the visitors. He knew who they were.

'God, Liam, you are a hard man to track down. We were looking for you all of yesterday. Where did you disappear to last night?'

'I was around.' Liam chose to be vague, as he did not know what the men wanted yet.

***

Gemma and Graham were now sitting in a speedboat, racing over the ocean. Finally, their holiday was about to begin. The capital city receded into the distance as they motored along. Another twenty-five minutes of this, and then... paradise.

A short while later and the boat slowed as it approached the prettily lit jetty. After pulling up and securing the boat, the crew helped the passengers disembark, where smiling staff were there to greet and welcome them. As their suitcases were unloaded, the party made their way to the reception foyer where cold towels and a refreshing drink awaited them.

The reception manager looked around, smiling.

'Welcome! Everyone OK? Good evening and welcome to the Sunset Resort, and welcome... to the Maldives!'

Gemma looked at Graham. Exclusivity had swung it for her. He smiled back. They would visit the Caribbean next time.

The manager had concluded his short introduction to the island and was finishing up.

'Restaurant is open for dinner when you are ready and remember... . no shoes, no news!'

A murmur of laughter from the new guests, some of whom had already removed their footwear.

***

The visitors looked at the man sitting in front of them.

'Liam, we'll get straight to it. We need you to come back to work. Our sister ship, sailing the Caribbean, had had the maintenance people and several crew go down with something. Only two engineers are still standing, so to speak. We need you to come back straight away.'

The two cruise-line officers were in a hurry. Liam did not answer immediately. He was thinking. Weighing it up.

'If it will help you to make your mind up, the company will pay you through, so it will be as if you had worked the whole time. You just had a few free days with pay!'

He had enjoyed the island life, but he had enjoyed the ship life more. Doing something. Seeing more of the islands. If he was honest, he had been drifting on the island, with no real purpose. It was great and relaxing, but you can have too much of even that.

'I need to cancel this house, and the car. There may be a penalty for that.'

'Well… let's see. We can go there later this morning.'

His visitors wanted to get this sorted quickly.

'OK. When does the contract for this finish?'

Liam wanted all the information.

'Around the end of May.'

'OK. Count me in.'

Liam had made up his mind. Time to go back to work.

Chapter 18

Detective Inspector Tonnick was now back at work after a relaxing sixteen-day Maldivian break. He was totally rested, and more than a little sun-tanned. He felt... healthy. His mind cast back to swimming with those green-tipped reef sharks, the night fishing where Gemma had caught the biggest fish, and the amazing villa they had stayed in, complete with its outdoor shower. He smiled, thinking about when Gemma saw the massive fruit bats overhead when she used that shower for the first time.

'Glad to be back?'

Raymond Gunne stuck his head around the door, smiling.

'It was amazing, Raymond.'

Tonnick pulled himself back to reality and focused on the current cases.

'The factory owner was arrested,' Gunne updated him, 'and they caught the arsonist. Most of the 'stolen' items have been recovered. It was an insurance scam. Case all but closed, just awaiting the conviction. They confessed.'

'That's good news. Always good to close a case. What else?'

The Lab manager looked him in the eye. Tonnick was looking back, hoping, pleading for information on the Jason case.

'Nothing. Sorry.'

Raymond Gunne noted the detective's disappointment.

'It will come eventually. We just need to be ready.'

'Yes… but there is still some information to gather. Name, where he went. Motive, even. I hate not knowing. This is unlike just about all of my other cases, and—'

'There's always some twist with serial killers,' Gunne cut in.

'This case is dominating your life, Gray. Relax, and be ready. That's it.'

Raymond Gunne left the office, and Graham Tonnick heeded his words. Yes… get stuck into the other cases.

He pulled over the case tray and called Max.

***

Liam felt a bit of déjà vu. For the second time, he was underway on a cruise liner, a liner virtually identical to the first one he had been on. Same crew quarters, same mess room, same engine room. There was only one difference, and it was a welcome one. He had been promoted to lead engineer in the maintenance crew, and with it, a small pay rise.

Someone had recognised his work and commitment to the company.

The routine was the same, but the cruise route was different. Liam was happy about that. See some new islands and sample more of the Caribbean. He had been away over four months; this was well into his fifth and as he told himself, it had shot past.

What's that saying? Ah yes... Time flies when you're having fun. Undoubtedly, Liam was having more fun doing winter Caribbean cruising than if he had stayed at home.

***

Detective Inspector Graham Tonnick was definitely not having fun. Despite it being spring, the air was unseasonably cold. He hurried to the coffee stand and took a hot cinnamon bun to have with his coffee, something he never normally did. The cinnamon reminded him of the plane trip out to The Maldives.

He got into his office and closed the door. He felt a little 'under the weather', maybe a cold or a chill — the seasonal weather back home was nothing like the heat of The Maldives. He switched on the computer and started to check emails. Nothing of any riveting interest. *Come on! Something... happen!* He smiled at his command and took a bite of the bun.

Looking out of his window into the main office he could see some of the team working on their current cases. Max glanced up as he looked over and raised his head in a sort of nod. The new girl was also hard at... something.

Lucy Downe had just been up to see her from the Lab, which always excited Max.

No Geoff, though. Wonder where he is? Tonnick tried to remember which case he was on… the school stalker, loitering outside the playground. Ahh so maybe he's gone to catch him in the act. His own case was another death, in a retirement home, but the staff did not think it was natural causes. There had been heated exchanges between a couple of septuagenarians, including threats from one to 'finish' the other. Now, that very outcome had occurred. The survivor was displaying wide-eyed denial and surprise, saying they were just verbally sparring, something they often did, and he could never kill his friend.

The preliminary staff interviews had thrown up one anomaly. While the care assistants agreed with the survivor that they were usually friendly, and it was inconceivable that he could have murdered the deceased, one of the catering staff, who took round the meals and cleared up the dishes and trays painted a very different picture, one of heated animosity and rivalry over one other female resident.

At that moment, the phone rang. It was the retirement-home owner.

'In connection with the death, we have been informed that money and valuables are missing.'

'Who informed you?' Tonnick needed to validate the claim.

'The daughter. She discovered his watch, ring and gold chain had disappeared. The watch alone is worth ten grand.'

'Wow — expensive watch.'

'Yes. A Calibre de Cartier. It is, and there's more... money has been taken out of his account.' The homeowner relayed the information. 'About twenty grand. The daughter tells me that the watch was a gift from his late wife.'

The detective sat up. 'Right. Thanks for that update.'

On thinking of something, he called the retirement homeowner back.

'One more thing. How long has that catering guy been working for you?'

'Let me check. Hold on.'

There followed sounds of cabinets being opened and records being pulled.

'Four months, two weeks. He's quite new.'

'Where was he before he came to you?'

There was a brief delay while the owner checked the records. 'Greenacre's Care Home, over on Orchard Street.'

Tonnick noted it all, then ended the call.

Detective Inspector Tonnick felt some progress with the care home case, but at the same time, his mind thought back to the stagnating Jason case, something he did ten or more times a day.

***

Coincidentally, Liam had a quiet moment and was thinking about Graham Tonnick at that same time. He had just finished his shift, showered and changed and completed the paperwork. Now he was relaxing with a coffee, and his mind cast back to his game with the detective. It seemed to trigger every time he spoke with Mandi. She did not talk about work much but nevertheless, her voice was forever associated with the detective. He got the feeling she was possibly drifting away. That was understandable, given that they had been apart for over four months and not the two weeks he initially told her.

Their last call had been largely superficial like she was just going through the motions. Liam was a bit thrown by that attitude. Up until that call, he thought they were solid and he was controlling the situation. Now, it seemed that Mandi was losing interest.

He brightened up when he thought about Tonnick. He thought about all his work last year. Liam smiled to himself at his description of his activities as 'work'. The clues he left the detective. The notes he sent to the team. The links the detective should have made. And yet, still, he did not seem to be any further on. Detective Inspector Graham Tonnick had had a frustrating winter while Liam had enjoyed work and play in the sun.

Liam one - Tonnick nil. He punched the air and said 'Yes!' out loud.

***

Tonnick was sitting in the reception area of the Greenacres Care Home, waiting to speak to the owner Gerald Holmes. He knew these places offered a service to those wealthy enough to be able to use them, but he also knew that they were very lucrative enterprises, in the main. Certainly, the building looked expensive, and the staff were well dressed and smiling. Tonnick wondered if the smiles were forced.

At that moment, Gerald Holmes appeared in the reception and came over to the detective. He greeted him warmly and suggested going into the meeting room for privacy. Refreshments were ordered and they sat down.

'How can I help you, Detective Tommick?'

'It's Detective Inspector Tonnick, but no problem.' He smiled, slightly. 'I am looking for some information on one of your ex-employees.'

'Can I take a guess at which one?' Gerald Holmes leant in.

'Be my guest.'

'Is the person of interest... Carl Walters?'

'What can you tell me about him?'

'He was not with us for too long. There was some trouble, and I gave him the choice. Resign or be dismissed. He quit, thankfully. Saved me a lot of paperwork.'

Holmes stood and walked to the telephone at the other end of the table

'Charley... Hi... yes, can you bring me the file record for Carl? Carl Walters. Yes, that's the one. In the meeting room, please.' He put the phone back in the cradle.

'I can't remember everything, so we can check the record. What's he done? Is he arrested?'

'Sorry I can't tell you. We are pursuing several enquiries at the moment. Tell me, what was he like?'

Holmes sat back down.

'He was friendly enough, and he did what we paid him to do. Trouble is, there was a suspicion that he was doing more than we paid him to do, if you get my drift… ?'

'What sort of extra work are we talking about?'

Tonnick never assumed anything. He remembered that adage… *if you assume, it will make an ASS of U and ME*

'Well… nothing was ever proven, but things went 'missing', to coin a phrase. Two of the residents spoke of missing money, and one lady said she could not find her diamond ring, though she suffered from dementia and her family was not sure it was ever in the home with her.'

'How much money?'

At that point, the door opened and the administrator arrived with the personnel record.

'Oh thanks, Charley. This is detective, err… Tonnick.'

It seemed to Tonnick as if Gerald Holmes was also suffering some memory problems himself.

'He's here to find out some information about one of our ex-employees.'

'Well… if it's that ex-employee,' she spat the words out as she pointed at the file, 'I say… nail him if you can. He's a no-good son-of-a-bit—'

'Thanks, Charley,' the owner cut her off.

After she had left, he opened the record.

'Yes… he was with us for four months only. His initial assessment was good but we had to monitor him after he started taking an unhealthy interest in some of the patients.'

'What do you mean, unhealthy?' Tonnick was genuinely curious.

'Oh no… nothing like that.' Holmes was a little shocked. 'Carl Walters started off chatting with the residents, but he always seemed to focus on the ones with infrequent family visits and who were suffering from Alzheimer's or dementia. Initially, we were OK with that, as interactions for the residents is good. But then, he became very close to two people here. Was spending a lot of time with them, so much so that his job was suffering. We had to reprimand him, and he took offence at that. Said he was just trying to brighten up the dull days for some of the guests.'

'So, what was wrong with that? As long as he did the day job properly, I can't think of any reason why you would not be happy that someone was making your residents happy.'

Tonnick was fishing for a response from the owner.

He got it.

'I can think of twenty-five thousand reasons.'

The detective looked up. Holmes was reading his notes in the personnel record.

'You asked how much money went missing. Well, that's it. Twenty-five thousand. That's how much money and also some valuables disappeared while Carl Walters was with us.'

Graham Tonnick stopped writing.

'And this was all reported to the police, right?'

'Well... err... no. The guests did not want to do that. Something to do with image and what the family would think. We kept a record internally, of course, but in any case, we could not prove that Walters had stolen the money. The two residents had memory loss issues and they could not remember if they had given money to anyone, so it became vague.'

'Where did Walters work before coming to you?'

Tonnick saw some leg work ahead of him to get to the bottom of the actions of Mr Carl Walters, catering assistant.

***

Liam was now well-settled on the second cruise ship and had enjoyed seeing the new islands. What cruise-goers forgot when they booked is... the ships simply go around the same routes, again and again. The guests only go around once, then they get off the ship, say their good-byes and go home. Every two weeks, Liam began the same route with new guests on board. He was still enjoying it. He had once again got off on every island on the cruise and had some souvenirs from each place to remind him of his travels.

He was still calling and speaking to Mandi, and once again, it appeared they were 'OK'. Whatever had caused her to drift was apparently over. He did not enquire. He started to make noises about coming home soon and she sounded excited. Liam felt some relief at this. Soon he would be able to catch up on the detectives' case. He laughed... the 'JASON' case.

His case.

***

For the first time in many months, Tonnick and Max were going out together. The destination was the home of the catering assistant who had spoken up about the death in the retirement home. Something was not right about his statement. They were headed to check out his accommodation and see if anything was out of the ordinary.

Tonnick pulled up and checked the address again. This was an upmarket area, not the sort of place for a lowly-paid catering assistant. The building looked pretty exclusive too. The detectives parked up and walked over to the reception foyer. The security guard momentarily asked what their business was but stepped back when they showed their badges.

After questioning the security, Tonnick learnt that the catering assistant had lived there for over five years. They had no idea of his occupation but thought he was working in the city, as he drove a very nice convertible.

Tonnick asked to see the car.

It was parked in his designated spot, an almost-new BMW drop-head in silver. Max noted the registration and the VIN and called in to run a check. The information came back quickly. It was not stolen. There were no outstanding violations, and there was no finance. The car was legit with the numbers that Max provided all checked out. The information confirmed the name of the owner — the catering assistant.

They photographed the vehicle, then thanked the security and departed.

'He's a catering assistant but lives in a better apartment than me. Max was shaking his head. 'Nice wheels, too.'

'OK... so how is he affording all that? On his retirement-home salary?' Tonnick was thinking out loud.

'Let's do a financial background check.' Max suggested exactly what Tonnick was thinking.

They headed back to the station. And once there, Max immediately called out for the financial background checks on Carl Walters.

The following day, a call came through. It was the initial result of the financial check. Tonnick punched the hands-free speaker button.

'Report is still being compiled, but I thought you would like to know about the bank accounts.'

'Yes, I do. What have you got?' The detective was impatient for information.

'Well… in his current account is his regular salary and it is a few hundred in credit.'

'Ahh OK.' Tonnick made another note, but he was disappointed.

'It's the other account that's more interesting.'

Tonnick paused and looked at the phone.

'Tell me.'

'Yes… this account is altogether more interesting. Irregular payments in, in cash. Large amounts in some cases. As of yesterday afternoon, over two hundred and fifty thousand in the account.'

The detective sat back and exhaled, something he always did when he knew there was more to it, but he was closer to getting to the truth. He had suspected the catering assistant was up to something. This seemed to bear it out, and although he had to cross-check for any other possible sources of the cash, he had a good feeling that Mr Carl Walters would be unable to explain this bank account sum away.

***

There were several developments in May.

As he already knew, Liam's contract would finish at the end of the month. He was ready for that, but it had been made official on the last day of April and he had received a formal letter notifying him of the date. No matter. He was now ready to go home. He drew a 7 x 5 grid on a sheet of A4 paper and wrote in the dates in May, then crossed off day one. His countdown had begun.

Carl Walters was in police custody. Enough evidence had been gathered, not least of which was the huge sum of unexplained cash in his second bank account.

Detective Inspector Tonnick looked back to the day when they finally confronted Walters. He was coming out of a downtown jeweller with a smile on his face. Tonnick laughed when he remembered how fast that smile disappeared when the officers cuffed him.

The Jeweller was not happy at having to give up the diamond ring even though it was stolen. He watched as the police and the suspect disappeared in the waiting vehicles. Walters did not protest his innocence, nor try to explain his actions. He said nothing. He just sat there staring straight ahead. Strong and silent.

He broke though, in the end.

In the interview room, when faced with the evidence, the bank account details, photos of his car and apartment, and a potted history of his employment, including the six other care home establishments he had worked at before the last two. In every case, there was a cloud over his employment. In every case, money and valuables had disappeared. Since he could not explain the quarter of a million sitting in his second bank account, it was assumed to have been ill-gotten.

It was the diamond ring that was the most damning. It belonged to the elderly lady in Greenacres, and Walters was selling it. Luckily, a photo of the ring had been circulated to the jewellery establishments in the city, and once Walters came in to sell the ring, the police were notified. That recovery was almost as good as the Calibre de Cartier watch which was found on the wrist of the suspect. When questioned about how he came by the items, he could offer no explanation. Even though the suspicious death at the nursing home had turned out to be from natural causes, the Detective Inspector knew that Carl Walters would be found guilty of the other charges.

He was looking forward to returning those items to their rightful owners once the case was concluded. He made a note to go and let them know that the ring and watch had been 'found'.

The third development was the most important to Graham Tonnick.

Finally, he and Gemma had set a date for the wedding, which would take place in late September. As he pondered the date and all the arrangements that had to be made between now and the big day, he couldn't help thinking that it would be better if no big cases were open around that time. That got him thinking, and inevitably, the case that had eluded him came to mind. The Jason case, and his burning question.

Where is he?

***

At that very moment, Liam was… in the engine room. He was carrying out the daily monitoring and checking regime. He ticked off the list of items on the clipboard as he went around. One other person was in the room, but he was cleaning up a small oil spill, which had happened during routine maintenance. No, no breakdown and no drama, Liam hated to admit it but he was looking forward to the end of the contract. He was getting bored.

He was certainly looking forward to meeting Mandi again. She seemed very happy to hear he was on his way back in June. Liam had hinted at a gift, which she made all the right noises over. He had carefully avoided telling Mandi exactly when he was returning, or where, or even how. Liam's defence mechanisms were still protecting him despite this extended break.

Yes, it was time to close this chapter and head back to reality. A six-month break. He laughed out loud. *I still have one more event to complete, thanks to the interruption that was Gary Poole, but they will surely have forgotten me.*

***

Graham Tonnick had not forgotten. A detective of his thoroughness, his tenacity, Tonnick saw the non-closure of the multi-murder case from last year as a defeat. The detective did not like to lose, and if he was honest, he was taking it personally. Detective Inspector Tonnick did have one thing going for him though.

He knew that Jason was coming back.

Once Tonnick had accepted that the 'JASON' referred to months, starting in July, and once he had read and re-read the last note saying he would be seeing Tonnick 'around'. The detective was 99% certain that the activity, or something, would be re-starting in two months, in July.

It was more than that though. Tonnick marvelled at how, sometimes, a chance conversation and a chance remark could put him and the team onto what would be their strongest lead in the case yet. The co-incidences had been high, but what had been discussed was still plausible.

He cast his mind back to a week earlier when he had been talking with Max and Mandi. They were discussing where Jason might have disappeared to. Home? Where was home? Or maybe home to his family home, if Jason lived independently. Or maybe, he was still in the area, living and working right under our noses? Max speculated that he might be out of the area, travelling around. On a couple of occasions, they had visited William Granger's house, but no one was there. On the last such visit, one of the neighbours told them they were wasting their time because he was still away with work.

Tonnick was thinking, yes, someone who is now away, and suddenly the murders stop. So... away for vacation, escape or away with work?

The detective was thinking out loud, in effect agreeing with Max that a complete break from the murders might coincide with work commitments or vacation.

Mandi cut in while writing up the notes of the discussions.

'Well, if that's the line of enquiry it might just as well be my boyfriend who did it. He had to go away with work and he's been gone for weeks. He's due back soon though.'

The talking had stopped. Mandi noted the last discussion point and looked up. The detectives were staring at her.

'What's up, guys?'

'When did your boyfriend go away with work, Mandi?'

She thought for a moment.

'Sometime in November, I think. Or maybe the start of December. I was joking, by the way… '

Tonnick moved closer.

'That's not weeks… that's months ago. Where did he go for this work?'

Mandi shrugged her shoulders.

'It was overseas, but I don't know where actually. He mentioned South America, but he was moving around. He left here a bit suddenly, but he did tell me he was going. Initially, it was only supposed to be two weeks. That's what he told me, anyway. We have kept in touch throughout the time.'

'Who does he work for?' This was Max, joining in

'Again, I'm not sure. No, let me correct that. I do not know. He has his own company and he's an engineer, I think. A mechanic.'

Tonnick was making his own notes.

'And your boyfriend… what's his name?'

'Michael. Mike.'

Tonnick looked up as if waiting for more. Mandi realised he needed the man's full name.

'Michael Kallin, boss.'

'OK. What do we know about him?'

'Only what I already told you. He had money, quite a lot of money, and he… well… he's fun to be with.'

'Where does he live? Did you ever go there?'

Max was curious. Mandi shook her head.

'I've never been there, and no I don't know the address. We always meet in some bar or restaurant. He has been to my place though.'

Mandi started to feel a little bit stupid. How was it she had never been? Why would she think that not going there was totally normal?

She looked at her two colleagues. There was a short silence as they looked back. She could tell what they were thinking.

Graham Tonnick broke the silence. 'OK. All is not lost. Call him tomorrow and get some detail on when he's coming back.'

JUNE

Chapter 19

It was late June and his Friday evening meet-up was ahead. At this time of year, it did not get dark until getting on for eight PM. Liam was looking forward to seeing Mandi again. Chatting on the phone, the odd skype call, were all well and good but person to person, in the flesh, that was the best. She had changed her hairstyle... that much he knew from the Skype calls, but he wondered if she had changed. Towards him, he meant. He would discover in the first few moments of their reunion and go from there.

By now, Liam had left his own house and discretely moved to a local Bed and Breakfast. When he returned home from the Caribbean earlier in the month, without telling Mandi, he learned from the neighbour that the police had called round. Liam thought there was still no reason to associate him with the murders, but as a precaution, he told the neighbours he was going away again and moved to a guesthouse until he could get information from Mandi. She of course knew him as Mike Kallin, not William Granger, so Liam felt pretty sure his cover was not blown.

They had arranged to meet in a downtown bar, one that Liam had not been to before, but that Mandi had told him was a really good place. Friendly people and a good atmosphere, and not too noisy. Liam had agreed without really thinking, but now as the taxi approached this uncharted territory, Liam's senses sharpened up. He started to look around, at the people walking this way and that, or just standing, on a call or waiting for somebody. Him? He tried to recognise anyone. He knew the detective's team, but none of them were on the streets as the taxi drove slowly past.

He looked down to the end of the street, where the bar was located, and his eyes scanned the line of cars parked on either side. Nothing strange about cars parked outside a bar, but then Liam's heart jumped. A large black van was parked on the end of the street. It looked totally out of place anyway but Liam had recognised it. It was one of the police's unmarked people carriers. Liam was suddenly on high alert. He scanned around, looking for any of the detective team, or any police officers lurking in the shadows.

There was nobody.

Still a little nervous, he asked the taxi to swing into the side road and pull up. He sat for a moment, thinking, then he told the taxi driver to keep the meter running as he was waiting for someone. That was not a lie. He was, but it was who might be with her that he wanted to ascertain. He had to look over his shoulder to see the entrance to the bar.

At that moment, a car that Liam did not recognise pulled up outside the bar. He suddenly focussed on it a hundred per cent when he saw Mandi getting out. She stood on the edge of the road as the car pulled slowly forward like she was waiting for someone. Liam looked on. She was. She was waiting for him, right? She was looking around, but his taxi was not drawing any attention to itself. A second car turned into the side road where he was parked. He did recognise this one.

It was Geoff's car.

He looked back once again. The car that had dropped Mandi had stopped on the side of the road with its hazard flashers on, and walking from it, towards Mandi, was Max. He saw Max look at the black van inquisitively and wave a thumbs up, and the van flashed its lights once. Ahh... so there was someone in the van, too.

Then both Max and Mandi looked straight at him. He froze. Max raised an arm and waved at him. Mandi was smiling. Liam turned around and stared at the seat in front. He'd been set up. Then he heard the approaching footsteps. Damn! I walked right into it. She knows and she's told them. They are here for me. He was rooted to the car seat.

'What do you want to do, boss? The meter is still running.'

The taxi driver snapped him out of it. He looked forward and his eyes met those of Geoff walking towards him from where he had just parked his car. The detective was peering into the cab. Liam looked out of the back of the car, again. This time, Mandi waved and gestured him to 'come on, hurry up!' Oh my God! They want me to get out and walk to them with Geoff. He went to unclip his seatbelt, but Geoff had not stopped and was now past the taxi and walking towards the bar. A few moments later, he was greeting Mandi and Max, as they walked towards the bar entrance. Liam breathed a sigh of relief and laughed. *You don't know how close you were to me!* He snapped the gathering on his mobile, then told the taxi driver to turn round and drive back down to the junction, with the bar on the opposite side. From there, he indicated to turn right and drive away from the bar, but a moment later he asked the taxi to drop him there and he would walk.

Something was bothering Geoff. A niggling feeling that he just missed something. He mentally retraced his steps. He had come by car to the stake-out location and had parked the car to walk the hundred yards or so to the venue. There were cars parked along the side of the road, and other people walking, some going to the same place that he was heading to. There was a taxi, and a customer looked to be either paying or at least talking to the driver. A young man.

Could it have been… ? Mike Kallin? No surely not but wait… it could have been. The man they were after was coming here to meet Mandi, after all. Geoff was at the door now. Mike should be inside, waiting. They went in, with Geoff hoping he was right.

Mandi lead the way, as they entered the bar, trying to not look too much like a posse of police. She quickly scanned the room but did not see Mike. They went further into the room, with one plain-clothed officer standing by the door, in case any attempt was made by the target to escape. They waited for a few minutes in case he was hiding in the restroom, but nobody came out. Geoff went to look in the restroom, just to be sure, but Max was already sure their target was a no-show. *Damn! Why not? Something had spooked him? Someone had tipped him off?*

He looked sideways at Mandi, standing a couple of meters away, and the briefest of thoughts crossed his mind, but just as soon as it had entered, it left his head. She was the one who initially raised the possibility that her boyfriend could be the killer and she was the one who had made the arrangements to meet in this bar. She had been at the forefront of all the arrangements and had kept everyone informed. Why would she do all that if she was then going to make sure he evaded capture? No... she would not blow the operation.

Max was sure of that.

***

Liam was pressed up against one of the trees that lined this street. From here, he had a clear view of the junction and the bar. He waited. It was now nearly ten minutes after he said he was going to meet Mandi and Liam was expecting the call.

It came less than two minutes later.

'Hi. Yes, I know. But I am not feeling well, so I went back home in the taxi. Yeah... sorry. I was just about to call you. OK… yes. You are right. I should have called sooner. Look, can we talk tomorrow, and fix up a date? OK? Sure, thanks, me too. I don't like getting sick. I don't know. Tummy upset and headache. Thanks. OK talk tomorrow. Love you.'

Liam finished the call but continued to wait and watch.

Within a minute of their call finishing, Mandi came out of the bar. She was accompanied by Geoff and Max. They stood outside the entrance for a few moments, as other team members who Liam did not recognise also exited the bar, making their goodbyes. A couple of them walked to the black van, got in through the side door, and the van left. Shortly afterwards, another unmarked car also departed, and Geoff said goodbye and started walking across the road to return to his car. He was looking for something as he walked, initially craning his neck to search up the street, and then looking around the other streets forming the crossroads. Liam knew what he was searching for.

He was looking for that taxi, the one he saw earlier. He was looking for Liam.

Max and Mandi were driving away from the bar. After a few minutes, Mandi broke the silence.

'Damn! How did he know? I'm not buying the 'I'm sick' story.'

Mandi was agitated. The stakeout was supposed to bring the suspect they believed to be Jason into custody, but it had been a complete waste of time.

'We don't know that.' Max was trying to be open-minded. 'It's possible what he says is true.'

'OK, let's go with that. So why didn't he call? We only found out because I called him. He may be sick, but it's also totally possible that he was watching the whole operation and realised what was going down.'

'I guess you will be finding out more tomorrow. Come on. This is not the end; it's just a setback. We'll get him.'

Mandi wished he sounded more convincing. She knew that her boyfriend had lied about when he had returned. His calls in mid-June had not come from abroad. She had underestimated him — he was smart, but then again, they knew Jason was smart, so maybe that pointed to them being one and the same.

**

Geoff was cursing. It had been Mike in that taxi, He was sure now. Mike, who they thought was also William… and Jason.

All he had had to do was stop. Stop and look closer. But he had walked past. Now their chance had gone. He imagined the dejected faces of his colleagues in the meeting room, later. Crazily, he thought about the cost of the wasted operation, not that he was responsible for the budget. Then he thought about the person who was responsible for the budget, and how he was going to react when Geoff told them all that, possibly, he had seen the suspect in a taxi outside the bar.

Geoff drove on in silence. He was not looking forward to the debrief.

***

Liam watched them all leave from his vantage point behind the tree. He knew he had been lucky. No two ways about it. Thanks to his inner senses, his honed defences, he had spotted that vehicle and that had triggered the alarm bells. That was it. One small piece of luck and being observant.

Liam thought about the alternative scenario. By now, instead of smelling the sweet air beside the tree, he would have been booked in at the police station, standing in front of that desk, and noting the smiling faces of Tonnick and Max, and then in all probability, sitting alone in a clammy, windowless holding cell, and from there to interview where it would only be a matter of time before the whole story would come out.

There was one other smiling face in that group around the desk that Liam was imagining.

Mandi Price.

Mandi with an 'i', his so-called girlfriend. She had been useful at the start but now she had gotten smart herself. It was clearly down to her that he had nearly been caught. There was no other link. He was away for six months and when he came back, the first date that was arranged with Mandi she had also invited all of her friends from the station.

Hah! Some date. He smiled. *But you still didn't get the better of me, Mandi. You, and Tonnick, and Max and the rest of you. I'm still free and you lose again.*

He thought further. She had been useful, yes, but now Mandi was no longer any use to him. She had become a liability. A clear message needed to be sent to Detective Inspector Graham Tonnick.

Liam corrected himself. She would be useful, for just one more time. His July target could wait and instead, he started to make a plan for Mandi Price.

***

'And Max, one more thing to arrange. Now, please. A search warrant for the home of William Granger. Let's find out what he's been up to.'

Tonnick was now impatient to move this case forward. They all were. Max made the call to set the warrant in motion.

The following morning, Tonnick, Max and three uniformed officers were outside the front door of Liam's home. They went through the motions of knocking, tapping on the window, and calling through the letterbox. The neighbour came out to inform them that William was back, from somewhere hot judging by his suntan. Tonnick thanked the lady, turned to the officer, and nodded in the direction of the door.

The officer stepped up, swung the 'big red key', as the battering ram was known, and broke through the door.

They immediately piled in, shouting 'Police! Show yourselves', while methodically entering each room and verifying it was empty. There was milk in the fridge, showing that someone was living there, *but where are you now*?

Then, finally, the search began of the home of William Granger.

The search was twenty-five minutes old , and nothing had been found of any interest. Max looked despondent, but Tonnick was still determined. There were not many places left to look. All Tonnick could think was *is it going to be another dead end*? They were not certain that William Granger was connected to the murders, but neither could they eliminate him.

At that moment, one of the uniformed officers called out. Tonnick and Max were straight up the stairs, and into the bedroom.

'What is it?'

'Here sir, under the bed, a loose floorboard. I lifted it… there are some papers in there, sir.'

'Can we get this bed moved out of the way?'

The other officers crowded into the small room, and between them, the bed was lifted onto its end. There near the skirting board was a small hatch in the floor, hardly noticeable. The small floorboard door was off it and Tonnick could see some bundles of papers.

He looked at Max, who stooped and picked up the top three bundles. With mounting excitement, they opened each bundle. House papers, photos of what was probably a young William Granger standing with an older woman and scribbled notes about bullying at work. Nothing immediately significant.

They reached the last two bundles, with hope more than anything. Max opened the larger bundle and began sifting through it. Old bank statements, pay slips from the Wilkins factory. He passed a larger paper, still rolled up, to the nearest officer to hold, as he needed both hands on the bundle. The officer unrolled the sheet, which revealed a birth certificate. Tonnick glanced over then stopped, transfixed.

'Yes! Here we are, boss. A list, mentioning Madeline, Jimmy Holt, Eddie, someone called David Nash... all the names apart from Poole. Boss... this surely links him to the murders?'

Tonnick was not listening. He reached for the certificate slowly, as Max looked up inquisitively. Attached to it was the faded photo of a small child and two adults. On the certificate were written the names of the parents Alice and James, but the detective wasn't looking there. He was looking to the right — to the name of the birth.

Tonnick stared for another few seconds, hardly daring to believe.

The name on the birth certificate read... Nicholas Roberts.

Tonnick was elated. The tide was finally turning on his nemesis case. He believed that Nicholas Roberts was William Granger. Further, William had a suntan, having been away. Mandi's boyfriend had also been away. He had disappeared from his home, and Mandi's boyfriend had, coincidentally, also vanished. Tonnick was sure Mike Kallin was the *alter ego* of William, probably created to gain information. Tonnick felt a secret admiration for the sheer audacity of this.

***

Back at the station, Mandi's research had identified David Nash as a psychiatrist, now retired, but who treated Nicholas in secondary school. She called and interviewed him. He checked records and told the detectives that Nicholas was a fantasist, making up stories and 'crying wolf' for attention. He had dismissed his claims and discontinued the visits. The other victims on the list were all connected with the loss of Nicholas' parents, or with the bullying. It looked like Nash was next on the list. Tonnick spoke to his boss to arrange surveillance.

A further breakthrough came when Tonnick had shown the photo of a young William to Mandi.

'Oh my god! That's Mike when he was a kid! He's much younger there but I am sure. It's Mike Kallin.'

Finally, it was all coming together.

William was Nicholas, was Mike, was probably… Jason.

***

His old SUV long gone. Jason watched from the driver seat of his nondescript replacement car as Tonnick and the officers entered his home. He was annoyed and transfixed at the same time. Dangerous to be so close and yet, compelled to watch what unfolded. He smiled to himself. Moving out had been another of his good ideas. The neighbour had kindly called him to say that the police were breaking in and he had rushed over.

Now, from his anonymous vantage point, he saw the detective triumphantly emerge about forty-five minutes later, holding his previously concealed papers. He cursed. *That was supposed to be secret. Damn. Now you know everything.* Liam was now on the back foot for the first time. He was sure a renewed search would start to locate him. He suddenly had nowhere to run. Even the B&B might be dangerous. Who had a recent photo of him? Wilkins never took one. His passport, but that was seven years old. There were no photos with Mandi; at least, she had not taken any. His mates in the pub had a couple but would the police get to them? Liam didn't know. Maybe they would now that they had worked out the links. *Damn!* He had not finished his work. There had been one more to go, but now, the police knew that name. He could have forgotten that one and not come back. If only he had stayed abroad.

Liam was making his way back to the B&B. He needed to sit and think with a coffee. Revenge number five, on his original list, was over, and that left him one option only.

His girlfriend. Mandi Price.

Once more, Liam formulated a plan in his head, the same as he had done five times previously. This one would be harder, but like the rest, Liam knew he had to go through with it to survive.

JULY

Chapter 20

Graham Tonnick felt like a massive weight had been lifted from him. Even though they still did not have their man, he believed they were now much closer. His boss had sanctioned the moving of the Jason case back to active, and the papers had been brought out of the corridor and back into the main office.

'I want a renewed effort to try and track down Rosemary Hill. Let's see what she knows. Also, let's speak with Granger's friends. Maybe there's an up-to-date photo on one of their phones.'

Tonnick was looking for a resolution.

'Everyone... listen... big jumps forward today on the Jason case. We know so much more now. Let's try to find out where he's gone. Start by looking at debit card use in the names of either William Granger or Nicholas Roberts. Max... make the arrangements, will you?'

They had failed to find Rosemary on their original searches to get background for the Chambers case. She lived out of town, some way away but their attempts to contact her had failed. Locating her had not been pursued because at the time, there was no known connection with William Granger. That had now changed. The older woman in the photo they had discovered was almost certainly her. Maybe she could give the info that would finally close the case.

**

Liam was setting a decoy.

He had found out where Geoff lived and now he walked casually past the home. Once he was sure there was no one there, he walked up to the garage and quickly wrote the letter 'J' in a circle on the door using the same pen he used for the letter on the car window when he had dealt with Eddie Fairley. He left the pen on Geoff's doorstep. *Yes. This will confuse them.*

Tonnick's team was in full mission mode and were contacting all the large hotels. Emailed details were sent to all and soon, the responses started to come in. Geoff ticked off each hotel and noted which ones had not replied, so they could follow up. There was an air of optimism with everyone was feeling positive that maybe, just maybe, the case was about to be broken.

**

Mandi got home late but happy. Finally, they were making progress. It had taken three weeks to contact, follow up and eliminate all the large and medium-sized hotels, but she knew… with every elimination, the chance of finding Jason's location increased.

As always, she did a check-round as she entered. The spare car keys were on the hall stand. She made a note to put them somewhere safer. The cordless house phone on the kitchen worktop, vacuum cleaner in the doorway to the second bedroom, stand light in the same place… but still, for the first time in ages, Mandi sensed that something was not quite right. Then she worked it out — there was no cat.

Where is he?

She smiled at the phrase, one used by Tonnick a lot, so much so that they had all started using it. Where was he? Where was Jason?

The cat was usually queued up for food, circling her ankles and walking between her feet, when she got home. Mandi called the cat, but there was no response. She went into the living room, but again — no cat. As she left the room, Mandi saw a box of papers out of the corner of her eye but she was desperate to find her cat so she ignored it. The papers can wait.

As she entered the bedroom, Mandi heard her cat faintly. Was it in the wardrobe? As she walked towards the wardrobe, Mandi was confused… that box of papers was in the wardrobe, not in the living room. She stopped, listened, and looked around the room. *Wait… where's the bedside lamp?*

She was distracted by a mewing sound from the wardrobe and barely heard the soft creak from the floor behind her. Her training and reflexes sprang into action, but… just not quite fast enough.

Mandi turned to look at a man towering over her, a man she recognised even in the gloom — her boyfriend. Then realised that she was looking at the murderer, realised that she was the next target, even as he swung the heavy lamp base against the side of her head.

Her last thought was, '*where is he?*'… *He is here, in my home*.

Her head spun, her legs gave way, and she crumbled to the floor, unconscious.

Liam finished securing the bonds on Mandi's hands and feet, the blindfold, the gag and the earmuffs. She was still out cold. Liam had jumped when Mandi's phone started ringing while he was securing her. He glanced at it and saw Max's name. He resisted answering it but when the phone stopped, he decided to muddy the waters even more. With Mandi still unconscious and immobile, he left her house with the phone and drove the short distance to the city refuse dump. After a quick check to make sure no one was watching, he lobbed the phone over the fence and then hurried back to the house. Good. Mandi was still out.

***

Geoff got home that afternoon home, parked and was walking towards the house when he saw the pen by his door. Cautiously, he checked for any signs of forced entry. He recognised the pen. Knew who it might be.

He called Tonnick.

'There's a pen on my doorstep — looks just like the pen used to leave Jason's calling card the last time. Yes, I'm outside. OK, see you shortly.'

Graham Tonnick was standing on the driveway twenty-five minutes later. They had entered the home, calling out as they checked the rooms. Satisfied that there had been no break-in, they went back outside.

'Maybe it was a coincidence?' Geoff was hopeful.

'Or maybe not.' Tonnick was pointing at the garage door. 'Call the lab.'

Back at the station, they had put Geoff under surveillance. It seemed he was the target, though they had not yet worked out why. Tonnick made arrangements for Geoff to move out of his home and into a safe house until Jason was caught.

Max reported still nothing in the search for Mandi. He suggested getting a location on her phone before the battery expired. Tonnick made the necessary call straight away. He looked around at Max and Geoff. The air of pessimism had returned. Just when he thought they were getting somewhere, yet another setback.

Further bad news came with the confirmation that none of the large or medium-sized hotels had any guests either presently or previously who matched the images and details provided. A complete blank. From being elated and positive, D.I. Tonnick was now looking at another potential victim, a missing colleague and a perpetrator who had once again vanished.

***

Mandi Price came to and could hear muffled noises. She had no idea how long she had been out. She knew she was somewhere else, not in her home — the smell was different. She was in pain from being restrained. She had been in this position, prone, over a settee or chair for some time and her joints were screaming. She was blindfolded and also cold. Though she had a throbbing headache, she sensed that someone else was nearby. The muffled noises grew nearer.

Without warning, Mandi felt pressure on her head, then her hearing cleared, as the mufflers were removed. A chill voice, that sounded vaguely familiar, instructed her not to move and not to speak unless asked a question. Then, the mouth gag was removed.

Mandi's senses were returning, as was her recollection of what had happened. She remembered seeing Mike, just before she was struck. She realised why she was cold — Mandi was without her blouse and trousers. The unseen voice was asking her questions about the case — where they were up to, what they knew, who they suspected? Instinctively, and perhaps because she did not fully understand the situation she was in, Mandi tried to avoid answering the questions. She started to answer with questions of her own.

Abruptly, her attacker's questions stopped and the gag was replaced. Then, nothing, for about ten seconds. Mandi was straining to listen for any sound when she heard a whooshing noise behind her and then intense pain on her back as the strap made contact. No other noise, apart from her heavy, frightened breathing. The strap was repeated another seven times across her back and buttocks. Then silence. Five minutes. Ten minutes of silence. It felt like a lifetime to Mandi, with tears rolling down her face and her back on fire. Liam was satisfied that she would now cooperate.

Once again, her head moved slightly as the mouth gag was removed again. Same questions, slow and measured. She responded fully and truthfully to them all. Now Liam knew he was the prime suspect. He knew what Tonnick knew. He knew everything.

He stood up, silently left the room and walked outside to his gate. With another indelible marker, he carefully wrote a 'J' in a circle on the inner face of the gate post. Then, with a look to the bedroom window, Liam put on some latex gloves and with a long sigh, he walked back into his house, to where Mandi was restrained.

Graham Tonnick was concerned that no one had seen Mandi. He instructed Geoff to go to her home again. While Geoff was following up, Tonnick and the rest of the team drew up the plan to circulate the photos they had of Liam to the smaller hotels, guest houses and B&Bs to locate him. This could be a large task if they had to visit everyone, so firstly they tried to narrow it down. They had already eliminated the larger hotels after an email campaign with photos, passport and details. Now they were on the next stage. Some smaller establishments had email, some did not. The team started the task of sending out where they could and drawing up a list of hotels needing a visit for those without an email address.

At that moment, a call came in revealing Mandi's phone location. Tonnick sagged in the chair when it was revealed as the city dump. Geoff called in to say no one there at Mandi's home. He could not see her car on the surrounding streets, so maybe she's had to go back for that family problem she had before. Geoff then suggested maybe she's had an accident and is in the hospital? Tonnick was straight on to that, requesting a hospital check on one Mandi Price. He grabbed his phone and together with Max, he set off for the dump.

It was the following day when the team got their first break in the search.

A small guesthouse emailed back to say that a person matching the photo and details had stayed there for three weeks but had left to go back to his office which was out of town. They described a single, well-built young man, a salesman, quiet, travelled light, with a small case and a laptop. He had paid cash. Max, who was handling this line of enquiry, got the name given, and home address which was about two hundred miles away. The proprietor told Max that the guest would be returning next month.

Liam had already left the guest house. One week earlier, he had made excuses that he had to go back home but would return. He moved to a second, slightly out-of-town guest house. He specifically chose this one because it had no internet. He told the elderly owner the same story — a salesman from out of town, trying to drum up new business.

***

Tonnick and his team were weary from the hotel checking program. The initial success with the first guest house had turned once again to frustration as no new lead had materialised. Tonnick's visit to the dump had at least not resulted in the recovery of a body, only a phone. *Jason playing games again?*

Tonnick made the decision to 'go public' with the search, putting out the passport photo and a composite of Liam in the hope that it would trigger someone to come forward. Following a talk with Mandi's parents, he also put her photo on the appeal. The team were on stand-by later that afternoon, as the pre-recorded appeal for information went out in the local news bulletin. Within five minutes of the transmission, the calls started to come in. Tonnick knew why the front desk got so agitated with appeals — so many hoax or crank calls, or well-meaning callers but no information to go on.

But then, a call came in that changed everything.

A small B&B, on the outskirts of the city, reported a man matching the images had recently registered there. The owner gave more details. He was a salesman looking for new work. Quiet guy, no trouble at all, but he does look like the photo in the appeal. Tonnick became focused. The 'salesman' story matched the first guesthouses' information.

Tonnick hardly dared to ask.

'Where is he now?'

'Oh… he's not here now… '

Tonnick was crestfallen.

'…no, he's out on his job, but he will be back later. He's still staying here!'

Graham Tonnick was not a man of outward emotion but no one could criticise him for what happened next.

He punched the air and let out a triumphant, 'Yes!'

Max looked up and smiled. Finally. We might even catch Jason. Like with the rest of the team, the name had stuck, even when it became obvious that Jason was not his name. William. We must call him William.

Max was still trying to locate Mandi. He had already contacted the out-of-town family, and no, she was not with them. Her car had also disappeared, even with a general 'locate' instruction put out centrally to find it. No useful information had come from the television appeal. The team had no home address for 'Mike Kallin', though they now suspected he and William Granger were one and the same. Her home was deserted, and the neighbours said she had not been around for a few days.

It was the last day of July, and Max had a bad feeling. Had something happened to her? It was one outcome. He did not want to believe it, but he had to consider all possibilities. He went to speak to his boss.

Chapter 21

Liam had had a long and stressful day in his home. He felt persecuted with no safe haven — even being at home was dangerous and the police might turn up at any time. He needed to move from the current B&B straight away. Get right out of town. He finished what he was doing, stepped back to admire his handiwork, and started to tidy up. He was rushing now; he did not feel safe in the house.

Liam had seen the TV appeal, with his passport photo and a more recent composite which looked pretty realistic. His details, including his name, and the 'Jason' moniker. He imagined people dialling the hotline number. That first guesthouse. June Davis. His bar friends. Who else? Not Mandi though. She would not be calling anyone. With a last look round, he left his home for the last time.

He was heading back to the new guesthouse when news broadcast updated progress in catching 'Jason'. The first guesthouse and a DIY store had apparently both come forward. Nothing else though. Liam resolved to grab his stuff and vacate the second guesthouse immediately.

As he turned into the road to the new guesthouse, he looked ahead and panicked. The guesthouse had two police cars, one of them Geoff's, parked outside and two policemen were standing by the gate. Liam pulled in and stopped. Damn! For the first time, Tonnick's team were ahead of him. He got out of his car and crept forward behind the line of parked vehicles until he was only thirty meters away. Five minutes later, Geoff exited the guesthouse, with another policeman carrying Liam's suitcase, notebook, and other personal items. He heard Geoff talking to the policeman who mentioned there's been no murder in July. Liam smiled for the briefest of moments. *Wrong again.*

Liam felt a moment of panic for the first time in a very long time. Again, he was not a hundred per cent in control. He had to get away from the area and think. Potentially, with the composite now out there in the public domain, and heightened interest from the public, he could no longer use hotels and guest houses. Sleeping in a car could lead to him getting caught. Friends were out, too, not that he had many. What about camping up in the woods? He liked the idea of solitude but there was a distinct lack of creature comforts.

Then, he had another idea. He cast his mind back — something he had done many times since his parents were killed. Back to the days of Nicholas. When he had those holidays by the lake. The boat. The fishing... and the cabin.

Once again, he thought about the family's holiday cabin in the woods. The memory was still strong, even though he had been quite young the last time he was there. This time though, he was not reminiscing. This time he was seriously considering it as a refuge. Assuming it was still standing, it could be perfect and best of all, no one else knew about it.

Liam remembered the drive there sitting in the back of his parent's car, along the main highway with only a rail line running parallel for company. Miles of the same road, until a landmark petrol station and shop. There was a small diner there too. The turning was not far afterwards.

He recalled that beyond the turning was a small town, with some commercial activity and farming, and there was a small railway station. This station was a transfer point, with one track continuing ahead and another separate track leaving the station and almost immediately arcing off at almost right angles. This track went to the coast. Jason knew this as his father had mentioned it several times, with a promise that *one day we will take a trip to the beach.* Was the cabin still there? Only one way to find out. Jason forgot all about the now-useless guesthouse and drove towards the main road out of town.

He was soon driving up that same piece of road as the one in his childhood. He had been on the road for about an hour and was looking for the petrol stop ahead. Mile after mile of monotonous driving, with nothing much to break up the scenery, and the occasional train passing on the parallel tracks.

Then Liam saw the road sign to Draize Cross, the name of the town that came after the turning for the cabin. It was where the trains changed if you wanted to go along the coast. Then, he came to the petrol stop, and next to it, the diner he had remembered. He was close now.

He resisted the urge to pull in. He had already collected some provisions and his priority now was checking on the condition of the cabin, and if it was habitable. The last thing he wanted to do was draw attention to himself.

With mounting excitement, he drove past the diner and cautiously along the road. There was light traffic only so he did not cause any hold-up. A few hundred meters past the petrol station, he thought he saw a slight opening in the thick hedge. This would be about where the gate was situated.

Liam pulled up to check. The hedge had grown up a lot since he was last here, and he did not really recognise anything. He got out of the car and cut through the waist-high grass. There were the remains of an opening but not the gate he hoped for. He was in the right place, he knew it, but the gate eluded him. Liam started to walk back along the hedge-line.

About fifty meters back, he found the gate. Of course, it was dilapidated, moss growing on the wood, one middle bar cracked but… here it was. He looked at the tall grass. The car should be able to drive through that, and beyond the gate, in the woods, the track was more manageable. He tried to open the gate and was surprised that it still swung, albeit creakily.

Once open, Liam decided to get the car off the road before exploring. He reversed back up the highway, then in low gear, he turned in and slowly moved through the tall grass. Finally, he passed through the gate. No need to close it… no one could see it.

He slowly moved forward.

An hour later and Liam was much more sorted out. The cabin, while old and musty, was weatherproof, the fireplace worked, and after tinkering with it for fifteen minutes, so did the diesel generator, much to his surprise. The diesel tank was over three-quarters full.

Lights, and the fridge all sprang to life. He started cleaning the kitchen using the materials he had brought with him. Half an hour later, he stood back and nodded his head. This was going to be OK.

Next, he went out to the outbuildings, and after checking the space, put something inside and covered it over.

Then he went back inside to complete the thorough cleaning of all the rooms. This was his new home.

AUGUST

Chapter 22

It was the first day of August and now the team was very concerned about Mandi.

The search for her car had yielded nothing. Officers had periodically checked the second guesthouse in case anyone showed up but this was also a blank, as were regular visits to her home. A house-to-house near Mandi's apartment had only thrown up that she was 'away' and even this was speculation — no hard fact. All they had was her phone, discarded in the city refuse dump, but thankfully, no body was with it.

After a lot of checking, the city monitoring contractor finally provided footage of a car with her plate, captured with the municipality CCTV system. They were able to plot a route as the Toyota moved around town. Geoff pieced together a timeline, terminating in the old part of town.

The team drew a blank at this until Tonnick looked again at the location and realised... this is the vicinity of William Granger's house.

Max and Geoff started speculating wildly — what if they were wrong about no murder in July? They need to go to the Granger house immediately. With mounting dread, Tonnick wondered what they were going to find. He was beating himself up on the case. *Why did I cut the surveillance on the house? Why did no one go back to check the place?*

He called the second guesthouse, the last location to see William. He was willing the answer to his question to be *Yes! He's been here,* or even *Yes! He's here now.* Instead, it was negative. Graham Tonnick felt his heart sinking, and started to visualise Mandi in William Granger's home, slashed on the kitchen floor, drowned in the bath, or hanging from the garage roof. This time, he did not think of *Cluedo.*

***

Thirty minutes later, Tonnick, Geoff, and Max were once again at Liam's house. All was quiet. Peaceful. There were no outward signs of any change. The detectives hesitated. No one wanted to be the first to break the spell. Finally, Tonnick tutted, retrieved the key from his pocket, marched to the garage, and opened the door. With crazy thoughts rushing through his head, he slowly opened his eyes and looked.

The garage was normal. Unchanged.

The relief washed over him — *so, she not hanging from the rafters*. Detective Inspector Tonnick was frozen with emotion.

'You OK, boss?'

'Yes, Max. You and Geoff. You go on in and check the house.'

He was leaning against the garage wall, his eyes closed.

Geoff and Max opened the front door and carefully entered. Everything seemed exactly the same as it was during the last warrant search. Apart from the steady tick-tock of the kitchen clock, the house was silent. It was disconcertingly quiet. Geoff looked at Max. *House doesn't want to give up its secret?*

They moved towards the kitchen. Again, it was the same as before. Scrupulously clean and tidy, Geoff had said the last time they were there it had the traits of OCD like it was never used. Everything was still exactly placed with precision and care. Max started to search the ground floor while Geoff had gone upstairs. A quick check in the bathroom. The airing cupboard. Even the laundry basket. Geoff smiled at the ridiculousness — the basket could not hold a dog; it was so small.

He moved cautiously to the first bedroom door and stepped inside. Again, it was peaceful and appeared to be unchanged. He was about to go further in when he heard Detective Inspector Tonnick calling from downstairs.

'Anything?'

Geoff came back out of the bedroom to talk.

'Nothing so far — just checking bedroom two, now.'

He entered the second bedroom. Again, there were no obvious changes. Under the bed. Nothing. Wardrobe... nothing. He looked up. *What about the ceiling void?* Geoff dragged a chair over and lifted the hatch... it appeared to be clear but it was gloomy and he couldn't see all the way back. He heard the others talking downstairs and went down to join them. They looked up questioningly, but Geoff shook his head. Detective Inspector Tonnick was relieved and relaxed. *Thank god, my premonition for once is wrong.*

Max was still looking around the kitchen, as Tonnick led the way back to the vehicle. It was as they walked towards the gate that Graham Tonnick's eyes were drawn to the gatepost... and stopped dead in his tracks.

Geoff walked on then stopped, surprised.

'What's up boss?'

Graham Tonnick pointed at the gate. Geoff came back and looked. They both stared in silence. Somewhat faded, but still clearly visible was... the letter 'J' in a circle.

They both turned back to the house, just as Max came to the door.

'He's been here. I missed it when we got here but here it is, clear as day. Look.'

In the sink was a dirty cup with a teaspoon in it, the remains of a coffee.

For a second — silence, only the kitchen clock, louder now. Then Tonnick started his own search, manically rushing around the house downstairs looking in cupboards and behind curtains. Under furniture. Max and Geoff exchanged glances.

Tonnick ran up the stairs, with the other detectives following him. This was different. This was one of their own. He burst into the second bedroom, looking in the same places Geoff had checked earlier. Max was on the landing as he came out.

'Did you look up in the roof space, Geoff?'

'Yes, in there, but not bedroom one, but it's not really a loft. There's space for cables and pipes. The ceiling would not support anyone going inside. It's a straight-through space for both. It's very narrow.'

The detective pushed past into bedroom one and looked up at the ceiling hatch. Geoff brought the chair and Tonnick jumped up to open the hatch. It smelled fresh. Nothing to see. He shined his torch in … nothing.

Tick tock from the kitchen clock in the silence.

Graham Tonnick looked down to his colleagues and they looked back.

'What are we missing?'

He climbed down, steadying himself on the wardrobe door.

'You checked under the bed?'

'Yep.'

'Curtains? That blanket box? In here?'

He was still leaning against the wardrobe.

The team looked at the blanket box. Tonnick tried to open the wardrobe door, which was stiff. It finally gave way and simultaneously he smelt the sweet, nauseating, pungent smell of death, from the cadaverine and putrescine in the decaying body.

He's snapped out of the daze by the shout from Max, who had turned back to him and saw the horror of the insides of the wardrobe. He slowly looked around the open door. Even as he started to look, he noticed the clear sealant used to seal the smell inside the wardrobe.

Mandi Price was there. Motionless, faded yet serene.

She was not nailed to the wooden frame; she was supported by the rail... not hung, but hung up, like a jacket. There was no blood, Tonnick noted, so she was probably killed somewhere else. Maybe her apartment? She has clearly been dead for some time because the skin was blackening and there was the fluid of decay beneath her. Max was already ringing Raymond Gunne. Tonnick made the call to update his boss.

***

The anger was mounting in the Detective Inspector.

Where. Is. He?

Tonnick was taking his daily journey back to his apartment. The tube was crowded, it was always crowded, but not busting at the seams as it did during rush hour. He was travelling later than usual and enjoyed a little space to breathe.

Now though, he was focused but frustrated. Again and again, his mind came back to the same question. *Where is he? We have so much but know so little. He's always one step ahead*. Tonnick thought of the warrants. The stakeouts. The guesthouse. No… the guesthouses. How has he evaded capture? He felt sick at the thought of six murders. Was he incompetent? Or was this Jason simply gifted in evasion? They had been slow to make the connections. To join the dots. Maybe in this area, they could have made a difference… but then again… what difference could they have made really? Still don't know why? Still not hundred per cent sure of what he's calling himself. Hell… we don't even have a recent picture. Jason could be sitting on this tube, in this carriage, right next to me and I would not know it — well, not know it for sure.

He's despondent that his one small victory has also been blown out of the water. He knew Mandi had been dead for some time, which meant… Jason did kill in July. The gate 'J' confirms it. 'J' for July — it was Mandi who had worked that out. Then another realisation — that kitchen clock was not electric… it was an old wind-up movement. Jason had been here, and the team had overlooked the obvious confirmation.

Tonnick was so preoccupied with the summation that he almost missed his stop. He glanced up and saw the doors open and his station name on the wall. With a start, he jumped up and dived out of the train, just as the doors started to close. He stumbled and almost fell as he exited, managing to regain his balance, and then he turned to see the train start to depart.

In a window seat in the same carriage, Liam stared out at the detective. Smiled as he saw the ungracious exit and the stress on his face. For a second, their eyes met but then the train was accelerating towards the next station.

Two of the detective team had been sent to Mandi Price's address, and they forced entry. The place was as eerily quiet as Liam's had been, which filled them with trepidation. Outwardly, it was a very clean place, but as they moved from room to room, closer inspection revealed that their speculation back in the station had become reality. In the bedroom, they found the lamp on its side on the bedside table, its heavy base with traces of blood, now long since dried.

A small pool of dried-up blood was on the carpet near the wardrobe. The two pieces of evidence seemed totally out of place in the neat apartment, like they had been planted there.

More worryingly, there was a faint smell of death. At a previous, unconnected team briefing, Detective Inspector Tonnick had asked how many had seen a dead body. About a third raised their hands. To those who had not, he explained what they should expect.

'Death. You will see it in this job. It's inevitable. But if seeing is one thing, the smell of death and decay is another. Once you sense it, you never, ever forget it.'

Another body to add to all those before? The smell was faint, but they traced it. In Mandi's wardrobe was another body.

The cat had died from starvation.

On hearing this back at the station, Detective Inspector Tonnick started to weigh up the significance of this. Owner and pet. Both dead. In wardrobes. Was there a hidden message?

***

Detective Inspector Tonnick was reading JASON's latest note, which arrived in the mail the following morning.

I got my eye on you, Detective Inspector Tonnick.
JASON

The team gasped at what was also included. With the note were photographs, either taken with a telephoto lens, or more likely at close range, of all the police team, and especially Tonnick… and his fiancé too. He stopped when he saw Mandi, Geoff, and Max standing outside the bar they had staked out. The picture that upset him the most was of him, on the tube, falling out of the carriage. He remembered speculating at the time that Jason could have been in the carriage. The guy had been right there, watching him.

A chill shiver ran through him, he thought of that saying 'someone just walked over my grave' but he was more concerned about the inclusion of his fiancé. *Does that mean she could become a target?*

Lucy called up to confirm the COD as asphyxiation and that Mandi had been dead for at least ten days. Lucy believed that she was bound up when she died, as she noted the ligature marks on wrists and ankles, and the lesions on her back. She had a fractured skull from the lamp base strike.

Chapter 23

It was four days after the discovery of the murder of Mandi Price and Tonnick was not much nearer to closing the case. An unexpected visitor to the station changed all that.

'Can I speak to Mr Tonnick, please?' The quiet unassuming lady stared expectantly at the duty officer.

'You mean Detective Inspector Tonnick… ?'

'That's the one,' she replied, with a smile.

Another nobody thinks she's going to be a 'somebody', he thought after she mentioned the JASON killings in response to his question as to the nature of her visit. Those public appeals were a double-edged sword, he thought. Yes… sometimes, sometimes, but not all times, genuine and useful information will come from it, but on the other hand… . the fame-for-five-minute brigade, the citizens desperate to feel important, and of course, the cranks.

Conflicting information told with wide-eyed sincerity, some agitation, and underlying aggression when told that this information was already known, or that information was already analysed and now discounted. Bare-faced fantasies dressed up as fact, with the associated expectation that the police would drop everything immediately and follow this 'breakthrough', and disappointment when it did not happen. Then some were coming forward for financial gain. 'Is there a reward? y' know, for information leading to... ' with some insinuation that they 'knew something'

And who has to field a lot of this? The desk. This desk. While the detective team take some calls, the brunt of it comes to and stops at the front desk. Bloody time waste, most of it.

The duty officer shook his head, and turned to the lady, still waiting patiently in front of him.

'Actually, he's not here just now... out on a case and not due back today.'

'Oh... ' She looked miffed, not disappointed like she was going to crack the case.

He chuckled. 'Shall I take a number? He can call you when he's free?'

He wrote down the number and name.

Then, Rose Hill, Auntie Rose, and most recently, a surrogate mother initially to Nicholas Roberts and latterly William Granger, turned and walked out of the station.

The duty officer glanced at the details again. So, Rose Hill... not from round here; he noted the address was a good hundred miles away. It's a cell number, though so she's probably not going home. He took the paper with those details and placed it on the keyboard of the detective Tonnick's desk PC and was immediately back on the front desk and into the next issue.

The contact details sat there all day, while around the room, there was frenetic activity for the current cases. Members of the detective team back working on the 'JASON' case walked right past without noticing it, much less picking it up and reading the detail.

If they had, and unlike the duty officer, they would have realised the immense significance of Mrs Rose Hill and the person she had raised. They had tried to contact Rose Hill a little while ago when they were piecing together the movements of Nicholas Roberts, but at that time they had not spoken directly. A message had been left, and this visit to the station was Mrs Hill getting back to them.

***

'Jeeez... how long has this been here?' Tonnick held up the note left on his PC. Everyone looked up. Blank stares all around — no one had noticed.

'It's a contact to us. From Rose Hill. Rose Hill? William Granger's guardian. Yes... that Rose Hill. We're all drawing a blank. No leads. The trail's gone cold, and she's been here. In this station. Asking for me. Why? Coincidence? Does anyone believe that? Oh my god... a breakthrough and we've wasted a day. Let's hope she's still around when I call.'

He reached for the desk phone and dialled the number. The ring tone could easily be heard because the room had fallen deathly silent. Everyone was looking at the phone, willing it to be answered.

It wasn't.

The call disconnected. He dialled again. The ring tone seemed to go on forever. A click. Disconnected again. Tonnick looked at the paper and the address. It was in another county. Not local.

'Maybe she's driving,' Max suggested. Relief around the room, a get-out. *Yeah, maybe* was in everyone's mind.

'Maybe she's changed her mind.' Tonnick brought them back to reality. He passed the paper to the girl sitting nearest. 'Keep trying the number, Gill. Shout me as soon as there's any answer.'

Gill reached for the phone, as Tonnick turned and walked towards the small office he occupied.

'Hello?'

The tentative voice muttered into the phone. It had been almost half an hour.

'Mrs Hill? Mrs Rose Hill? You came to the police station today. I'm Detective Gill Stevens. I believe you were asking for Detective Inspector Tonnick?' Gill's voice was calm but in the incident room, she was frantically waving for someone, anyone to fetch Tonnick.

Rose Hill started to repeat that she needed to speak to Detective Inspector Tonnick on an urgent matter.

'I'm trying to locate him for you, but is there anything I can help you with?

'It's all right, Gill. I'm here. Give me that phone.' Graham Tonnick appeared suddenly and walked purposely towards the phone, trying to sound firm and calm. He was churning with anticipation.

'Mrs Hill? Graham Tonnick. Thanks for coming by the station today. Are you still local? I'm prepared to come to you or to meet somewhere if you prefer not to return here.'

The detective's voice sounded polite, but no one could miss the air of desperation behind it. He did not even know what she wanted but he felt he had to meet her face-to-face. He was scrambling for a pad and pen as she replied, and then the call ended.

***

They had driven as quickly as the traffic would allow, the thirty miles to a small coffee shop which Tonnick did not know but which Max did. When that came to light, Tonnick wondered what his subordinate might be doing in such a place, to be familiar. They pulled in. There was only one car outside. That makes it easier. No third parties getting in the way of, well, who knows what they might be getting in the way of? Tonnick smiled. This lady must be mid-fifties. All the same, it could be a trap, so he warned Max to be sharp before they left the car.

Rose Hill was sitting at a table in the middle of the shop. The barista looked happy that she now had not one but three customers when usually at this time there were none.

She came across to take the order.

'Americano. Milk on the side. No sugar.' Tonnick was a man of routine. He had this same coffee every day of his life. Max ordered a Mocha and a biscuit. Tonnick lingered his stare at the detective next to him, just enough to make his displeasure known, then turned to the lady sitting opposite him.

'What can I get you, Mrs Hill?'

'I'd just like some water please.' The voice was a little faltering like she was nervous.

'So, Mrs Hill... you came by the station today, asking for me. What's it in connection with?' Tonnick jumped straight in.

'I think you know.' The voice was clear now. 'Let's just wait until the order comes, then we can have privacy.' She glanced around conspiratorially. Tonnick looked around the empty shop too but nodded in agreement.

'I have a lot to tell you but I don't know where to begin,' Rose began, once they had got their drinks.

Tonnick suppressed his impatience. 'Just start at the beginning,' he suggested. 'Who or what are we talking about, Mrs Hill?'

She stared at him and for a moment Tonnick thought he had blown it. He took a mouthful of coffee, and glanced at Max, working his way through the biscuit. He wished he had ordered one too now.

'Nicolas Roberts,' she said, finally. 'That was his name, his real name until he changed it, but you know him as 'Jason'.'

Even though both men knew the name and history, they shuffled excitedly in their chairs. Hopefully, some new information to add to what they already had. 'Do go on, please.'

'He has this other name, did you know? '

Tonnick was about to say, 'really?' but before he could, Max, who was playing along, had already spoken.

'Which is?' he asked, not looking up.

Tonnick looked sideways at Max, willing him not to blow their best and only lead.

'What can you tell us about Nicolas?' Tonnick tried to sound upbeat almost chatty.

'OK, I can see you are playing dumb, so let's try another way. What do you want to know about this person you say you never heard of?' Rose Hill sounded a little exasperated. She was not ready for the response. Both men stopped and looked at each other

'Where is he?' they said in unison.

Rose Hill pulled the chair closer to the table, took a sip of water, and began to tell them everything she knew.

As the afternoon wore on, they learned that William Granger had been overseas working, and yes… confirmation that he had changed his name from Nicholas Roberts to leave the terrible past behind him.

The information confirmed that their prime suspect was also the son of the parents killed by the drunk driver. The factory connection with Chambers, who was that driver. Madeline Torrey the school teacher, the affair, the workmates & schoolmates, and the bullying. The taxi driver condoning it all, and his son in the same gang, led by Jimmy Holt, that did the bullying at school. Tonnick already knew that Gary Poole had foolishly tried to blackmail William, at least, according to the note they had recovered on the body, and he too had paid the price. Jason's note seemed to confirm it. Poor Mandi had probably blown it with that stakeout and revealed she was trying to catch him. The dismissive psychiatrist David Nash had been on the list too and he had had a lucky escape. Rose confirmed that William had been upset with his assessment. As a finish to the revelations, she then provided Tonnick with William's two mobile phone numbers.

There was now only one common factor tying them all together... Nicholas Roberts, or as he was now, William Granger. Tonnick had stopped calling him Jason. It was right at the end of the interview that Mrs Hill mentioned what later turned out to be a key piece of information.

'He was such a sweet boy. I remember his early childhood, the holidays they took in the cabin. He was so happy, fishing and being out on the lake with his father. Then that was all taken away by a drunken driver.'

Tonnick had stopped writing. He looked at Max.

'Tell me about the lake, Mrs Hill.'

'...And the cabin.'

***

William Granger had gone to ground. Completely disappeared. They had checked his house and the guest houses. They had visited all his known friends and colleagues. They had tried a public appeal and it had got nowhere. William Granger, AKA 'JASON' for so long, was still out there.

But now, they could track William via his phone and they had a new lead. A new location. Tonnick was positive again, for the first time in a long time. This could just be the place he was hiding out.

***

The following day, Liam had come back to the city on the train. To check the service before he used it for the last time on the return journey and because he did not want to be caught in any car that might be on a wanted list. His original Ford SUV was long gone but now, he had also abandoned his replacement car. It was a cheap, anonymous Japanese model, but he knew that sooner or later, it would be found, and the connection made. He was better off without any car.

He was also preparing to leave the city for good. All the loose ends were pretty much tidied up during the day and now only avoiding Tonnick and his team remained. He smiled as he visualised Tonnick reading his last note and seeing those photos.

I'm still one step ahead, Graham, and in a couple of days, I will be gone forever. He grabbed the small bag of groceries from the backstreet supermarket counter and walked towards the railway station.

Ten minutes later Liam entered the bus terminal that was adjacent to the railway station. He walked straight into the gent's toilets and locked himself in the last cubicle. Liam waited until he could hear no one outside the door, then he switched on his mobile, placed it at the back of the cistern, still visible to the next user, and exited the restrooms.

He did not buy a bus ticket. Instead, he walked out of the bus station and straight into the train station next door. He had purposely delayed turning on his phone until the train service he wanted was only twenty minutes away. Liam went straight to the ticket counter and bought his ticket. All he had to do now was wait twenty minutes for the train. He used the time in the station shop.

Tonnick got the call from the phone company, telling him that the phone they were monitoring had just been turned on. He noted the phone's GPS location they gave him and headed straight for the motor pool with Max.

At last, at long last, we are closing in on you... William.

Chapter 24

Tonnick had enlisted the help of the uniformed officers to close in on his target. The police team, under the control of Inspector Smith, approached the wooded cabin just off the highway with feverish excitement. They did not know what to expect. They had watched the place for almost twenty-four hours with no movement of any kind, so the decision was taken to go in.

They drove down the access track, with trees lining the route. These were not formally planted trees, and were in effect, the forest. The track had been carved through it. As the place had been empty and forgotten for so long, the forest had started to reclaim the road area. Some quite sizable new growth made access at times difficult, but the team noted that some of the worst areas had been cut back — someone had been here before them, and recently.

The other effect of the dense tree cover was that it was gloomy. The canopy blocked out a lot of light, adding to the suspense. As they came into the clearing where the wooden cabin stood, the trees parted slightly, casting those crepuscular rays over the property, dappled sunlight as the trees swayed in the breeze. There were three outbuildings, the police Inspector noticed.

'Everyone. Stay sharp. We don't know who, if anyone, is here.'

The SUV pulled up outside the wooden, single-story dwelling, and the second police car parked at the end of the driveway, between the trees preventing any escape by vehicle. Everyone disembarked and gathered outside the front door.

One man turned to observe the outbuildings, while two police officers went around the back of the cabin.

Then came the moment to try entry. Could he have booby-trapped the place? The thought ran through the Inspector's mind.

'Everyone ready?'

He raised his hand to the door and knocked twice.

There was no sound, apart from the wind moving the trees and some birdsong. The forest completely blocked out the noise of the nearby highway. It was like they were all in the middle of nowhere.

He knocked again.

A loud bird call came from somewhere behind the outbuildings. They all looked around. Had something disturbed it? An officer walked briskly across to check. Thirty seconds later, a shake of the head. They turned back to the bungalow. Again, Smith knocked. Three times, and louder this time.

After what seemed like an age, but was in reality about fifteen seconds, he again raised his hand, and took hold of the door handle, a round wooden knob. Slowly, he turned it. The door gave way, it wasn't locked, and with a push, it opened inwards.

They were greeted with… nothing. No person, at any rate, but already, they knew someone had been there. It did not smell musty and derelict. There were no cobwebs, no feral animals using it as a home, scurrying about. There was a distinct smell though — one that every officer in the team knew only too well.

Coffee, and a fry-up.

There were glances between the police team. Someone had had breakfast here. But when? Today? They moved cautiously inside. The place had been cleaned up. The floors were swept, and the bench cushions looked to have been washed or wiped, at any rate. The windows sparkled. Whoever was here, was here long-term.

The team fanned out through the building, which was not that large. The Inspector took a seat on one of the small sofas in the sitting area off the kitchen, by the fireplace. He noticed that although the place was old, the floors were solid, and did not creak. The well-made building stood the test of time, he thought. Soon after Smith started to hear the 'clear', 'clear' as each room was checked.

'OK, we're looking for anything identifying who is here,' the Inspector stated to the team, 'anything personal. Wallet. Passport. Correspondence… anything. Also, anything that makes us think the person is still here or will be returning here.'

The team began a meticulous search of the cabin.

At the bus station, Tonnick was evaluating the situation. They knew that the phone, recovered from the lost-and-found was Liam's phone, conveniently left where it would be found. Yeah... a diversion. A buying of time. But that still left his whereabouts now. They had checked the bus routes out of the terminal for the last hour. All were long distance and if he was on any of them, he was a 'captive audience' until the first stop.

Graham Tonnick did not believe that Jason would commit to that. He must know we could easily catch up with any of the buses. *They are speed limited; we are not.* Then... car transport. We knew all the details on his car though we could not find it; he could still have attempted to disappear on the roads. Of course, the idea of using the car could be a scheme too, again designed to throw us off the scent. Without a different driving licence, he would find it difficult to rent anything — we had circulated his two names to all the rental companies. We did not know if he had a motorbike but his aunt had said before that he detested them, so... probably not.

It had been a real breakthrough when she told us about the weekend retreat place, back at their meeting in that obscure coffee shop. That and when she provided the photos, which backed up the one we got from his passport. He suddenly remembered he was yet to ask Max about his connection to that coffee shop. So many things going round in his head. He was amazed his long-suffering fiancé was still on board.

He was looking at a map on the wall of the terminal. It showed places of interest, and how to get there. Bus. Underground. Taxi. Train. He stopped looking as he considered that. The train station was next door, and trains were not limited in the way buses were. No traffic either. They were fast and efficient.

***

Inspector Smith's mobile rang while he was in the kitchen. It was Tonnick, looking for an update.

'Well, there's no one here now but there has been, and recently,' Smith told him. 'We're looking for identification of who it is as we speak.'

Graham Tonnick's heart fell as he heard 'there's no one here now', so much that he barely heard the rest of the sentence. Damn, we missed him again. In his mind, there could only be one person occupying the property — William Granger.

'OK, I'm on my way there, shortly. Just one more avenue of inquiry here, to follow up on. Please keep me posted,' was all he could manage in response.

At the bungalow, they found clothes in the bedroom, and the bed had been slept in. A fire had burnt in the living room and there were toiletries in the bathroom. The kitchen revealed a fridge full of food, all recently purchased. Everything added up to someone living there.

But who? There was nothing of a personal nature. Nothing to tie the occupancy to Jason or indeed, anyone.

'Take a look in those outbuildings,' the Inspector called, 'and look down by the lake, too.'

A couple of the team set off.

Inspector Smith sat down on the kitchen chair, somewhat deflated. So much here but still they could not tie it to the killer. As so many had done before him, he posed the question in his head.

Where is he?

'Sir, please come and see this. I think we've found what you are looking for!'

The officer had stuck his head around the kitchen door.

Smith jumped up from the seat and walked quickly out of the bungalow, following the officer towards the outbuildings.

'It was in the last one,' the officer continued, 'we could not get in at first because it was locked... a new lock I might add. Then it was covered over with rubbish and stuff.' They came around the open door.

There, behind the boxes and tools... was a car.

It was not locked. The keys were in the ignition. It was fully fuelled and clean. There was nothing else in it, but it was definitely out of place in the current setting.

Smith called Tonnick.

'What do we know about his transport? We have found a vehicle.'

'He has a car, a Ford SUV.' Tonnick imagined the Inspector looking at a Ford then confirming it to him.

'Well, we found a car,' Smith continued, 'but it's not a Ford. It's an old Toyota.'

Tonnick's senses prickled at that, but he was not crestfallen. He knew Jason did not have a Toyota, but he knew someone else who did.

'Corolla? White? What's the registration number?' He asked. When the answer came, he knew.

The battered Toyota had belonged to Mandi Price.

The Inspector made a decision to pull out, then called Tonnick. They agreed to meet at the petrol station just down the main road. He called one officer over and asked him if he smoked, then gave the man brief instructions and told him to grab some water from the SUV.

He shouted out to the others to load up and vacate immediately.

***

The train slowed as it arrived at the transfer station, Draize Cross. Jason always felt, when travelling on the train, that the slow down was interminable. At no more than a crawl, the train pulled up to the station platform and stopped. Jason breathed out, slowly. He was almost free.

The tannoy announced the station name, and for people heading to the coast to disembark and go to platform two. Jason saw a few people standing up and stretching, collecting their belongings, and of course, checking their phones. He had little with him, just a wallet, money, the few groceries and his new phone which had yet to be used. The battery was still out of it, of course.

Jason had been fascinated to learn that phones could still be tracked even if they were switched off. It was not an easy or commonplace practice, but he was not taking any chances. The only way to stop this was battery removal... then that smartphone became just a very expensive paperweight.

He glanced down at his ticket... Seatown. The coast. His ticket went all the way, but he was not going to Seatown. This was his stop. He thought again about Detective Inspector Tonnick, even assuming he had got to the train station, and checked the records, and pinpointed him in the station, and seen his ticket purchase, and noted the final location, and set up an intercept at Seatown. Even if he had done all of that, and it was a stretch to imagine that all those ducks were in a row, Tonnick would still be barking up the wrong tree. He got up in a leisurely way, and glanced out of the window, onto the platform. He was almost surprised to see... nothing untoward. Just normal station activity, passengers moving here and there, the station staff standing and... watching the train?

He stiffened. Surely not. After all his careful planning. How could anyone... ? Two of the staff walked across the platform, towards the train, towards his carriage. Jason's heart was pounding. No. It's not going to end like this. He looked around frantically. Both connecting doors in the carriage were unobstructed.

Resisting the urge to run, he walked, as calmly as he could, towards the door furthest away from where the station staff were approaching the carriage. He reached the door just as the door at the opposite end opened. He was through. Had they seen him? He did not wait to find out but walked briskly to the next connecting door and passed through it. He looked back. No one was following. Slowly, he edged towards the exit door and looked out.

Two carriages down, several station staff were gathered around the door, nearest to where he had been sitting. Jason saw one man enter the carriage, the same coach he had just been sitting in. *Thank goodness I moved; thank goodness I was alert,* Jason was telling himself.

Moments later, another staff member reached into the open carriage door to help the passenger who had been receiving the medical care. The wheelchair was lifted off and the patient was pushed away by the nurse.

Jason was still on a nervous high but managed a laugh, as much as anything to diffuse the tension. The platform was all but empty now and the train was making ready to leave. Jason stepped out onto the platform and immediately walked across to the fence. He leaned against it, pretending to look at something on his dead phone.

With a shrill whistle, the train moved off under its diesel-electric power; at this speed, there was hardly any rail noise, just a steady acceleration.

Chapter 25

Tonnick made his way back to the car. He was sure that Jason was not flying anywhere. But a train? Yes. Maybe. No need for ID to buy the ticket. It was regular and could get you away quickly.

He arrived at the train station only minutes later and went straight to the ticket office. He showed the ticket seller a photograph of Liam that he had got from Rosemary Hill.

'Who wants to know?'

The ticket office seller was not just handing out information. Tonnick cursed under his breath as he pulled his wallet out and showed his identification. The seller looked at the photo again.

'Yeah, yeah I think so. Young man. No baggage. He paid cash, I think.'

'You think?'

Tonnick suppressed his rising temper.

'Well, it would be easy to check. The CCTV is right there,' the seller said, pointing at the camera.

'Well, what are we waiting for?'

Tonnick was already reaching for the office door.

'Let me just call my supervisor.'

The seller was in unknown territory and was seeking support. Tonnick exploded.

'Get this door open and show me the bloody tape. Now!'

***

Tonnick was now in the CCTV booth in the train station offices and the supervisor was helping him review the video feeds. Of course, with so many people using the station and buying tickets, this was taking time. They were back over twenty minutes and focusing on the counter where the ticket seller said he remembered the man in the photo.

'Wait! There!' Tonnick jumped forward and touched the screen.

'That's him. I'm sure. 12:33 minutes, twenty seconds. OK so we know he's on a train, but which one?'

He looked across at the supervisor who was smiling.

'That's easy. We can cross-reference the time stamp to ticket sales. Will take a couple of minutes.'

They played the tape back to where William was requesting the ticket and they saw the operator make the ticket printout. He noted the time stamp.

'Right... got it. Follow me.'

The supervisor passed down the hall and entered another office. He began tapping keys on a terminal. Tonnick waited behind him, hardly daring to breathe.

'OK, it's clear. No other ticket sale went through in that timestamp range. He bought a through ticket to the coast. Seatown. It's a big local fishing port and they—'

'OK! I have what I need thanks,' Tonnick cut in. He got up and made for the door.

'The train changes at Draize Cross,' the supervisor shouted after him. Tonnick raised a hand in acknowledgement as he was running out of the offices. He reached for his phone and called Max.

'Meet me outside the railway station with the car. We are hot on his trail. He's pulling a fast one with that family retreat; it's another red herring. We need to step on it but this time... I think we are going to get him!'

Tonnick had filled the details in to Max and had called Inspector Smith to update him. They agreed to keep the lookout at the lake cabin, just to cover all bases.

Tonnick sat in the car, as Max drove towards Seatown, and recapped. His passport details, in both names, was circulated. The plane was out. They had his car details under surveillance and now, they knew about the Toyota. At one time, it seemed pretty obvious that Jason would turn up at the family retreat at some point. There was one officer on watch to make sure they were aware, if and when he did return. But now, Tonnick believed that Jason was bolting to the coast, probably to get on a boat and get away. The officers had continued to refer to Liam as 'Jason', even though they now knew his real name, and Tonnick had gone back to doing the same.

***

William exited the station and looked about. No police. No security. Nothing. Just a nice day. He checked for a taxi but there were none, just a few cars parked up... day trippers to the beach probably. William did not mind and in truth, as he thought about it, it made sense not to use a taxi or indeed... anything. It was not far to the bungalow, maybe five miles and he was in no rush any more. He would walk it. He decided to cross the fields surrounding the station access just in case anyone came looking. He thought he would try to go the whole way over country... keep off the roads. Again, he reasoned, there was no rush at all. Even assuming they had found his phone and assuming they had thought he had used the train, they did not know about the family retreat. Hell. No one did. It was abandoned. They would probably think he was heading to the coast to flee.

He set off, walking along the station's access road and came to a pedestrian footpath, set off the road behind a hedge. Perfect! Liam dipped behind the hedge and started a slow walk along the path. He did not see anyone as he got to the end and reached the main road. He looked left and right; there was one car coming so he stepped back down the path, waiting until it passed by then swiftly crossed the road and walked along the verge. The grass was tall, the municipality was probably due to trim this at any time but their delay in doing so served Liam well. Another car approached and before it came into view,

Liam crouched down in the grass, head bowed and motionless. The car went straight past.

Liam could see ahead that the verge was running out, being replaced by a roadside hedge, but just before it did there was a field gate. He scrambled along the verge and quickly entered the field, using the military way of passing a gate, reaching over, leg over and flipping his body as he supported his weight with his hands. He landed on two feet and immediately moved behind the hedge and looked around. No one could see him unless they were in the field, which was very large. Liam remembered that modern farming had used economies of scale — machines getting bigger and needing larger and larger fields to work effectively. This had meant the destruction of miles of hedgerow and all the associated wildlife that lived in it. Liam listened. Yes. Silence. No birdsong. They were right.

He spied another gate diagonal to the direction he wanted but it was not too far so he set off towards it, reaching it some ten minutes later. On the other side was another big field but this one was planted with what looked like a cereal crop, not grass. He could see the next gate on the opposite boundary, and another gate next to it on the roadside so he made his way towards them.

***

In the car, detectives Graham and Max were making good time. They had taken a shortcut on a small diagonal single-track road that came off the motorway, cut the corner and linked up with the main road heading to Seatown.

Tonnick checked the train timetable again. He had done this three times already. He looked at his watch.

'We should be there five minutes before them.'

'As long as we don't hit any traffic.'

Max wanted a get-out clause if there were any hold-ups. Tonnick considered that.

'Better step on it now, while we can. I would love to be there ten minutes before them, minimum. C'mon Max… let's go!'

Max accelerated marginally and settled at a new, faster pace.

He looked out of the corner of his eye. Tonnick was bolt upright… in fact, he was leaning forward slightly, eyes wide open. He thought, *as if he was going to get there slightly ahead of me…* they were on the road towards Seatown and making good time and silent in the car. Max hoped he was not going to sit like that for the rest of the journey and as if by telepathy, Tonnick sat back, with a sigh. Max passed a comment, more for conversation than anything.

'Dunno why people would take the train… this is a great drive down to the coast and trains are expensive. OK… you have no roadworks or accidents, but you do have to change trains at the station back there which adds time, and when you get there, no way to travel around if you don't have a car.'

He waited for any response from his boss.

Although he did not reply, Tonnick had heard his driver, and was thinking as he absent-mindedly looked on the GPS on his phone, looked at the train route, the changeover station, the sights along the…

'Oh my God!'

Max looked over. Tonnick was white like he'd seen a ghost. 'No… no… no… NO!'

He was looking at the transfer station on the GPS.

Max pulled over. 'What up, boss?'

'You see the transfer station here? See it?'

'Yes.'

'And see what's also near to it? About five miles from it, in fact? We missed the location because of that shortcut.'

Max looked, but Tonnick was already pointing. The motorway. The fuel stop and… . The abandoned cabin that Inspector Smith had checked out earlier.

They looked at each other. It was unsaid but they were both thinking the same thing. A double hoax? William was going to the coast? Or the cabin? Or… neither? Tonnick was on the phone immediately.

'Hello. Inspector? Graham Tonnick. Listen… he may be doubling back to the cabin so tell your man to stay sharp.'

'If he's going there… we will know about it. What are you going to do?'

'We will carry on towards the coast, to cover that off.'

'OK keep in touch.'

'You too.'

The phone clicked off.

'Well? What are you waiting for? Get us to Seatown quickly!'

Max gunned the engine and sped off once more.

***

Just over an hour later, Liam walked purposefully down the dirt track which accessed his childhood weekend holiday home in the country. Carefree days spent with his parents. Now his parents were long gone, but he was not going to let that cloud the day. It had all been dealt with.

On the hill between the cabin and lake, a watchful pair of eyes focused, on hearing the footsteps, the owner of those eyes crouching lower to avoid being seen yet craning to try to see who had arrived.

Liam felt elated. Here, he could finally relax. He was certain that no one looking for him knew about the cabin. This place had not been used for years and he believed it was forgotten. Until Liam, or William or was it Nicholas? He laughed, or even… Jason… had rediscovered it and made it his base.

When he came around the last corner and the main road was no longer in view, he could have been anywhere. No sound from the road. Just the birds in the trees, the insects buzzing around. It was true what people had said about the bungalow in the past — you almost get cut off from the modern world around you. Liam would settle for just being cut off from reality. The terrible reality of what he had done, what he had had to do.

But now, it was over, finished. The demons had been put to bed — well actually, he had missed one minor player in his scheme, but he was prepared to let that one pass and two additional ones which was a necessity to survive. The wrongs in the main had been righted. He could, at last, get on with the rest of his life.

Elated, yes… and relieved. Relieved it was finished and that he had not been caught. He walked towards the house, no, the cabin, he reminded himself, and went in through the front door. He suddenly realised that, apart from that sandwich on the train, he had not eaten properly for nearly two days. He suddenly felt very hungry.

On the hill, the lookout cursed to himself. He had missed identifying the person who entered the bungalow. He decided to wait for a little while to try and get a positive ID, before calling his boss. He did not want to blow the operation or incur the wrath of the Inspector if it was not their target.

***

After starting the generator, Liam went to the fridge and took out a steak pack he had bought about five days earlier. Should be all right — it was still in date, just. He had vegetables, too. With all the food out on the kitchen table, he set about preparing a meal. He could make fries! And some other boiled veg. and the steak. He remembered having a bottle of red wine, tucked away for when this day finally arrived.

He prepared the veg first because the steak would be very quick even though it was going to be pan-fried. Broccoli, carrots, fried onions. He sliced the onions then half cooked them, to be finished with the steak. Next, he heated some oil and when hot he placed his prepared, dried potato fries into the pan. He had seen somewhere on a YouTube channel about double-frying the fries, or 'chips' as the chef referred to them, and he decided to try the same technique for his. Once he had done the first 'frying' and lifted the fries out to drain, the other vegetables were put on to cook in a little salted water and then… the steak.

A little butter in the pan, then he seasoned the meat with salt, cracked black pepper, and crushed garlic. 'Ha-ha no problem for the garlic,' he thought, 'I'm not meeting anyone today!' He was smiling and happy, doing a mundane chore, except it wasn't a chore. He loved cooking. He put the steak in, and turned it around in the pan a few times, then added the onions back.

While he was waiting for the steak, he undid the screw-top on the wine. It made him think of his dad, here in this very house, opening wine — no screw-tops back then. Just the 'pop' of the cork followed by the tasting. It was like a ritual. He looked back at his bottle, reached for a glass, and poured a small amount into it. He swirled it around then took a mouthful. Yes… that was very good and it had not even had time to 'breathe'.

Time to turn the steak over, another sizzle as the raw side made its acquaintance with the hot oil. He stirred the onions, then picked up his glass and drained it. Next, the fries went back in for the second 'fry'. Everything was coming together.

William had enjoyed the meal, helped by two glasses of wine, and was at peace. What to do next? He thought of taking a nap but he did not feel tired and he wanted to sleep well later. He looked out at the lake. The boat was pulled up on the shore under a tarpaulin. He had already checked the boat and it was fine. In remarkably good condition considering the time that had passed. So... a little rowing, and... yes why not? A little fishing too. Just like old times.

He left the kitchen and went to the bedroom to change into some shorts and a T-shirt. Then armed with the fishing tackle, a jacket, a blanket, a bottle of water and some snacks, and a plastic carrier bag to bring the catch home, he walked towards the shoreline.

As he did so, he walked across a piece of open, well-lit ground, with no bushes or trees to hide him.

He pushed the boat into the water, chucked the oars in, and climbed aboard.

With measured strokes, the boat made its way around the little bay in front of the wooden bungalow. Soon the bungalow was out of sight.

In the trees, on the headland overlooking the bungalow and the boat, somebody had watched his movements through that well-lit area, and the boat's subsequent disappearance and was now reaching for his mobile phone.

Chapter 26

In the car, they were almost at Seatown. Tonnick's phone rang. He snatched it up.

'Yes? Yes. Oh really? Only got a clear look when he left the bungalow? OK, that's OK… How long? OK, we're on it.'

He frantically motioned to Max to turn the car around. Max braked sharply and set off back the way they had come.

'Will call you when we are close.'

He sat back in the chair, then looked at his driver.

'Damn it! This was a waste of time. He's there. Max… he's at the cabin. Smith's observer just called. Apparently, our target has gone out fishing in the boat. He was at the bungalow for some time but there was no positive ID until he went out on the lake.'

'How fast can we get back to that station and the bungalow?'

'Just over an hour, give or take'

'This is it. Let's go get the son-of-a-bitch.'

Max was already heading back but now he was driving with purpose. To bring the case to a close.

***

Liam was ecstatic. He had not fished for... how many years was it? And now... two fat trout in the bag. He would cook one of them later. He was happier now that he had been through the last ten years. He rowed the boat into another small inlet and jumped out, the cool water pleasant on his skin. He laid out the blanket on the grass under a tree just up from the beach and settled back with his snacks and water in the dappled sunshine. Looking out across the lake. He was thinking about the future, thinking about the relief he now felt. It was a release. No more getting himself worked up over past wrongs, no more fretting and stressing over if a particular part of his many plans was going to work, and always whether he was going to get caught. No... it was all done, all finished and no, he did not get caught. Here he was, about to start his new life. He had run rings around them all. He chuckled as he remembered Graham Tonnick falling out of the carriage and onto the platform. He imagined the Detective Inspector's face when he saw a photo of that very incident, how close he had been, and how 'Jason' had once again been one step ahead.

He was always one step ahead.

He was putting the events of the last twelve months out of his mind and pretty soon he dozed off into a happy sleep.

***

Liam awoke an hour later. *Wow, I must have been tired after all,* he thought to himself. It was still warm and sunny. Liam looked around him. He looked at the boat bobbing in the water, secured by the rope he had tied to a tree. The bay itself, and the trees surrounding him. It was a private spot. He smiled again. He liked this newfound freedom. Then he remembered the trout tied in a net and dangling off the boat in the water.

Moving in a leisurely manner, he collected up the rug and his snack wrappers, took another swig of water, which by now had warmed up, and ambled towards the boat. There was not another person to be seen on the lake. It was like… like Liam was the only person left in the world. Just the distant sounds of woodland wildlife behind him, and some waterbirds out on the lake itself. No animals. No motors.

No people.

Liam did not want a world without anyone to talk to. He loved open spaces, and if he was honest, he could get a little claustrophobic. He liked to be able to pass the time of day with other people, but again, over the years he had got used to long periods of solitude.

He pulled the boat back to the shore and put in his few items. Then he untied the rope from the tree, gave the boat a gentle push into the free water of the lake, and scrambled aboard. For a moment, he just let the boat drift, as he lay back and looked up to the sky. Some songbirds were overhead. Now that's real freedom, he thought, but... this drifting boat is a close second. Again, he smiled.

Liam felt the weight of the last year lifting from his shoulders as he relaxed and looked forward to the rest of his life.

Liam continued to drift. Now he was well out on the lake at least 200m from the shore. He felt the sun on his face, the first signs of sunburn, and sat up. For a moment he was disoriented. He understood how sailors could lose their way — all the lake looked the same, whichever way he looked. Then he saw some familiar trees and a stony outcrop. He had passed them as he set out earlier in the day. They were near the cabin.

He sat forward on the middle bench, and taking up the oars, began to row towards home.

***

On the freeway, Max had driven with purpose and was now approaching that same lake. Tonnick called the Inspector as they arrived at the cabin location. Within five minutes they were all gathered at the end of the trail by the main road.

'Any update from the lookout'? Tonnick needed real-time info now.

After a brief conversation on the radio, he answered

'He's still out on the lake. Been a while now, he's got to be coming back soon, right?'

There were nods all around from the assembled officers, and Tonnick also went along but then stopped suddenly.

'Wait a moment. How long has he been out there?'

'Coming up ninety minutes,' this reply from one officer, assigned as the operation coordinator.

'An hour-and-a-half? So, possibly, he's given us the slip again. Suppose he did not intend to come back here? Suppose instead he left all these clues here for us to conveniently 'find', and meanwhile once again, he planned something else?'

Smith's face clouded.

'Yes... instead of coming back here, what if he simply rowed on to the other side of the lake? What's over there? Anyone?'

'A hiking trail, some forestry company access tracks... '

The coordinator was referencing his notes. Tonnick stiffened.

'What about a road? I assume there is one?'

'Yes.'

'Right so... do we have anyone over there?' Tonnick sounded like he was speaking to a group of teenagers.

Smith turned and gave some orders. Two of the officers ran back to the carpark where their vehicles were.

'Got it covered now, and they can easily check that road.' He sounded less than convinced himself, and that was not lost on Graham Tonnick.

'OK let's hope he's not beaten us again.' He also sounded unsure.

They all stood around at the roadside and there was an uncomfortable silence as they realised this might be wasted time. No one seemed willing to move down the trail to the bungalow. It was like they were frightened of it. Frightened of what they might find. Nothing? A cleanout? Or a note —another note? Laughing at them in a stupid yet clever riddle.

Once again, Tonnick felt sick.

They had moved to positions around the bungalow, and ten minutes passed in near silence, with everyone deep in thought about the current situation, then a call came to say the officers were on the opposite side of the lake, but there was no sign of Liam.

The Inspector looked crestfallen but then his phone rang again.

Smith became alert, and Tonnick was leaning in for the message.

'Action stations! He's rowing towards this inlet! Remember. Radio and phones to silent. Move!'

Tonnick gave the command, pushing his hands out to clear the police from the bungalow. He and Inspector Smith took up a position behind the sheds, where they could see everything.

Five minutes later and they heard the sounds of a boat arriving. Then they heard the boat being dragged up the shore, then things being collected from it, and finally heavy breathing as the person walked towards the cabin.

At last, at long last… William Granger came into view.

Tonnick tensed up, and Smith put a hand on his arm. Their eyes met and he mouthed, 'Not yet, Graham.'

Liam entered through the main door and the detective watched him through the windows as he put everything down on the floor and walked into the kitchen. They continued to watch, mesmerised. Their quarry was right there in front of them. Surely he could not get away this time? No… they had far too many officers surrounding the cabin

They continued to watch as Liam appeared to be preparing food. They saw him go back to the stuff he had left on the floor, then return to the kitchen with a bag, from which he removed a large fish. He moved to the sink and they guessed that he was cleaning it, ready to be cooked.

One of the team moved from his hiding spot and Smith motioned him to be still; it was almost time, but not yet.

They watched as Liam continued to busy himself in the kitchen, then he seemed to tidy up and put lids on the pans, before leaving the kitchen and into the rear of the house. Tonnick and Smith gave him a minute, then they moved towards the bungalow. As they got nearer, they could hear Liam singing, presumably in the bathroom — he must be showering. Tonnick told Smith to be ready at the side of the house, then he moved to the door and turned the handle.

Slowly, he opened the door into the small vestibule before entering the open plan living room. Despite the windows, the room was a bit dark but that suited Tonnick. He moved quietly to the far corner, in the shadow, and sat down in an armchair to wait.

After ten minutes the door from the bedrooms into the living room opened and Liam walked through in a towel. He moved straight to the kitchen to check the pans, then poured himself a glass of white wine from the fridge and turned on the gas to cook the trout.

All the time, Graham Tonnick continued to watch him.

Liam was looking forward now to the rest of his life. Everything had been perfect in the end. The trust fund was going to take care of him, and he would live here for a bit, then move right away and buy a place in a new location, maybe a new country.

He took another mouthful of wine and turned the trout over in the pan.

What must they be doing now, he wondered. Probably chasing after that bus. He smiled. He had led them a merry chase and he had beaten them all. He turned the trout again. It was almost done. He reached for the wine bottle and poured himself another glass.

He looked out of the window, at peace with himself when the silence was abruptly broken.

'Hello, Jason.'

Liam froze, looking out of the window. He did not turn; he already knew who it was. Outside, he saw uniformed officers approaching the bungalow. He looked down at his dinner, now cooked, and reached for the bottle of wine again. He topped up his glass, almost to the brim, picked up a fork and pulled the skin back from the fish. The fork slid into the delicate flesh, and he brought it to his mouth. It tasted wonderful.

Tonnick remained motionless, watching.

Finally, he spoke,

'I'll allow you that, so enjoy. Where you are going, you will not be getting trout or wine.'

Liam wanted to take another fork-full, the first had tasted so good, but already, it was sticking in his throat when he tried to swallow. He gulped at the wine, coughing.

Finally, he gave up and slowly turned to the detective.

'What happens now, Graham?'

'Put that fork down, drink up your wine, if you want it, then face the counter and put your hands behind your back.'

'Is this how it ends?'

Liam was in shock and on autopilot, his world, and his carefully worked-out future, abruptly terminated.

'Yes, Liam. I'm afraid it is.'

At that moment, Inspector Smith and three other officers entered the bungalow. Detective Inspector Tonnick stood up and walked towards Liam, cuffs in hand. A moment later, Liam had been cautioned and was being led out to the waiting police car. His clothes followed in a bag.

Graham Tonnick smiled to himself. He hated an unsolved case. Hated loose ends. He wished Mandi could have been there to see this. With Liam apprehended, finally, he could close the book on the 'JASON' murders.

He reached for the mobile to call Gemma.

'Good news, Gem! I will not be late home. I have closed the case and we are going out for dinner tonight, no arguments.'

He looked at the cabin's kitchen, now abandoned.

'I fancy some fish.'